TAUNT HER

Rebels of Sterling Prep Book 1

CAITLYN DARE

Edited by Pinpoint Editing

CHAPTER ONE

Ace

I look around at the only home I've ever known and feel conflicted. It's a shithole, but it's our shithole—the only place I and my brothers have ever called home. And if I wasn't convinced that this move would benefit them, it wouldn't be happening.

They throw their bags into the trunk of their heap-of-shit car without a word. Dread sits heavy in my stomach as I move on autopilot, as if we aren't about to leave our home. The feeling isn't an unusual one, nor is the fury that fills my veins on a daily basis.

Our uncle should have been here ten minutes ago to take us away to start our new life in Sterling Bay. Maybe he's decided we're not worth it after all. Chance would be a fine fucking thing.

I'm just about to tell them to give up and go back

inside when the crunching of gravel by the trailer park entrance hits my ears.

Fucking great.

A black town car with equally blacked-out windows comes to stop in front of the three of us.

"I hope he's not planning on staying long, that thing'll be on bricks in minutes," Conner mutters, his eyes locked on the driver's door.

We haven't seen our uncle in years, not since he left us with our shit show of a mother. It seems family only matters when his hand has been forced by the state.

I'd have quite happily been my brothers' guardian for a year, but apparently an eighteen-year-old with a rap sheet like mine isn't a responsible enough adult to look after others.

The door opens and I lean to the side to get my first look at the man who abandoned us to this life instead of fighting for his family, but the guy who stands isn't one I recognize.

"Who the fuck are you?" I bark, much to the guy's irritation if the widening of his eyes is anything to go by.

"I'm your uncle's driver. He sent me to pick you up."

"Fucking brilliant." The laugh that accompanies my words is anything but amused.

"If you'd like to put your bags in the trunk, I'll take you home."

Home. *This* is my home.

My body tenses, my fists curling at my sides, as I step up to the man. He already looks totally intimidated by his surroundings, and I delight in him taking one step back as I approach. Slamming the door as I go, I stop him from an easy escape should he feel he needs it.

No motherfucker, you've probably not dealt with anyone like me before.

The scent of his expensive aftershave fills my nose, and it only makes me want to hurt the privileged asshole that much more.

"Let's get a few things straight." I don't stop until I'm right in his face, so close I see the fear in his eyes. Now *that's* something I can work with, something I can feed off like a fucking leech. "Firstly, that place you're meant to be taking us to is not our home. It'll never be our home. And second, we're not getting in this fancy-ass fucking car. Where the hell is James? I thought he was coming to collect us."

"He's been called out on business."

This is a fucking joke. First he demands we move into his pretentious mansion—blackmails me into it when he knows it's the last place in the world I want to live—and then the motherfucker can't even be bothered to turn up himself. He's probably too good for this place. No wonder he looked down his nose at us all those years ago and turned his back as fast as he could.

"He will be home later to greet you."

I stare at him, no emotion on my face and a storm brewing in my eyes.

"If you could just get in and—"

"Un-fucking-likely. We can make our own way."

I told James as much when he instigated this whole thing in the first place, but he insisted. Probably because he doesn't want my brothers' rust bucket sitting in his fancy driveway and bringing the tone of the area down.

"I really don't think—"

"I don't give a fuck what you think, *Jeeves*."

All the blood that was left in his face from when he

first stepped out of the car drains away, and he swallows nervously.

"D-do you want to f-follow me then?"

"Marvelous, Jeeves. What a fantastic plan," I mock, mimicking his posh British accent.

The second I take a step back, he scrambles into the car as quick as he can. Fucking pussy.

"I can't believe he sent a car," Conner mumbles as my brothers join me, and together we watch the town car roll slowly down the dirt track.

"Really?" I balk. "James isn't our savior, Con. You think he'd even be taking us in if it weren't for the court deciding I'm no good..." I swallow the rest of the words. Of course, no one would trust me with my brothers. Apparently, the fact that I've raised both of them since we were just kids doesn't matter.

My chest tightens.

"It'll be okay, Ace." My brother squeezes my shoulder. "A fresh start could be just what we need."

"Yeah, whatever." I shrug him off. "We should probably get going." There's nothing left for us here.

Conner gives me a weak smile before following Cole to their car. It's an ancient Ford they somehow manage to keep running despite the fact that it should have been scrapped at least ten years ago. Cole doesn't even spare our trailer a backward glance as he climbs inside and guns the engine. I'll need to keep my eye on him; he's always been a quiet kid, but lately he's been even more brooding.

They follow Jeeves' lead before I throw my leg over my bike and rev the engine. The vibrations instantly help to cool me off. The anticipation that I'll soon be flying down the coastal road helps to push my ever building anger over this fucked-up situation down a little more.

I gun the engine once both the town car and my brothers have disappeared from sight and take one last look at this place. It's dark and dingy, like Hell on Earth. But it's our home... *was* our home. We're moving. Heading over the border to the rich side of town. Like we're ever going to fucking fit in there.

Dust and gravel fly up behind me as I speed off to find my brothers' taillights somewhere up ahead. We know roughly where James lives, but I've no idea which of the insanely pretentious houses actually belongs to him. Probably the biggest one, knowing that pretentious stuck-up prick.

I catch them just before the road opens up and the bright blue sea appears in the distance. I guess that's one good thing about where we're going: the girls on the beach. It's just a shame they're all going to talk like Jeeves, as if they've got a spoon permanently stuck in their pouty mouths.

"Fucking hell," I mutter to myself as I follow the two cars up a long ass driveway. It's not until the very last moment that the actual house appears. It's a huge place on a hill overlooking the ocean. The kind of house I've only ever seen images of in magazines, or on the TV when the piece of shit worked.

Images of the parties we can have here start to fill my mind. Maybe this place won't be so bad after all. I can get off my face and attempt to fuck some rich chick looking to take a walk on the wild side... in every room of the house.

Parking between my brothers' car and a flashy Mercedes, I throw my leg over my bike and head in the direction I just watched Jeeves walk into the house. He obviously thought against helping with our belongings. Wise man. He's learning quickly.

With our bags in hand, we climb the stairs to the double front door. It's a damn sight different to the one on our trailer that swelled up so bad in the summer we had to crawl out through a window, and that allowed the wind and rain to come inside during any storms.

"Holy crap," Conner gasps as we walk into the entrance hall of all entrance halls. I swear to fucking god that the only house I've seen quite this lavish is the Playboy mansion. I'm half expecting scantily-clad women to pour through the doors for a welcome party at any moment.

Sadly, the only person who emerges from one of the many doorways is Jeeves.

"Would you like a tour?"

"Or a fucking map," Conner mutters. Cole, however, stands totally mute and looking bored out of his skull. I know he's taking everything in, though. It's how his brain works.

"Just point us in the direction of our rooms. I'm sure we can figure the rest out ourselves. We might be from a trailer park, but we're far from stupid."

"I'm well aware of that. I'm William, by the way."

"I would say it was nice to meet you, Jeeves," I spit, curling my lip in disgust, "but in all honesty, it wasn't."

"Right, well. You can get to your rooms via this staircase, but you do have your own at the other end of the house. If you'd like to follow me."

For once, the three of us do as we're told and trail behind him until he comes to a stop at a slightly less audacious staircase, although it's still much grander than any I've seen before.

"At the top you'll find four rooms. Each has a fully stocked en suite, but if you need anything extra please speak to Ellen. You can usually find her in the kitchen, which is directly behind the main staircase, and she'll see you have everything you need."

"How about an ounce of weed and a few bottles of vodka?"

He stares at me as if I'm going to laugh at my own joke. It's not a fucking joke. I'm going to need that and then some if I'm meant to live here.

It's only a year. You can do this for a year for your brothers.

"If that's all, I'll leave you to find your feet." He spins on his heels and fucks off as fast as his legs will carry him.

"Shall we do this shit then?" Conner asks as we all stand like statues at the bottom of the stairs.

"Fuck it." I move first, but they're not far behind me.

I take the furthest door from the stairs, and the one I'm fairly sure will have the best view. I might be here for them, but they can fuck off if they think they're getting it.

"Fucking hell," I mutter, walking onto the insanely spongy cream carpet and looking around at my new digs. This one room alone is about double the size of our trailer.

I dump my bag on the window seat and look out at the ocean beyond, exactly as I'd hoped. Staring out at the perfect postcard view, I hope its calmness will somehow transfer into me. No such luck, because when I turn and take in the room around me, the need to smash it up is all-consuming.

I don't want to fucking be here.

I want my old life. My shitty trailer. My state school and dead-end opportunities.

Pulling my cell from my pocket, I sync it with the speakers I find on the sideboard and turn it up as loud as it'll go. This house might be a mansion, but I'll make sure Uncle fucking James knows we've arrived.

Retrieving the packet of smokes from my bag, I pull one out and place it between my lips before falling down onto my bed. I can only assume there's a no smoking rule in a place like this. I smile as I light up and blow smoke right into the center of the room.

I didn't follow any rules before, so like fuck am I about to start.

I can't hear anything over the sound of my music, so it's not until the door opens that I realize someone wants me. Looking up, I expect to find my brothers, but instead Uncle James stands before me in his sharp three-piece suit, slicked-back hair and clean-shaven face.

"What do you want?" I bark, turning away from him and lighting up once again.

"I was coming to see how you were settling in, but I see you've already made yourself at home."

"What the fuck?" I seethe when the cigarette is plucked from my lips, seconds before it's flicked out the window.

He pulls up the front of his perfectly pressed pants before sitting down on the edge of my bed. If he's trying to look authoritative, then he needs to try fucking harder.

"A few house rules are in order, I think."

I scoff but allow him to continue so he can list his challenges, because you can bet your sweet ass I'm going to breaking each and every one just to piss him off.

"No smoking in the house. You want to kill yourself with those death sticks, then you do so outside. You will not bring any drugs or drink into this house. If you want friends here, you can use the pool house. I've set it up as a den of sorts for the three of you. That's your domain."

"So we can smoke, drink, and do drugs in there?"

"No. There will be no parties, no girls, nothing that will cause any trouble of any kind."

"If you're not looking for trouble, then you invited the wrong guys to come and live with you."

"You are no longer in Sterling Heights." He frowns. "Things are different around here. I think it might be important for you to remember that."

"Whatever."

"School starts in two weeks. Your uniforms are already in your closets. I suggest you familiarize yourself with the place before the hard work starts, because there is no way you're not graduating this year," he jibes, knowing full well that I fucked up what should have been my senior year last year. Not my fault that someone had to earn some goddamn money to support my brothers.

I look to the other side of the room as if his mere presence is boring me.

"Dinner will be served in an hour. I expect you all to be cleaned and dressed appropriately." I see his gaze from out of the corner of my eye drop to my ripped jeans and oil-stained shirt. "My girlfriend and her daughter are coming to welcome you to town, and I shouldn't need to tell you that you will be nice to both of them."

Well, doesn't that sound like a fucking fun way to spend our first night in Sterling Bay? A nice, cozy family meal with the man who only wanted us when we had no parents left in this world.

He makes out like he wasn't aware of what our lives were like.

He's a fucking liar.

"An hour. I've already warned your brothers. We'll be waiting."

I do shower and change—not because he told me to, but because I fucking stink, and to be honest, I can't deny that the rainfall shower in my en suite wasn't appealing. It was a shit load better than the open pipe we had in the trailer.

Wearing a different pair of ripped jeans and a slightly cleaner shirt, I step out into the hall at exactly the same time both Cole and Conner do. They're dressed similarly to me; it seems they took Uncle's warning about as seriously as I did.

The sounds of voices direct the three of us toward the dining room. My curiosity as to what hides behind each door we pass is high, but I don't look. I don't want to seem like I care, because I really fucking don't, I'm just intrigued as to why a man who's always lived alone needs so many fucking rooms.

As we join them, all conversation stops and three heads turn our way. I know our uncle is here but don't pay him any mind. The brunette, however, captures my imagination quite nicely.

He might have warned me about no girls already, but he didn't mention one who clearly already spends time here.

He walks over and wraps his arm around both the brunette and her mother. "Ace, Cole, Conner..." He grins like the cat who got the cream, and I fucking hate it. "This is Sarah, my girlfriend, and Remi, her daughter."

CHAPTER TWO

Remi

"Hello, boys," Mom sing-songs. "It's nice to finally meet you. James has told me all about you."

"He has, has he?" One of the boys slides his narrowed gaze to his uncle. His tone is cold, icy even, sending a shiver skittering up my spine.

A beat passes, then James clears his throat. "Ace," he warns, flicking his head to where Mom and I are standing.

According to Mom, Ace is the eldest. He and his twin brothers lived with their mom until she died suddenly. Since they had nowhere else to go, and the twins are still minors, James offered to take them in.

"Hey," Ace replies, his eyes gliding down my body and back up. Another shiver works its way through me, only

I can't decide if it's a nice one or bad one. Ace looks like he either wants to throw me down on the table and do very bad things to me, or murder me with his bare hands.

It's unnerving.

He's unnerving.

They all are.

But then, what did I expect? Kids from Sterling Heights aren't like kids from the Bay.

"Hi, I'm Remi," I say. "I go to Sterling Prep, so we'll all be in the same class."

None of them look pleased about that.

"Shall we get seated?" James motions for us to move to the table. As always, he pulls out a chair for Mom, and as always she makes a scene of getting situated. I swallow a frustrated huff. I love her something fierce, but I wish she had more backbone. My experience with guys may be lacking, but I know my worth, and I'll never rely on a guy for anything.

Before I can take the seat next to Mom, one of the twins slides into the chair. The other twin takes the one opposite, leaving two empty seats between them.

Ace watches me, a faint smirk tugging at his lips. Whichever chair I take, I'm going to be stuck between him and one of his brothers.

Just perfect.

"I don't bite," the twin sitting nearest teases, grinning up at me. "I'm Conner."

He seems friendlier than his brothers, so I take the seat beside him, trying to ignore the way Ace's leg brushes mine when he finally sits down.

Just then, Ellen enters the room with a tray of drinks. "Dinner will be served shortly," she says, pausing when she catches sight of the boys. "Oh my, you must be Ace, Cole, and Conner."

Her eyes run over the three of them as she steps back. "Now, you two must be the twins," she says, pointing between Cole and Conner. "Which means you must be—"

"Ace."

My body tenses when his hand lands on my thigh. Hard. Possessive. As if I'm a piece of property he just claimed.

What the hell is he doing?

I swat his hand away, resisting the urge to stamp my heel into his boot.

Asshole.

"Oh, you boys remind me so much of... never mind." Ellen hurries off, leaving a tense atmosphere lingering in the room.

"So, boys, are you excited to start at Sterling Prep?" Mom beams at them, and I can't decide if she's trying to make it easier on James, the boys, or whether she's just oblivious to all the tension.

Ace leans back, casually throwing his arm around the back of my chair. His hand brushes my shoulder and I bristle. "What's not to be excited about?" he drawls.

"Oh yeah," Conner chuckles. "We're real excited, Sarah. All the new *friends* we'll make." The way he says it sounds so dirty.

"Boys, please..." James lets out a heavy sigh, running a hand over his jaw.

James has been good to us over the years. He's been there, in the background, helping us and offering Mom a shoulder to lean on. But it was after she got out of a bad relationship a few years ago that James offered her a job at his company. She spends almost as much time there as he does, so it's hardly a surprise they finally crossed the line from friends to lovers. At least, I think that's what this is.

I suppress a shudder. That is one visual I don't ever need.

"It's okay, James." Mom flashes him a warm smile. "This is an opportunity for us all to get to know each other."

"Sarah's right, Uncle J. Don't you think he's right, Ace?" Conner smirks.

"Hell yeah, I can't wait to get to know you better." His finger ghosts over my shoulder, and I jerk forward.

Something tells me he isn't talking about getting to know my mom.

"Remi, sweetheart, is everything okay?"

"It must have been a bug or something." I cut Ace with a scathing look. "Excuse me, I need to go to the bathroom."

I leave the five of them in awkward silence. I need air. I need to get away from Ace Jagger for a second. He's unlike any guy I've ever come across. And when you grew up next door to one of the most popular boys in Sterling Bay, that's saying something.

But Ace and his brothers aren't like the guys from around here. They're rough around the edges with a darkness that shadows them like a thunder cloud.

They're probably in a gang. I've heard a lot of the kids from Sterling Heights are.

I make my way to the bathroom at the back of the house. Ellen's soft voice fills the air as she sings a tune. Locking the door behind me, I stare at the girl in the mirror. The same long brown curls frame her face and big brown eyes. The same freckles dust her sun-kissed nose. But something is different. The smile she wears no longer reaches her eyes.

It hasn't for a while.

Senior year is supposed to be the time of my life. Homecoming. Prom... Graduation. But nothing is the same anymore, and the thought of putting on the charcoal blazer, royal blue tie, and pale gray knee-length skirt that all the girls insist on rolling up to skim their ass, fills me with nothing but dread.

After waiting long enough, I wash my hands before slipping out of the bathroom, only to walk smack bang into a solid chest. "What the—"

"Easy there, Princess." Ace smirks, his hands gripping my shoulder a little too tightly as he holds me at arm's length.

"Get the hell off me." I jerk back but he stalks forward, forcing me further into the bathroom.

"This isn't funny," I say firmly, despite the ratchet of my pulse.

"Do I look like I'm laughing?" His pierced brow rises. "I thought we could *get to know each other better,*" he mocks.

"Oh my god," I breathe, disbelief clinging to every syllable. "Just who the hell do you think you are?"

Ace steps closer, and I edge back. He thinks it's a game. It's right there, glittering in his frosty blue eyes.

But I know guys like Ace, guys who think they can just take whatever they want without consequence, and I have no interest in becoming his sparring partner.

My back hits the counter, and my hands shoot out behind me to steady myself. He leans in, putting us face to face, and I'm sure he must be able to hear the gallop of my heart in my chest.

Calm down, I mentally demand.

Moving closer still, he inhales deeply, and my breath catches. "You smell so fucking good."

"Ace..." I suck in a harsh breath. "Let. Me. Out." The words leave my lips through gritted teeth as I try to maintain some control, but it's futile. Ace holds all the power, and he knows it.

His mouth curves into a wicked grin. "Scared, Princess?"

"Stop calling me that." I'm not a princess, not like most of the pretentious spoiled girls in my class.

His hair is unruly, falling over his eyes a little. The sudden desire to push it away washes over me. I internally groan at myself. I'm such a cliché, letting myself fall under the bad boy's spell.

"Move or I'll scream."

Ace moves his mouth to my ear, his warm breath dancing along my neck. "Screaming only makes it sweeter."

Without thinking, I shoulder him out of the way and dart around him.

"I'll be seeing you around, Princess," he calls after me. I glance back, scowling, but it only fuels Ace's rumble of laughter.

I march out of there, wondering what kind of hell I've landed myself in.

I barely eat. Between Conner's innuendos and Ace's proximity, I feel nauseous.

"Is something wrong with your chicken, sweetheart?" Mom asks, frowning at all the food left on my plate.

"I'm just not hungry, sorry."

"If it's going spare, do ya mind?" Conner reaches for my plate.

"Jesus, Conner, show some manners," James scolds him. "If you want more, I'll have Ellen—"

"It's fine. He can have it." I push it toward him and he digs in, like he hasn't just cleared his own plate.

My eyes flick to Ace. He and Cole are having some kind of silent conversation. I allow myself a second to look at him, *really* look at him. The dark hair, piercings, and tats peeking out from under his t-shirt and running up his neck make him look scary, but I know better than to judge a book by a cover, and I find myself wondering about their life in the Heights.

"Maybe you should take a photo, it'll last longer," he whisper-hisses, his intense gaze settling on my face. Mom and James are deep in conversation. Business talk, no doubt.

Cole barely cracks a smirk at his brother's attempt to get under my skin.

"Actually, I was looking at your tattoos."

"You like ink?" He seems surprised.

"I like art."

He studies me like I'm a puzzle he's trying to solve but quickly averts his eyes.

Okay, then.

Ellen breezes into the room and begins clearing away the plates.

"Thank you, Ellen," James says. "It was lovely."

"Clean plates all around, the best compliment a cook can ever have." She turns her attention to the boys. "Now, who wants dessert?"

"Dessert sounds great." Ace walks his finger up my thigh again, keeping his attention ahead.

I roughly grab his fingers, bending them backward. He lets out a garbled sound, tearing his hand away. Shooting him a saccharine smile, I cross my legs, putting as much distance between us as possible.

"So, Cole," Mom says. "James says you play football."

He shrugs, grunting some inaudible reply.

"Are you any good?"

"He's going all the way to the NFL, baby." Conner slaps his hand down on the table.

"Con," Ace warns, and the two of them share a look.

"Remi's friend Bexley plays for the Seahawks. He's the quarterback." Pride fills her voice, as if it somehow matters.

"Bexley? What the fucking kind of name is Bexley?" Conner barks out a laugh.

"The Danforths are one of the wealthiest families in the state. Bexley is following in his daddy's footsteps and going to Stanford next fall. I'm sure Remi will introduce you all."

The three brothers stare at my mom like she's lost her goddamn mind, and I'm beginning to wonder if she has.

Ace and Bexley becoming friends... yeah, never going to happen.

"I can hardly wait," Ace deadpans.

"I spoke to Coach Miller just last week and he's looking forward to seeing Cole at practice."

"You got him on the team?" Conner chokes out. "Cole... playing for the Seahawks?"

"Well, I assume he'll have to try out like any new player, but yes, I pulled some strings."

"You *pulled some strings*?" Ace's tone makes my blood run cold. I glance down and notice his hand curled into a tight fist against his thigh.

"Ace," James releases an exasperated breath. "This is a good thing. Cole has real potential..."

"Potential?" he spits. "What do you know about Cole's potential?"

"Ace, man," Conner says tightly.

"The Seahawks are a good team. Cole has a real shot at making his mark. But you've got to work with me here." James' expression turns pleading.

Ace hesitates, and I can sense his torment. Something is going on here, something deeper than just three boys plucked from the Heights and dumped in the rich end of town. Ace has made no attempt to hide his disdain for his uncle. Conner seems to think everything is one big joke, and Cole... well, I haven't quite figured him out yet. He's barely spoken two words.

"You think you can just—"

"Ace." Cole shakes his head slightly, his eyes saying everything he isn't.

"Fine." The eldest Jagger brother shoves his chair back and stands. "I need a smoke."

Of course he smokes.

I bet he rides a motorcycle and carries a knife, too.

We all watch him stalk out of the room.

"I think as far as first dinners go, that went well."

Conner grins at me, and I can't help but smother my own smile. He kind of has a point.

"I'm going to get some air too." Cole excuses himself and takes off after Ace.

"You'll have to excuse my brothers. We're not exactly used to all... this." Conner glances down the table.

"It was perhaps premature on my part to expect you all to do this."

"Oh, I don't know," Mom covers his hand with hers, "I think they did okay. So Ace is retaking senior year?" she asks.

"He is." James grimaces. "It's not ideal to have them all in the same class, but it is what it is." He shoots Conner a knowing look.

"Why did he flunk last year?" The words spill out before I can stop them.

"That is a story for another day." James dabs the corner of his mouth, throwing his napkin down. "Why don't we move this into the sitting room? I'll have Ellen serve us dessert there." He and Mom get up and make their way into the adjoining room, leaving me with Conner.

"So your mom and my uncle, huh?" He runs a hand through his hair. It's dark like Ace's and Cole's but has lighter tips. Out of the three of them, he looks the one least likely to eat me alive.

"Yep."

"Are you around here a lot?"

"Sometimes, when Mom insists I come."

"I see." His lips thin, and I wonder what he's thinking.

"Why?"

"Oh, no reason." Conner stands up, looming over me. "Just watch your back, yeah?"

He walks away and leaves me sitting there.

I want to believe it's a friendly warning, that Conner might be a Jagger brother you can trust, but something tells me it isn't a warning at all.

It's a threat.

CHAPTER THREE

Ace

"Why don't you have the night off? Go and do something fun," I suggest to Ellen after pulling the refrigerator open and grabbing a bottle of water. Something tells me she's never done a single fun thing in her life, but who knows... tonight could be the night.

"Oh, no no. I need to clean out the pantry."

Okay, so she's even sadder than I thought. Noted.

"It's Friday night. Go home."

"But..." I raise an eyebrow at her and press my lips into a thin line, a move that works on almost everyone. Apparently I'm scary. *Use what God gave you,* Mom used to say. So I do, scaring the shit out of people on a daily basis. Or at least I did when I was in Heights. Fuck knows what the rich folk around here will think about me.

"Okay, okay. You're right, I do need a night off. My pussy misses me terribly when I work a late shift."

I scoff, just about managing to cover my amusement at her statement, although one look at her innocent face is all the evidence I need to know she's talking about a cat. Great, we left the most notorious trailer park in Heights, and now we live with a cat woman. How the mighty fall. It's a good thing she's leaving, because what's about to go down in this house would give her a fucking heart attack.

"You go home and stroke that pussy." I suppress a chuckle. "We'll be fine here."

"You'll call me if you need anything?"

"Sure," I lie. I'm not sure why, but Ellen seems to think we need someone. To be looked after. She clearly didn't get the memo about us looking after ourselves for the past fuck knows however long.

I leave her collecting up her things and shoot a message to my guys. I told them this was happening about ten seconds after James announced that he was going to be away on business this weekend.

His warning about no parties was a distant memory as I handed out his address to every fucker I know.

We've been here almost two weeks, and it's the first time he's left us alone for more than a few hours. I was starting to think he didn't trust us.

Sadly, his little princess hasn't been back. It's a real shame. I was looking forward to having some more fun with her, but we all know she's on borrowed time. School starts next week and there will be no running.

She'll be right there for the taking.

The perfect prey.

The ultimate pawn in my games.

"We're all set." I throw my brothers a bottle of vodka each and a baggie of weed. "No more than that," I say, staring at Cole. If he's got tryouts for the Seahawks on Monday like James implied, then he needs to be sober and focused. "And no fucking pills. You hear me?"

"Yes, Dad," Conner mutters with a two fingered salute.

I still at the mention of Dad, and something cold runs through my veins, reminding me of all the truths I need to uncover during my time here.

"The guys will be here within the hour."

I take my own bottle and blunt to the front door. I drop my ass to the stone steps and light up. Fuck the pool house. This is going down in the main house tonight.

The first few shots of the vodka burn down my throat, but after the third... or fourth, I no longer feel it.

I flick the end of the blunt to the gravel of the driveway as lights make their way up to me. A smile twitches at my lips. I really fucking need this.

"Jag," Dean calls the second he pulls up in front of the house. "This place fucking suits you, man."

"You think?"

"Fuck yeah. The drug lord needs an appropriate mansion." I laugh at his idiocy as other cars pile in behind him and people spill out onto the driveway, heading for the house. Bottles clatter as they carry them inside to get the party started. Someone I don't recognize drags a set of speakers from his truck, and they disappear inside to set up.

Kelsey, my regular hook-up, saunters up to me dressed as she usually is: in very little. She steps into me, her sweet scent filling my nose, but, unlike previously, it does little for me.

"Hey, baby. I missed you," she slurs. One of her hands slides up my chest and slips around the back of my neck while the other descends for my cock. My fingers wrap around her wrist before she gets to my waistband.

Taking her chin in my hand, I move her face so I can stare into her eyes. They're dark and blown. "Fucking hell, Kels. You're meant to be getting off that shit."

"Yeah, I was. And then you left."

"You're not mine," I snap, pushing her away. She stumbles but doesn't fall. Shame. She's always thought there was more to us than I ever let on, but she was a way to pass the time, nothing more. "Lay off the hard shit, or find your way back to the Heights." She's taken things too far one to many times, and the last thing I need is to find her OD'd in the pool.

"You need a drink and to lighten up," she complains. "Find me later when you need some action." She winks, but it's not appealing in the slightest. Her lifeless blonde hair is doing nothing for me right now. I've got my sights set on a certain brunette.

Music booms as more people flood into my uncle's house, and, after a few moments, I join them.

Falling down onto the opposite end of the sofa to where Conner has some girl grinding on his lap, I lift my bottle to my lips before pulling out another blunt.

Now this is a much better way to use this house.

Something smashes out in the hallway, but like fuck if I care enough to go and check it out.

"Donny is really missing you, man," JJ says, dropping down beside me and thankfully cutting off the view of my brother's tongue delving into that hussy's mouth.

"So I've heard," I mutter, thinking of the messages I've had from my boss asking when I'm going to come and do another run for him.

I fucking need to. I'm skint, and like hell am I going to use a cent of the money James has given us.

I was building up a nice little nest egg for the future until a fucking ghost from my past turned up and used my one and only weakness against me.

"Give me what I want, or I'll go about it another way." Even the memory of his voice sends a shiver down my spine.

Our father. Cunt of the century, and a man we all thought was fucking dead. Turns out he was just lying in wait for the perfect opportunity to ruin my life.

"I'll be back," I promise JJ. "Just got some shit to deal with here first."

"What the fuck kind of shit could you need to worry about here?" He looks around at our lavish surroundings as the sound of something else breaking fills the room "Well, maybe aside from that."

"Fuck that. I don't give a shit about this place. It's the motherfucker who owns it that needs my attention."

JJ's brows furrow. He's probably thinking the same as everyone else in Sterling Bay: James Jagger is an upstanding citizen of the community and a prestigious businessman. If any of that means *liar* and *master manipulator* then yeah, that's good ol' Uncle James all right.

He's covered his tracks well, I'll give him that. But he seems to have forgotten one thing.

Me.

And I'm out for his motherfucking blood.

I'm not entirely sure how it happens, aside from the fact that Conner is involved, but sometime after midnight, the house begins to empty as everyone stumbles their way across James' perfectly landscaped yard and towards the beach beyond.

Flowers get trampled, and bottles and half-smoked cigarettes and blunts get thrown every which way as we descend. No one gives a shit, and I fucking love it. I'm already pumped to see his face when he gets back to this disaster. I only wish I could be a fly on the wall when he gets the inevitable phone call about the out-of-control party in his beloved mansion.

The last thing I'm expecting when we eventually get down to the shore is to find another party in full flow. Only this one is a little different.

They're drinking out of solo cups instead of bottles of liquor and, as far as I can see—or smell—there's nothing illegal going on. It's just a group of kids hanging out around a bonfire like a bunch of fucking boy scouts. Oh, and one more thing... they look preppy as fuck.

All heads turn our way as we come to a stop before them. Some guy wearing a blue and white Seahawks team jacket stands. I know his type immediately: privileged jock asshole. The one who thinks he's hard. The one who thinks he can defend his school's honor or some shit.

He's got perfectly slicked-back blond hair and blue eyes. He's such a fucking cliche it actually hurts my eyes to look at him.

"What the fuck do you want?"

I step forward, not because I don't think anyone else

will, but because it's high time I made my mark. I've been to—or crashed—plenty of Bay parties over the years, but I'm fairly sure I'd remember this preppy fucker if I'd seen him before.

"For you to get out of my fucking face," I taunt, closing the space between us.

Hunger for the imminent fight filters from behind me, whereas when I look over the douche's shoulder, all I see are terrified wide eyes.

These fuckers need to be taught a lesson.

Ace Jagger is about to take over the motherfucking town, one rich douchebag at a time.

My fingers twitch. It would be so easy to pull out my knife and do this properly.

"We're just hanging out down here. You're the ones gatecrashing. But I hear that you Heights scum have a thing about crashing Bay parties. Probably because we can afford better alcohol."

"Nah," I say with a laugh. My lips curl, but I'm anything but amused as I bare my teeth at him. "Your bitches have tighter pussies."

"Motherfu—"

"Bexley, stop."

That voice.

A slender hand lands on the asshole's shoulder before familiar dark curls appear, followed by her huge, brown eyes and full, pink lips.

I look between the two of them. Of course the princess would be with the captain. If I didn't already want to take the motherfucker to the ground, then I fucking do now for having her touch him like that.

Innocent little Remi might have no idea, but she belongs to me now, and no one touches what's mine.

"Move, Remi," I warn, closing the space between us. "Rexley and I need to have a little chat."

"It's Bexley, asshole. And you'd better fucking remember that."

"Is that right?" I taunt, "because I'm pretty sure the next name your girl there moans will be mine."

Remi moves just in time for Bexley to cock his arm back, ready to take a swing at me. Sadly for him, he's not aware that I've fought guys like him almost on a daily basis back in Heights, and I'm faster. Much faster.

My knuckles connect with his cheek before he even attempts his first punch. Girls scream, including Remi, and a few of his team members step forward, although as my guys move, they suddenly look like they could be about to run.

Fucking bunch of pussies.

Grabbing Bexley by his collar, I stare down into his panic-filled eyes. "The Jaggers are in town now. You'll learn your place."

"Fuck you," he spits seconds before my head connects with his nose, making him scream like a little bitch and blood cover his jacket.

He comes at me, but he's no match for my strength or speed. In only minutes, he's on the floor, writhing in pain, bleeding and crying like a baby.

A couple of his pussy ass teammates drag him off as my guys wait behind me to see if they're going to need to get in on the action. But it seems that the rest of the Seahawks are a little more switched on than their captain, because they stay put.

That doesn't mean I can't see the need to fight back in their eyes, though. They want payback for this, they're just not willing to when I have half of Sterling

Heights standing behind me. Our reputation clearly precedes us, and rightly so, most of the motherfuckers standing behind me wouldn't bat an eyelid at the chance to hurt a Bay kid.

Turning my attention to Remi, I watch as she stares at me with wide, terrified eyes. I step toward her. She takes one back, and another, her pace quickening until she stumbles in the sand and ends up on her ass. I straddle her waist, her entire body trembling beneath me. I gather both her wrists in one of my hands and lift them above her head before dropping the other to the side of her head and gazing down at her. She refuses to hold my stare. Instead, she turns to the side defiantly.

Taking her chin between my bloody fingers, I squeeze until I know it'll pinch and turn her so she has no choice but to face me.

"Look at me."

It takes her a second, but eventually she concedes.

"You need to watch who you hang out with, princess." I trail a finger from her rosy cheek all the way down her neck and to the swell of her breasts. Her breath catches and her skin breaks out in goosebumps. "Decide whose side you're on tonight and either fuck off or come back to the house with me."

Her body trembles again, but this time it's not with fear.

I know what she's going to say—it's written all over her face before the words pass her lips—but I'll give her this one chance. Next time, I'll just take what I want, because a broken Remi is going to get me the answers I need.

CHAPTER FOUR

Remi

Ace stares down at me, making my heart thump violently in my chest. My body is hot and restless beneath him, but it's only anger.

That's all it can be.

"Get the hell off me." I buck against him, but he holds my wrists firmly in his grasp.

"Say the magic word, Princess," Ace taunts. Blood coats his knuckles and splatters his wife-beater. I can't believe he just did that. Bexley's nose is broken for sure, I heard the crunch.

"Tell me you're not with that preppy fucker?"

"Jealous?" My lip curls. I don't know why I omit the truth, why I even consider sparring with him, but he brings out something buried deep inside me.

"Oh you'd love that, wouldn't you?"

Something sparks in his eyes, flecks of silver streaking across his soulless blue gaze.

"Shit, Ace," a voice calls, but neither of us move,

locked in this strange standoff. "What are... whoa, is that the princess?" It's Conner. Ace glances over his shoulder and I use his distraction to my advantage. Shoving my fists into his shoulders, I dig my foot into the ground and slam my body upwards.

"Motherfucker," Ace grunts, rolling off to the side. I sit up, barely able to contain my laughter. I didn't mean to catch him in his balls, but I can't deny it gives me a strange sense of satisfaction.

Conner moves closer, offering me his hand. I take it, letting him pull me up. "You might want to put some ice on that," I say to Ace, who looks ready to kill me with his bare hands. Once he can stand again, anyway.

I snicker again, and Conner explodes with laughter. "Shit, Princess, we sure underestimated you."

"Tell your brother to stay the hell away from me." I don't stick around to hear either of their replies as I march across the beach toward the path leading over the sandbanks to my house.

Some party.

I didn't want to come tonight, but Mom ran into Bexley earlier and he mentioned it, and Mom being Mom hounded me until I finally gave in. Besides, I knew Hadley would be here, and she's about the only girl left at Sterling Prep that I can stand to be around.

"Remi, wait up," her familiar voice drifts over to me, and I stop. She reaches me, a little breathless as if she ran over here.

"You should go back to the dorms, Hads," I say.

"What the hell was that? Bexley is—"

"Bexley had it coming," I grumble.

She smothers a snort. "Yeah, he did. God, he's such a self-involved, righteous asshole."

And this is why I like Hadley Rexford. Despite being on the cheer team, she doesn't buy into the whole school hierarchy bullshit.

"So that's Ace Jagger, huh?" There's a lilt in her voice that has me frowning. "Oh, come on. We've all heard the news by now. The Jagger brothers have moved into town. Did you meet them already?"

"Something like that," I murmur.

"And you and Ace are what, exactly?"

"Nothing," I deadpan. "We're nothing. I barely know him. Besides, have you seen the guy?"

"Oh, we all saw him." Her brow quirks up. "He's really something."

I glance back to where I left him sprawled out on the sand, clutching his junk. But there's no sign of Ace or Conner.

"It's late," I say, desperate to get off this beach.

"I'll walk with you, if that's okay?"

"Sure, why not." The two of us walk side by side, the soft sand giving way under our feet.

"Bexley will be out for blood once school starts up," she says.

"Something tells me Ace isn't going to worry about a guy like Bexley."

"I still can't believe he did that. And did you see some of his friends?"

We'd all seen them. Tatted, pierced guys who looked like they belonged in some motorcycle club, not at a bonfire party in the Bay.

"What's their story, anyway?"

"You care?" I throw back at her.

Hadley isn't a gossip. She doesn't live for school cliques and classroom politics. She mostly keeps herself to herself. If it wasn't for her being in the cheer team, she'd be invisible.

"No, I don't care," she chuckles, "but you've got to admit, it's the most exciting thing to happen in the Bay since Krystal Gavin had an affair with the vice principal."

"Scandalous," I mock.

Krystal is a girl a couple years older than us. She and the vice principal back then got caught exchanging dirty texts. He was fired, and she was shipped off to her grandparents in Pasadena to finish out senior year there.

"You know, senior year is going to be a hell of a lot more interesting with the Jagger brothers around."

"Don't remind me." I press my lips together.

We hit the path leading away from the beach. There's a row of beach houses lining a quieter section of the Bay. Mom and I live in the end house. It's by far the smallest, but it's ours, and it has the best views of the ocean.

"Well, this is me," I say as we reach the spot where the path splits.

"See you at school Monday?" There's a glimmer of hope in her eyes. Like me, Hadley doesn't fit in. But unlike me, she never has. And I'm not sure which one of us has the better deal.

"I can hardly wait." Sarcasm drips from my words, but it doesn't faze her.

"It's senior year, Remi." She gives me a weak smile. "Who knows, maybe things will be different this year."

I want to believe her, but I learned to stop wishing for things a long time ago.

"Good morning, sweetheart." Mom greets me with a mug of coffee as I pad into the kitchen. "How was the party?"

"You should probably ask Bexley."

"And what is that supposed to mean, young lady?"

"He and Ace got into it." There's no use in lying to her, she'll find out soon enough. The Danforths are one of the most well-known families in Sterling. They live behind us in one of the houses lining what we locals call 'Palm Tree Avenue.' Technically we're not neighbors anymore, but we were for my entire childhood. When my mom and dad separated, Mr and Mrs Danforth insisted on helping us. I think they secretly hoped that, one day, me and Bexley would fall hopelessly in love and ride off into the sunset together. But that was before.

Now the Danforths don't look at me and see their future daughter-in-law. They look at me and see a charity case.

And I fucking hate it.

"They were fighting? I find that hard to believe," she scoffs. "Bexley is such a good boy."

"Bexley got his ass handed to him."

"Oh my... well, boys will be boys, I suppose. There's going to be an adjustment period for everyone."

"Adjustment period... sure thing, Mom," I grumble beneath my breath as I slide onto the wooden bench and watch the waves roll in from the window.

"So, would now be a good time to tell you I invited them over for breakfast?"

"You did what?" I gawk at her, sure I misheard, because there's no way, no fucking way, she invited Ace Jagger and his brothers to breakfast.

At. Our. House.

Guilt fills her expression. "With James away for the weekend, I wanted them to feel at home, you know?"

"Mom, really?" I let out a heavy sigh. "This is our house. After... I just thought you'd be more careful."

"Sweetheart." Mom gives me a sad smile. "I know they're a little rough around the edges, but they haven't had it easy..." She hesitates, staring out at the ocean.

"What happened to them, Mom?" I find myself asking. Because no way can someone be as angry and sadistic as Ace without some kind of deep childhood trauma.

I should know.

"I don't know the whole story, baby. James seemed very distressed when he told me he was taking them in. But I do know that Ace... he found her."

My breath catches. "H-he found her?"

Mom nods. "Overdose. Apparently Maria never really recovered after their dad died. She turned to drugs and alcohol and Ace was forced to grow up overnight to care for his brothers."

"Wow, I didn't know..." My voice trails off. I can't imagine what that must have been like for them. It's no wonder he seems so... damaged.

"So now you know why I want to make them feel as welcome as possible. Sterling Bay is like shark-infested waters." Mom's lips thin. "They're already going to be swimming in uncharted territory without us making it more difficult on them."

"Nice visuals, Mom," I chuckle.

"I'm just saying, it wouldn't hurt for you to try to be nice to them."

She begins plating up a stack of pancakes just as Ace appears at the French doors.

Crap.

I'm still in my oversized holey Rolling Stones t-shirt with untamed bed hair. But before I can make a run for it, Mom has opened the door and invited him in. "Ace, we're so happy you could join us."

"Conner didn't give me much choice."

Just then, Cole and Conner enter our small kitchen.

"Something smells good," Conner rubs his stomach, wearing that easy smile of his.

"Yeah, it does." Ace's eyes darken on me. I grab the glass of orange juice Mom poured me earlier and drink it down.

"How's the hand?" I raise a brow, and he smirks.

"It was worth it."

Asshole.

"Remi told me you were fighting." Mom cuts Ace with her best stare. "That's not going to win you any popularity contests."

"I'm not looking to make friends, Mrs—"

"Sarah. You can call me Sarah. Now come on, make yourselves at home. I made pancakes and bacon, and there's fresh fruit."

"This looks great, Sarah." Conner wastes no time sitting at the table and helping himself to four pancakes. I push the syrup toward him. "Thanks," he replies.

"Nice place." Ace doesn't sit. Instead, he takes an apple and hovers by the door.

"Oh, it isn't much, but it's ours, and the view is worth its weight in gold." Mom makes sure they all have a drink and some food before she finally sits down and loads her own plate.

"Does James go out of town a lot?"

"Your uncle works very hard." Pride glitters in her eyes. "A lot of his clients are based out of Silicon Valley so he has to take the occasional trip here and there."

I glance over at Ace and his eyes immediately snap to mine.

"Remi, sweetheart?" Mom's voice pulls me back to the moment, and I blink over at her.

"Sorry, what?"

"I asked if you could pass me the syrup."

"Oh, sure thing."

"Can I use your bathroom, please?" Ace asks.

"Of course. It's up the stairs, last door on the left."

"Did you take a breath?" I ask Conner, who already has a clean plate.

He grins at me. "I was hungry."

"I can make another batch of pancakes." Mom gets up.

"Mom, you don't have to do—"

"Nonsense." She waves me off. "The boys are our guests. I can't have them leaving here still hungry, Ellen would never let me live it down."

Conner leans back in his chair, throwing an arm behind his head. "What did you think of the party last night?" His lips curve.

"I think you and your brothers need to do a better job at blending in."

"Not likely." He chuckles. Cole sits quietly beside him. He's eaten his food, but he hasn't said a single word.

It's unnerving, but in a totally different way to Ace.

With Ace, what you get is what you see. He's bold and gives zero fucks. He'd eat you alive if you let him get too close. But Cole is a silent threat. Quiet and calculating. He's the kind of predator you would never see coming.

"I'm sure you'll find your feet. Sterling Prep is a good school." Mom catches my eye, and I narrow my gaze at her. She lets out a small sigh. "Okay, so some of the kids can be..."

"Total assholes?"

Conner snickers while Mom stares at me in disappointment. "Remi, that isn't fair."

"Really? You really want to do this now?" I glance at our guests.

"I'm just saying you need to give people a chance, sweetheart. They used to be your friends."

I shoot up and edge toward the door. "I'm going to take a shower."

"I'm sorry," Mom calls after me, but I don't look back. I've already heard enough.

Climbing the stairs two at a time, I reach my bedroom door only to find it ajar, which is weird because I always keep it closed. Old habits die hard.

"Hello?" I say, grabbing the handle and pushing it open.

"Busted." Ace smirks at me. He's sitting on my bed, scoping out the place like he plans to come back tonight and steal all my worldly goods.

"Get. Out." I don't even bother with pleasantries. Ace has a serious issue with boundaries, that much is apparent, and I'm not in the mood to play games.

Of course he completely ignores me.

Standing up, taking the air with him, Ace stalks toward me. Only this time, I stand firm.

Amusement flashes in his frosty stare.

"Why are you here?" I ask.

"Because mommy dearest invited us over. Dumb move, by the way." He drags his bottom lip between his teeth, releasing a small breath. He smells like cigarette smoke, stale liquor, and bad choices.

"She's just being nice."

"More like stupid. She just handed me the keys to your kingdom, and I can't wait to watch you fall."

"Really?" I scoff. "You get girls with those cheap lines?" I edge back, but Ace grabs my arm, anchoring me in place.

"Word of warning: I always get what I want, Princess." His eyes burn into mine, scorching me to the bone.

"I know you're hurting, and I know you probably don't want to be here," I say, "but that doesn't mean you can lash out at everyone around you."

He jerks back as if my words physically slap him. "What did you say?"

"I said, I know you're hurting—"

One second he's standing in front of me, the next he's right in my space, his nose almost touching mine.

He's so overwhelming, I can hardly breathe. But I can't back down.

I won't.

I made a promise to myself a long time ago never to be weak again.

Even if I am in way over my head.

"You don't know the first fucking thing about my life," he grits out, his anger poisoning the air around us.

I don't reply. I can't. Tears burn the backs of my eyes, but I won't cry. Biting the inside of my cheek, I hold his murderous gaze. It's a war of wills, a battle neither of us wants to surrender.

He cracks first though, the corner of his mouth tilting slightly. "Oh, I'm going to enjoy this."

My brows pinch with confusion, but I smash my lips together, refusing to ask what he means.

Ace moves around me to the door, and before I can stop myself, I glance over my shoulder.

He's still there, watching me.

A predator stalking its prey.

"See you soon, Princess." His smile grows.

Wicked.

Arrogant.

Dangerous with a capital D.

And I know senior year just got a hell of a lot more difficult.

CHAPTER FIVE

Ace

When we walk back into James' after what was probably the most enjoyable breakfast of my life, it's like an entirely different house to the one we left earlier. The smashed bottles, empty cans, and cigarette butts no longer litter the floor and every available surface. Instead, everything is back to how it used to be. It's a show home once again.

"What the fuck?" Conner asks, crashing into my back when I stop abruptly, not able to believe what I'm seeing.

"Apparently, money can buy happiness. This is fucking epic."

I nod as Conner sidesteps me and heads toward the kitchen. How the fuck he can still be hungry after the number of pancakes he put away earlier god only knows.

I glance at Cole, who stands silently beside me, taking in the scene.

"Neat," he finally says before pulling his cell out and disappearing toward our staircase to hide.

"You need to spend the weekend making sure you're ready for Monday."

He glances over his shoulder and narrows his eyes. I don't need his words, I know he's telling me to tone it down a notch and let him do his thing. But my brother needs to realize the only reason I'm here right now is for him and Conner, to ensure they have a decent shot at life. There has to be something good that can come out of this. Chances are, I'll still end up in prison, with or without this place. But my brothers? They've now got the world at their feet and enough money around them for all their dreams to come true. And I'm going to make fucking sure they do. Starting with Cole.

"Get changed. Grab a ball. Meet me in the yard."

He rolls his eyes but moves to do exactly as he's told. He's been on the wrong end of my fists more than once to know it's in his best interests to just listen to me.

There may only be a year between me and them, but never doubt that they know who the oldest is around here.

At hearing voices in the kitchen, I come to a stop just out of sight. It wouldn't be out of the question for James to have returned early. He knows all about the party, or at least I'm assuming he does after the twenty-five missed calls and handful of texts demanding that I call him. But I'd like to think he'd have heard us by now and would already be attempting to rip me a new one. If he thinks I'm going to do what I'm told over text, then he really needs to realize who he's invited to live in his house. He might have been absent for most of our lives, but I thought he knew the kind of kids he was dealing with.

"This smells incredible, Martha," Conner says as the sweet smell of more pancakes hits my nose.

"Martha?" Ellen asks, sounding confused. It's a common thing where Conner is concerned. Some random ass shit falls from his mouth at times.

"Yeah, Martha. Like the legend that is Martha Stewart."

Ellen chuckles. "Well, I don't know about that, my dear. But I do my best."

"Your best? You saw this place this morning. That's some mad fucking skills you're rocking to get it whipped back into shape so fast."

"I have my ways."

"Apparently so," I say, marching into the room, gaining both of their attention the second I do. "But what I want to know is why? Why not leave it for us to deal with? For James to find?"

Ellen looks between the two of us, a sympathy in her eyes that I don't want to fucking see.

"It was the right thing to do. I know you're just settling in, trying to find your feet. I expected it." She shrugs and turns back to her batter.

Conner's brow creases, but he soon accepts her words, whereas I'm suspicious as fuck. No one does something nice like that just because. There's always a motive. Always.

"Would you like some pancakes?" Ellen asks, looking at me.

"No. I'm going to help Cole with practice. Maybe

you'll join us when you've finished filling your face," I bark at Conner before marching from the room.

As I walk down the hallway toward the back of the house, Cole's feet thunder down the stairs, and when he catches up to me he's wearing his old Heights jersey and has a ball tucked under his arm.

"You're going to be the best damn player this town has ever fucking seen, you hear me?"

He nods before running ahead to warm himself up.

Part of me expected James to turn up at some point, but by some miracle we got through the rest of the weekend without him reappearing. After helping Cole, we spent the rest of our free time in the pool house on the Xbox James set up for us.

I should really have gone back to the Heights to pick up some work, but the temptation of just hanging out with my brothers before we're forced to spend our days with the preppy stuck-up kids of this town day in, day out, was too strong.

By the time Monday morning rolls around, I'm almost ready to get on my bike and fuck off back to the trailer park. I stand in front of the closet with just a towel wrapped around my waist, staring at the ridiculous uniform I'm expected to wear.

I've never worn a uniform or conformed to anything in my fucking life, and I'm really not happy about suddenly doing so now.

Throwing the towel onto the bed, I drag a pair of boxer briefs up my legs and snap the waistband into place. Blowing out a really fucking frustrated breath, I reach for the clothes. A grey pair of pants that would probably look right at home on someone's ninety-year-old grandad with how high the waist is. A baggy white shirt, a blue tie with the school crest on it, complete with a seahawk in the middle, and a grey fucking blazer with blue trim.

If it weren't for those two motherfuckers down the hall, I would never be seen dead in this shit. I don't give a fuck about the fact I didn't graduate when I should have. It's not like I had any need for the fucking diploma. The gang I've been drug running for doesn't exactly require qualifications. All they want to know is that you can defend yourself and that you're willing to do whatever it takes to get the job done, even if you end up with blood on your hands.

"Fucking hell," I mutter, shoving my feet into the offending fabric and fastening the button around my waist.

This is total bullshit.

After running some wax through my hair, I stand in front of the full-length mirror strapped to the wall in the bathroom and can't help but laugh at myself. I'm like a walking fucking contradiction. I'm wearing preppy rich douche clothes with my tatts showing on my neck and down my forearms where I've rolled my sleeves up. There's absolutely no doubt in my mind that I'm going to stand out like a sore fucking thumb.

A loud crash sounds out throughout the house before footsteps pound up the stairs.

Oh goodie, Uncle James is back to wish us well on our first day.

I pull my bedroom door open with a smirk firmly in place on my lips.

"Is your fucking cell phone broken, boy?"

I make a show of pulling it from my pocket and checking it. "Nope, looks perfectly fine to me. Excuse me, I've got somewhere I need to be."

He stands aside before my shoulder crashes into his as I pass, but his hand grips onto my upper arm. His fingers dig in but not enough to actually cause any pain.

I turn on him. My eyes narrow and my lips purse as I go toe-to-toe with the man over twice my age. He's tall, but I'm taller, and it's painfully obvious to him as he's forced to look up at me.

"Problem, *Uncle?*"

"You will not throw any more parties here. I very clearly told you the rules, and the first thing you did the second my back was turned was break them."

"Huh." I tilt my head to the side as if he's just asked me some important question. "Funny, because I have no idea what you're talking about."

"I won't put up with your defiance, Ace."

"What are you going to do?" I taunt. "Send me back to the Heights?" His face pales. "Nah, I didn't think so. For some fucked-up reason you suddenly want us here."

"I've always—"

"Cole, Conner," I bellow in his face, cutting off whatever he was going to say. "Let's go. We wouldn't want to be late."

They both emerge from their room dressed exactly like me: loose ties, sleeves rolled up, the lot.

A smirk pulls at the corner of my lips.

Sterling Prep is not ready for this.

After making our way from the house and leaving James exactly where he was, Cole and Conner climb into their car, but I decline their offer of a lift and throw my leg over my bike. I have a suspicion that at some point during today I'm going to need to make a swift exit to avoid taking a preppy douche out on day one. I couldn't give a fuck about getting kicked out, but I need my brothers settled before I fuck up too much.

We're some of the last to arrive, clearly not as excited about the first day of the school year as others. Audis, Mercedes, Porches and other insanely expensive cars for teenagers to drive litter the parking lot.

All eyes turn our way as Cole and Conner's clapped-out engine sputters into a space before the rumble of my bike follows.

It's just like Friday night on the beach with everyone looking our way like we're new animals at the zoo.

The second I kill my engine, I light up a blunt, needing something to chill me the fuck out before I drive back the exact same way we just arrived. I thought I was done with classes, homework, and school fucking gossip, but the way we're still holding everyone's attention, I think we're going to be the hot topic of conversation for some time.

The rolling countryside that surrounds the school buildings offers me little reprieve before I turn to where I know all the students are staring at me. I spot the football team in their jerseys. Almost every one has a cheerleader hanging from their shoulders. All eyes are on us, but I don't see the captain anywhere. He's probably still at home, crying over his broken nose and black eyes.

"Come on then. Let's get this show on the road," I call to my brothers after flicking what's left of my blunt to the gravel beneath my feet.

Together the three of us head toward the entrance.

The grand, over-the-top buildings looming before us are a million miles away from those at Sterling Heights, which were mostly dirty grey and covered in graffiti—most of which I'd put there over the years. Everything about that place was dark and smelled of death and destruction. This place, however, is like something you'd see on a documentary visiting old English manor houses. Everything is perfect. The grass looks like it's been cut with fucking scissors, the buildings are a spotless cream brick, and all the giant windows seem to still be intact.

Silence falls around the students as we pass. My skin burns and prickles as their eyes run over every inch of me.

The guys who think they're something all take a step forward like they have a fucking chance if they were to stand up to me, while the girls flick their hair and lick their lips like we might be fucking interested in their rich, stuck-up pussies.

I think not.

Just before we approach the reception building, a dark pair of eyes catches my attention. She's hiding in the shadows, but still I see her.

Our eyes hold for the briefest of moments before she averts her gaze and turns away from me.

You can hide all you like, Princess. I will find you.

A petite lady in a baby pink twin set scrambles from behind her desk as Conner and Cole slam the doors back on themselves to announce our arrival.

"Oh, hello. I'm Miss Peterson..." Her voice is quiet, almost like a mouse as she looks between the three of us like we might be about to squash her with our bare hands. It's totally doable and probably wouldn't take much effort, either.

"Just give us our schedules and we'll be out of your hair, Mrs Peters."

"It-it's Miss Peterson, actually."

"Of course it is." I roll my eyes, dropping my hands to my pant pockets and rocking back on my heels, getting impatient as fuck.

"Principal Vager is waiting to meet the three of you."

"Great. Lead the way."

She hesitates. "You... um... might want to..." She tugs at her sleeves, too scared to actually tell us what to do.

"We're good, thanks."

"O-Okay. T-this way then."

She knocks the giant walnut double doors before a deep voice calls out for us to enter.

His office is massive with an impressive hand-carved desk that gives him a view of the sea in the distance. Bookshelves line the other walls and are filled with vintage looking books.

"Ah, the Jaggers are here," he announces almost sarcastically, and it puts my back up immediately. "We've heard a lot about the three of you."

"All good, I hope."

He scoffs but holds my stare. "I'm sure that you'll soon find yourselves at home here in Sterling Prep."

"You think?"

Both Cole and Conner take a seat at his desk when he gestures for us to do so, but I refrain from following orders. It's best he learns from the get-go that that's not how I do things.

Walking over to one of the bookcases, I run my finger over some of the spines. I stumble upon a collection of Shakespeare.

Pulling one out, I flip it open and discover what I

was expecting. First editions. It says a lot about our dear leader. More fucking money than sense.

"I would just like to run through a few things, a few ground rules if you will, and then we'll go over your schedules and you can begin your new life as Sterling Prep students." His eyes run over the three of us, and I already know what's going to come out of his mouth before he says it.

"First, I think we should discuss how we expect our uniforms to be worn."

CHAPTER SIX

Remi

"Did you see them? I heard Principal Vager almost peed his pants when he called them into his office."

I roll my eyes at the girls behind me. It's all I've heard all morning, and it's only second period.

Did you see them?

Did you check out their tattoos?

What do you think they're doing here?

I heard they're in a gang.

Unsurprisingly, the Jagger brothers are the hot gossip on everyone's lips. Girls are already hatching master plans of seduction, and Bexley and his football friends are no doubt plotting their revenge. And here I am, trying my best to stay under the radar.

The door to AP English flies open, and Mr Triskin

lets out a startled cry. "This English?" Ace steps into the room, and I swear you could hear a pin drop.

"Crap," I mumble under my breath. I was praying we wouldn't share any classes, but I'm hardly surprised.

It's like the universe just loves torturing me.

"You're late." The teacher stands, letting his glass-rimmed gaze look over Ace.

Someone snickers, and I find myself smiling along with them. It is quite amusing. Ace stands at least a foot taller than Mr Triskin. He's shed the school-issue blazer and rolled up the sleeves on his crisp white shirt. Dark, menacing tattoos snake up his neck and run down his arms like twisted vines.

"Holy. Crap. He's fine," Lylah Donovan groans from behind me, and her girlfriends all snicker.

I tune them out. I know all about how strong Ace is, how scary and intimidating he is.

"Something came up," Ace replies around an easy smile. I frown. He seems different. Still as scary as hell but more chilled.

Then it hits me.

He's high.

Jesus, he really does give zero fucks.

"Find a seat, Mr Jagger." Triskin looks ready to blow.

I glance around, relieved to find no empty desks next to me. The last thing I need is to spend the next fifty minutes with Ace within breathing distance. My relief is short-lived though, when he stalks right up to me. I lower my eyes, refusing to play whatever game he has up his sleeve today.

Lylah and her friends can barely contain their excitement. "You can sit next to me," she says in a dulcet tone that makes my skin crawl.

To my satisfaction, Ace doesn't acknowledge her.

"Mr Jagger, we don't have all day." Mr Triskin lets out a frustrated breath.

"You," Ace barks at the kid at the next desk over. "Move."

"I... uh, yeah, sure." He slinks out of the chair to the nearest empty desk. Ace drops down beside me, stretching his leg out to the side so that his boot kisses my desk.

I ignore him, forcing myself to stare ahead. Triskin is talking about this semester's focus, but listening is an impossible task. Ace's eyes burn into the side of my face, intense and suffocating.

"Stop," I breathe, glaring at him.

A smirk tugs at the corner of his mouth. His eyes are half-lidded and cloudy.

Yeah, he's definitely high.

But even in his inebriated state, it's like he sees me better than anyone else in the room.

"Make me." He leans toward me.

I can hear Lylah and her friends whispering, drawing their own conclusions about Ace's interest in me.

Great, just what I don't need.

"Hey, Ace," Lylah whispers seductively.

I watch out the corner of my eye as he glances over his shoulder. "Yeah?" he says.

"You should come hang out with us tonight at Surf's."

"Am I supposed to know what the fuck that is?"

"It's the beachside diner we go to sometimes."

"Will Remi be there?"

I swallow the urge to groan. He isn't making this

easy. It's only the first day of school, and already he's painting a target on my back.

"Remi?" Lylah says with mild disgust. "Why the hell would she be there?"

"I am sitting right here," I hiss.

Of course, Mr Triskin chooses that exact moment to stop talking. "Miss Tanner." He glares at me. "Is there something you'd like to share with the class?"

Lylah snickers.

"No, sir," I say with saccharine enthusiasm, "but I think Lylah had a question for you about the work."

"Bitch," she whisper-coughs.

"Miss Donavan, I'm waiting. Or perhaps you'd like to join me after class?"

"N-no, sir. Everything is fine."

"As I suspected. Now, if it's not too much trouble, how about you try paying attention to the rest of class. Who knows, you might learn something."

Lylah gasps, which is ironic since everyone at Sterling Prep is intelligent enough to breeze into an Ivy League school of their choosing. And if they're not, you can bet that mommy and daddy are paying enough tutors or writing enough checks to make it happen.

The rich and entitled... oh, how it must suck to be them.

Another few minutes pass. Lylah is drilling holes into the back of my head, but it's nothing I haven't already experienced a hundred times before, unlike Ace, who is so still and quiet I wonder if he's asleep with his eyes open. He hasn't written a single thing in his notebook.

I'm doodling Jane Eyre's name when I sense Ace shift closer. "How about we make a deal, Princess?" His voice is a low whisper in my ear. "You take this class for me, and I'll repay you."

My eyes slide to his. He isn't just watching me, he's trying to ensnare me in his trap. I don't want to succumb, but I feel myself falling.

"*Repay* me?" I hiss. "Trust me when I say, you have nothing I could ever want."

He raises a brow, a lazy smirk breaking over his face. "Is that so?" Ace leans closer, his big body shadowing mine. "Because I could've sworn I felt your tight little body hot and needy beneath me the other night after I taught your boyfriend a lesson not to touch what's mine."

People are watching. I feel their licks of curiosity brushing up against me.

"Ace." It's a growl on my lips. "Whatever game you're hoping to pull me into, just stop." *Please*. The word teeters on the tip of my tongue, but I swallow it.

"Mr Jagger, please give Miss Tanner some room."

"But she smells so fucking good," he drawls, causing the room to break out in uneasy laughter.

Anger zips up my spine. The kids of Sterling Prep don't need any more excuses to make my life difficult, and yet, whether he realizes it or not, Ace is handing them all the ammunition they need.

"Mr Jagger." Triskin sounds pissed now, his face burning with indignation. "This is your last warning before I remove you from my class." Silence falls over the room and Ace does nothing more than stand up and saunter toward the door.

"Change of plan," he says to a wide-eyed Triskin. "I'm hungry,"—his eyes lock on mine, setting off a wildfire in my veins— "and this shit is boring."

And just like that, he walks out.

Taking my final shred of dignity with him.

"Remi, wait up." I turn to find Hadley walking toward me. She's in her blue and white cheer outfit, her honey-blonde hair pulled into a high ponytail and her face made up to perfection.

I don't know whether I envy her or despise her.

Her expression falls flat, and I know I've done a crap job of hiding my disdain. "Sorry, I know..."

"It's fine," I say. "I get it." She had no choice to be on the cheer team, the same way I had no choice about being here.

Hadley's smile returns. "I just wanted to make sure you're okay? I heard Ace cornered you in English."

"News sure travels fast." It was only lunch.

"They're the talk of the school. Conner is in my math class. He seems funny. Although he did do this thing with a pencil that Mr Faiman did not appreciate."

The hallway grows restless, everyone pointing and staring at something. I crane my neck around Hadley and let out a groan. Bexley and the football team are making their grand entrance. Kids start calling out, cheering on their beloved Seahawks.

"Get 'em good, Bex," someone yells, inciting another round of raucous cheers.

Bexley's face is a mess. There's tape across his nose and dark purple bruising around both eyes. But in his blue and white jersey, it only makes him look the part.

"Holy shit, he looks ready to kill."

Bexley Danforth is your all-American guy, a trust

fund baby born into a world of privilege and power. He doesn't have to work for a single thing; it all lands right at his feet, gift-wrapped with a bow. As if that isn't enough, the football gods themselves have blessed him with a record-breaking throwing arm. He's one of the best quarterbacks in the state.

And he's looking at me like I kicked his favorite puppy.

"Hads, Remi," he greets us as his teammates spill around him.

"Hey, Bex," Hadley says. "I'll leave you two to talk."

I shoot her a look that says, 'please don't', but she's already gone, disappearing into the sea of kids all headed to lunch.

"Does it hurt?" I ask him.

"Not as much as it'll hurt Jagger when we get him back," he grinds out.

"Are you sure that's a good idea? Going after Ace, I mean."

Bexley releases a frustrated breath, placing a hand at the locker beside my head. I know what he's doing; he's giving me no chance of escape.

Asshole.

"Don't tell me you like the guy? He's a piece of shit Heighter that doesn't belong here."

"Wow, you really are a judgmental prick."

"Remi, come on. The guy broke my nose and for what? To make his mark? Please." He scoffs. "He's a fucking liability. I can't believe they let him transfer here."

I press my lips together in defiance. It's not that I want to defend Ace, but I don't want to side with Bexley, either. That ship has long sailed.

As far as I'm concerned, they can both go to hell.

"All I'm saying is, do you really want to start a war with someone like Ace Jagger?"

Bexley's expression darkens. "He came to *my* party and broke *my* fucking nose. This is Seahawk territory, and he'll get what's coming to him."

And that is precisely why I no longer have a membership for the Bexley Danforth fan club. He's everything that's wrong with this world, and it makes me sick.

He makes me sick.

"Did you forget I no longer hold the required qualifications to be in your little club? Or are we just going to pretend that isn't an issue?" I bite back, so over his pretentious bullshit.

"Come on, Remi, you know it's not even like that." He runs a hand down his face.

"Yeah? Try telling that to Michaela and her band of bitches."

"You know I love it when you get feisty." He inches closer, his expression softening. "Go out with me. Just say yes. Come on," his voice is low and husky, "you must have thought about it. It'd drive Michaela crazy."

My heart sinks. Bexley has been after me for a while now, but not because he wants me. No, that would be too simple. He wants me because I don't want him.

I never have.

I just want my friend back. I want the Bexley who used to try and teach me to surf for hours in the summer. The Bexley who held me when my dad left, who let me sleep in his bed because I hated my mom's boyfriend and couldn't stand to be under the same roof as him.

I miss *that* Bexley.

But that boy is gone, replaced with a young man who looks at me and no longer sees his friend but a challenge.

A prize to be won.

"You're thinking about it, aren't you?" Hope glitters in his baby blue eyes.

"Actually," I say coolly, "I'm thinking about what happened to the boy I used to know. See you around, Bex." I shoulder past him, and don't look back.

The rest of the day passes without any drama. I heard Ace took off after leaving Triskin's class—someone saw his bike speeding out of the parking lot. He'll never last at Sterling Prep, but then, maybe he never planned on it.

I still can't figure out why James is so set on them coming here. They've spent their entire life in the Heights. Asking them to forget their roots and play nice with a school full of rich kids seems unfair... or completely stupid.

Whatever.

I have bigger things to think about, like the text I got earlier from my sorry excuse for a sperm donor.

Throwing some books in my locker, I slam it shut and make my way outside. I walked to school today. It takes me about thirty minutes along the coastal path, but I enjoy the fresh air, and it means I don't have to listen to Mom try and coach me on how to *fit in*. The path takes me parallel with the football field, where the team is busy practicing. I spot Bexley and a few of the other seniors. It looks like they're giving shit to some of the new recruits.

Oh crap.

My eyes widen at the sight of Cole Jagger going toe-to-toe with Hayden, Bexley's best friend and the star running back for the team. Even from where I'm standing, I can feel the hatred sizzling between them. Cole is an outsider, and despite the blue and white jersey and standard issue shoulder pads he's wearing, there's no disguising that he's different.

"Jagger," the coach yells, and the tension evaporates.

I let out the breath caught in my throat.

First Ace going up against Bexley, and now Cole going up against Hayden. This isn't good. But it's not my problem.

My cell phone dings, and I dig it out of my pocket.

Dad: Please, Remi. It's just dinner.

Me: But it's not just dinner. It's dinner with them. With her.

Dad: It's your first day of senior year. I'd like to hear how it went.

Me: It was fine.

Dad: Please don't make this any harder than it needs to be. Dinner at Surf's at six-thirty or I'll call your mom.

Bastard. He knows she's my weak spot.

Me: I hate you.

Dad: I know. See you at six-thirty. Don't be late.

His words coil around my heart and squeeze, turning my blood to molten lava. The last thing I want to do is have dinner with him, but every few months, he does this: demands I spend time with him. Only spending time together is never just him and me.

It's me and them.

His family.

The one he chose instead of me and mom.

Della, his wife. Farrow, his step-son. Pacey, their son, and Michaela Fulton, his step-daughter.

My step-sister.

And my ex-best friend.

CHAPTER SEVEN

Ace

Sterling Prep is exactly as I'm expecting it to be—full of self-righteous, privileged assholes. I turn up to my math class late, thanks to Principal Vager and his long-winded way of laying down the law to the three of us. Does he really expect us to follow any rule he puts in place? Rules are basically challenges to guys like us. Tell us no and we only work harder to prove some motherfucker wrong.

The teacher is expecting me and immediately directs me to my seat before continuing with whatever the fuck he's explaining to the class. I don't think he realizes that from the second I entered, all attention left him in favor of following my every move across the room.

As I make my way to the back, the whispered gossip starts to fill my ears.

Did you hear that he's killed someone?

Shot between the eyes.

He dragged his brothers with him into a gang.

He killed his own mother.

The rumor mill is already getting out of hand, although the worse it gets only works to my advantage, making people even more terrified of me. Something I'm more than happy with, especially if it means they keep their distance. I have zero intention of befriending any of these assholes. I just need to do my time and get out as soon as possible. Prison would have been fucking easier than this shithole.

Falling down onto my seat, I don't get a chance to pull anything from my bag, even if I had any intention of doing so, because someone slides over to me.

"You must be Ace Jagger. I've heard so much about you," a blonde wrapped in a cheer uniform almost purrs as she all but forces herself onto my lap.

I stare at her in disbelief as she openly checks me out and thrusts her tits in my face. "I'm sorry, can I help you with something?" I grunt, lifting her from my lap and depositing her back on her feet.

"I just wanted to introduce myself I'm M—"

"Not interested."

She looks me up and down. I think she's expecting me to tell her that I'm joking.

I'm really fucking not.

A preppy, wannabe cheerleader really isn't my type.

After dismissing her, she skulks back to her seat, but at no point do I lose her attention, nor do the rumors about me cease. By the time the teacher dismisses us, I've just about had my fill of bullshit, so the last thing I need is to hear some more fucking lies about me and my brothers.

I heard he had a gun on Friday night. He was going to kill Bexley.

I wait until we're out of the room before grabbing the gossiping motherfucker by the collar and pinning him up against the wall. A few gasps sound out from the students around us, but no one dares to do anything to stop me.

"You want to say that to my face?" I ask as the guy pales and trembles beneath my hold.

"I-I'm sorry, man. It was just what I heard," he whimpers like a little pussy.

I lean forward, getting right in his face. My breath races over his skin, and his eyes fill with tears.

"So you weren't there?" I ask. My voice is calm, cold. Exactly as I like it. It unnerves my victims, and I like surprising them when they least expect it. It's the best part of something like this.

"N-No. M-My friend said..."

"Your friend's a bullshitter."

"O-okay."

As I tighten my hold on him, his eyes widen in fear. "Think about this the next time you open your mouth." I throw him to the ground, and he goes down like a sack of shit.

Standing over his body as he tries to scramble away, a smirk pulls at my lips. "If you want to know the truth, I had a knife, not a gun. And unless you want to be on the other end of it next time, I strongly advise you stay the fuck out of my way."

He visibly shakes as I step away and in the direction of the nearest doors. Digging the spare key for my brothers' car from my pocket, I cross the parking lot and jump inside. I want to leave. The temptation is strong, but I can't. Not yet.

I pull a blunt from the glove compartment and light up. The tension starts to leave me almost instantly, and I sink back into the seat with the memory of her shocked eyes staring at me from a distance earlier.

My thoughts turn to home, but as much as I might want to be back there, I know this place can offer Cole and Conner so much more. Cole has a real chance at a football career if he gets a starting position with the Seahawks. He's good enough, and if James has pulled some strings like he says he has then he should have a solid chance.

Conner has never said much about his future. I think, like me, he never even considered anything outside of our circles in the Heights. We were born into that world. It was an unspoken rule that we'd just continue with that life. He's clever though, more so than Cole and I, and I know he has a bright future ahead of him if he can just make it through this year without fucking it up.

By the time I've smoked my blunt, the second class of the day has long started. But I figure there's no time like the present to meet my next teacher, and am I glad I do when I find none other than Remi sitting quietly in the center of the room.

I may not have made it the entire way through AP English, but I learned enough to know that I'm getting to her.

It was obvious I was affecting her when I pinned her up against the wall in her bedroom on Saturday morning, but from the second she reluctantly glanced at me, I watched her eyes darken with interest.

It seems Miss Tanner is going to make my life easy for me. Give it a few more days and she'll be begging for me to break her.

After marching out of that fucking place, I spend the rest of the day riding around town and ignoring texts from Donny. He wants me to check in, and I just want some fucking space, a chance to catch my breath after the last few days.

I've got nowhere to go. The idea of sitting back in a classroom listening to my dear new classmates gossiping about me doesn't really fill me with joy, and I can't go home. I've no doubt my absence has already been reported, and James is once again on the warpath.

What the fuck is he really going to do about it? Send us back where we came from? I doubt it. He clearly wants us here for a reason. And I'm going to find out. Starting with getting to his precious Remi.

I don't have any intentions of accepting the invitation from the annoying bitch who was giving Remi hell in English earlier, but a couple of hours after school is finished for the day, I find myself pulling up to a seafront parking lot.

There are Sterling Prep kids everywhere. They might be out of uniform now, but I can spot their arrogance a mile off. Climbing from my bike, I head over to the row of storefronts looking out over the sea, just on the off chance that she might be here. After the way the girl was talking to her, I doubt Remi accepted her invitation either.

To my surprise, as I walk toward the surf shack the first person I spot at the window seat is her. She stares down at her still full plate with her shoulders sagged in defeat and ignoring everyone around her. Her discomfort is palpable. I glance at the others around the table. There's an older couple but the woman isn't Sarah, two younger kids, and then my eyes land on someone familiar.

Her.

And she's still wearing the fucking cheer kit. She laughs at the man sitting opposite her, all the while playing with the children who are giggling beside her. Everything about her is the polar opposite to Remi.

I look away before I'm caught staring and give her the wrong idea. If I wanted her then I could have had her this morning. But my eyes soon find their way back to Remi, trying to figure out why she's so fucking miserable while everyone around her laughs and jokes.

It's as if she can feel my stare, because not five seconds later, she looks up. Our eyes connect for the briefest moment, long enough for me to register the shock in hers, before she looks back down again.

I take that as my cue and fuck off, but I very quickly decide this isn't going to be the last time I see her today.

Instead of going back to my uncle's, I take the short journey to the house by the beach that Remi shares with her Mom. There aren't any lights on when I pass, so after parking a little down the street in the hope I'm not spotted, I walk back toward the modest house. Its size is nothing in comparison to James', and it makes me wonder how Sarah can afford for her to attend Sterling Prep.

I don't bother with the front door, it'll only cause suspicion if any of the neighbors see, so instead I go straight to the back. The door is locked, but when I stand back and try to figure out how to get inside, I find an open window with a trellis leading up to it. I'm pretty sure it's her bedroom window, too.

I smile to myself. It's almost like she's giving me an open invitation.

After giving my makeshift ladder a tug to ensure I'm not going to go crashing back to the ground halfway up, I start to climb. I'm proved right when I poke my head around the frame and find her purple bedroom inside.

Bingo.

Making quick work of throwing my leg over the ledge, I let myself in. Her scent assaults me immediately, and my mouth waters with my need to know if she tastes quite as sweet.

I look around her space, much like I did the other day. She's got a couple of photographs of her and Sarah at the beach. There's one of another girl, both of them in their Sterling Prep uniforms. I make note of her face, just in case I can make use of her at some point. She obviously means something to Remi for her to frame the photograph. I find no evidence of any of the people she was with tonight. Clearly none of them are important in her life.

I flick through her school books that are sitting on the side. Noticing that we share more than just AP English, I pull my cell out and take a few photographs of the shit I missed today. Getting bored, I pull a few of her drawers open and rifle through her belongings like the fucking creep that I am, but aside from her panties, I don't find anything of any excitement.

It must be almost an hour later when the front door slams shut and footsteps thunder up the stairs. I push myself to the edge of her bed and wait to see if it's her or Sarah. I really fucking hope it's the former.

My heart begins to race as the steps get closer. Time seems to slow to almost a stop as I stare at the door, willing her to walk through. I'm desperate to hear her shriek of surprise once again. To see the widening of her eyes and the fear that creeps into them.

Fuck.

I need to watch as her chest heaves when I'm too close to her.

She's too fucking tempting for her own good.

Just like I was hoping for, the handle twists and the door pushes open before she emerges. I'm given a few seconds to take her in, as she doesn't notice me immediately.

Slamming the door behind her, Remi falls back against it. Her hands come up to cover her face as a sob erupts from her throat.

I stand, fighting my need to announce my presence, but her bed betrays me and squeaks when I shift. Her hands fly from her face, her eyes red-rimmed, full of tears and utterly terrified as she screams bloody murder.

"Whoa," I cry, racing over and pressing my palm down over her lips to stop her alerting anyone who could be within earshot.

Her eyes remain wide, but her body relaxes slightly when she registers that it's me.

Interesting. Who else did she think it would be?

Tears continue to stream from her eyes and splash

onto my hand. I watch as they drop, too intrigued to know what, or who, put them there.

Something crackles between us as we stare at each other, but at no point do I attempt to remove my hand.

That is until her lips part and she sinks her teeth into my middle finger.

"Fucking bitch," I grunt, pulling it away and inspecting the damage.

"Get the hell out." Her voice is weak, and I've no idea if that's because she's too emotionally exhausted to deal with me or because she doesn't really mean it.

Either works in my favor right now.

"Why are you crying?

"None of your business." She pushes from the door and puts some space between us. She can try all she likes, but her room isn't all that big, so she'll have a hard job escaping me. Especially when I know I can get to the door before her.

"Who were you having dinner with?"

"None of your goddamn business. You need to leave. If Mom finds you here, she'll—"

"She'll what? Tell me exactly what you think she's capable of." I take a step toward her and she takes one back, only she doesn't get very far because she's backed herself into a corner. Perfect.

"W-what do you want?"

"I thought I made it clear earlier."

She swallows and draws my eyes down to her long, slender neck. I bite down on my bottom lip as I close the final bit of space between us.

I stalk towards her and place my palms against the wall on either side of her head, caging her in.

"The only thing you made clear was that you don't

give a shit about anything. That stunt you pulled didn't impress anyone."

"That wasn't a stunt, Princess. I don't set out to impress anyone. Like me, hate me, I really don't give a shit."

"That's a shame, because I really fucking hate you."

CHAPTER EIGHT

Remi

Ace stares at me, indifference glittering in his eyes.

He means it.

He really doesn't care.

The things people say about him, what they whisper when he walks past them down the hall, how they point and stare like he's an exhibit at the zoo.

I envy him.

I tell myself I don't care, that their opinions of me mean nothing, but it's a bitter pill to swallow when I used to *be* them.

Every day, I tell myself Michaela is welcome to my father and his cheating scumbag ways, but I'm the daughter left to watch from the sidelines while they play happy families.

Every second of every minute, I tell myself none of it matters, but I know it's a lie.

"You're saying one thing, Princess..." He leans in, running his nose along my jaw. A shiver works through my body. God, why does he affect me so much? *Perhaps it's because you've never been touched like this.*

"But your body is telling me something different."

"I have no idea what you're talking about." My voice quivers, betraying me. Ace must hear it, because a smirk graces his devastatingly rugged face.

"I bet right now," he breathes the words over my lips, "if I touch you right here..." His hand skates to the apex of my thighs. Thank god I'm wearing jean shorts, "you'd be wet for me."

"You can't say stuff like that to me," I grit out.

His brow quirks up. "No? Wouldn't your boyfriend like it? How is good old Bexley, by the way?"

"He's not my boyfriend."

"What a shame."

"Yeah, and why's that?"

"Because," he slides his hand up the side of my neck, letting his thumb brush over my pulse point, "I was really hoping to get under his skin when I mark his girl."

"What the—"

Ace's mouth crashes down on mine, hard and demanding. His tongue invades me, licking furiously at my own. I fight against his grip, trying to push him off, but I'm completely at his mercy, trapped between the wall and his overpowering body.

His teeth rake my tongue as he slides his hand around my throat, holding me in place. It shouldn't feel as good as it does, but the harder he kisses me, the more

I drown in the sensations crashing over me. Drown in *him*.

Before I know it, I'm no longer fighting him, I'm submitting. My hands curl into his t-shirt, twisting and pulling him closer, *needing* him closer. I've been kissed before but nothing like this.

Never like this.

It's hot and frenzied, and the way Ace consumes me leaves little room for me to think. It's like he's turned a switch and all of the emotions, the hatred and bitterness festering inside me, just melt away.

And I want more.

God, I want more.

I start kissing him back, pressing up on my toes to meet him kiss for kiss. He chuckles against my mouth, letting me know he senses the change in me. But I don't care. This feeling of complete abandon is addictive.

"I thought you'd make me work a little harder to get a taste of this." Ace's hands glide down my spine and grab my ass, hiking me up against his body. He's rock hard at my stomach, sending a bolt of lust shooting through me.

Fuck, what am I doing?

"Stop," I cry suddenly, slamming my hands into his chest. "Just stop."

Ace lifts his head, staring at me through hooded eyes. "You think you get to call the shots here?"

His hand returns to my neck, his grip a little tighter—not enough to hurt me, but enough to make my pulse spike.

"You marked me, Princess." He holds up his finger, a bead of dried blood crusted over my teeth marks. "So I think it's only fair I get to mark you."

Ace rips the neckline of my T-shirt down and licks the curve of my breast. A reluctant moan spills from my lips, but god, it feels good. My fingers dive into his hair to yank him away. This needs to stop. It's wrong.

He's wrong.

"Ace, st—" It comes out a garbled moan as he bites down hard, soothing the sting with his tongue.

"Now we're even," he says, backing away, dragging his thumb across his bottom lip as if he's savoring every last taste.

I glance down at the little crescent-shaped teeth marks, freckled with red and purple where the blood has rushed to the surface. "You bit me," I say with utter disbelief, as if the last few minutes didn't happen.

"You bit me first, princess."

"You need to go," I bark, slipping out from between him and the wall. "Now."

"That's how you want to play it?" Amusement glitters in his eyes.

"Ace, just go, please."

He holds up his hands. "Fine, but this isn't over."

I keep a safe distance as he grabs the door handle. "This... me and you," he waggles a finger between us, "it's only a matter of time."

"Arrogant much?"

"Deny it all you want, but you felt that just now. You let me kiss you, let me brand you with my teeth."

My body trembles with anger because he's right. He's fucking right. I did let him kiss me.

I *wanted* him to kiss me.

Because not only does Ace Jagger terrify me, he also intrigues me, not to mention the fact that he's even more of an outsider at Sterling Prep than I am.

Like it or not, Ace reaches something inside me.

Which is exactly why I can't let him pull me into whatever *this* is.

"Goodbye, Ace," I say calmly. "Don't let the door hit you on the way out."

A sly grin lifts the corner of his mouth. "Oh, you and me, Princess... we're going to have some fun."

I watch him slip into the hall, a strange feeling washing over me. I want to believe it's outrage; regret and shame at what just happened between us.

Ace Jagger is a menace, and I hate him.

I do.

But as I run my fingers over the fresh bite mark on my chest, it doesn't feel like hate at all.

Thankfully, my school issue shirt covers the bite mark. It might be hidden, but it's branded on my soul.

Ace Jagger bit me.

He really is as crazy as some of the rumors flying around school say. Still, there's a tiny part of me that flushes every time I think about the way he just took control and commanded my body. It should freak me the hell out—*he* should freak me the hell out—but I can't forget how weightless it made me feel.

How free.

I've never let anyone touch me the way Ace touched me, not since *him*.

I shudder, locking the memories away. He doesn't have power over me anymore. I fight day in, day out, to make sure of it. But it's exhausting, dragging around the sins of your past with you.

Ace made it all go away.

I'm more messed up than I thought, if Ace's rough treatment of me actually made me feel... good.

I suppress another shudder. I need to stay out of his way, because something tells me he'd chew me up and spit me out before I even knew what was happening.

Mom is sitting in wait downstairs. "So," she fights a smile as I enter the kitchen. "How was it?"

"How was what?" I reply, making a beeline for the coffee maker.

"Really?" Her brow lifts.

"Fine. I survived."

"Remi..." Sadness creeps into her expression. "It's senior year, baby. Don't you think it's time to put all that behind you? Make some new friends, rekindle friendships with old ones... go on a date or two, maybe?"

Coffee poured, I sit down at the table. "Do you have any idea what it's like for me there?"

"Sweetheart, it's a good school. One of the best in—"

"State. Yeah, I know that, Mom. But I'm not one of them anymore." Michaela made sure of that after she stole my life.

At first, I thought getting a new step-sister would be fun. I mean, Mom and Dad's separation sucked, but I was getting a sister. Until I walked into Surf's and saw Michaela sitting there with my dad's arm slung around her shoulder.

That day, I gained a step-sister and lost my best friend.

"She knew, Mom," I say, swallowing down the betrayal.

It still hurts even after five years. "All along she knew and never said a word. Then she acted like our friendship meant nothing." Pain rages inside me, but I refuse to let it out. My hands tremble as I grip the mug of coffee tighter.

Michaela stole everything from me, and she did it with a saccharine smile and cold heart.

"It's been five years, Remi. You need to let it go. I don't want you to look back one day and see how much time you wasted being angry and bitter." Her smile weakens. "I know things were hard, and I know I wasn't always the mom you needed, but I'm trying, baby. I am."

"I know, Mom. I just can't pretend to be someone I'm not."

She gets up and comes over to me, placing her hand against my cheek. "I'm not asking you to be someone you're not, Remi. All I'm asking is that you embrace senior year. Make new friends. Try new things. You're almost eighteen; it's time to start living, sweetheart."

I offer her a small nod. It's the best I can do. She doesn't get it. How could she when she doesn't know the whole story?

"I should probably get a move on, James will be here any minute." Mom smooths her hair down and grabs her purse off the counter.

James seems to genuinely care about my mom, and I'm pleased for them. I am. But I can't help but wonder if she feels the same or if she's out to prove something.

"Oh, and sweetheart," she says as she reaches the door, "the boys offered to give you a ride this morning, isn't that sweet of them?"

"Boys?" I choke out.

"Yes, Conner and Cole. I might have let it slip that you walked to school yesterday."

"Mom," I grumble, unimpressed at her attempt to railroad me.

"I know they're a little rough around the edges, Remi, but they're James' nephews and I'd really like for us all to try and get along."

"I enjoy the walk, and it's such a beautiful—" Wind howls at the French doors, and Mom shoots me a victorious smile.

"Looks like a storm is blowing in. Gotta run, love you." She blows me a kiss before spinning on her heel and disappearing into the hall, but I hear her final words loud and clear.

"Tell the boys I said hello."

"Princess, your chariot awaits." Conner grins as I close the door behind me. He's leaning against the rust bucket of a car he and his brother share. Cole hasn't bothered to get out, but I'm hardly surprised.

I let out a groan, but the sound of rain hitting the asphalt drowns it out. Pulling up my hoodie, I jog over to the car. Conner yanks open the back door and I slide inside.

"Hey," I greet Cole.

"Hey."

Okay then.

Conner climbs inside, shaking out his hair and sending water droplets flying everywhere. "We wondered if you'd show."

"Didn't have much choice, did I?" I say.

"You don't drive?"

"I got my license, I just don't have a car yet." It's an expense we don't need right now, and no way am I going to accept one from my dad.

"Well, she isn't much," Conner runs his hands around the cracked leather steering wheel, "but she's ours, and she's never let us down yet." He fires up the engine and the thing splutters to life, a cloud of black smoke rising into the air.

"Good to know." I stare out of the window, watching the storm lash down over the Bay, as Conner takes the coastal road to school.

Sterling Bay is such a cliché, a quintessential Californian coastal town, with its palm tree-lined streets and beautiful mix of Spanish colonial, Art Deco, and beach houses. But it's a cutthroat community wrapped up in a pretty bow. Wealth, money, and power are the driving forces behind some of the most influential families in the state.

I try to imagine what Conner and Cole must see. Do they see a rich man's paradise or something else entirely?

Maybe they don't care.

Ace sure as hell doesn't seem to.

Sterling Prep looms up ahead. Back in sixth grade, I'd been so excited to start here. Me and Michaela were going to take on the world together. Then everything changed.

She changed.

And as a result of her betrayal and my father's treachery, somewhere along the way, I changed too.

"So where's good to get fucked up in this place?" Conner asks as he pulls into the parking lot. "Ace said something about Shark's?"

"You mean Surf's?" Jealousy licks my insides. Did he go there and meet Lylah after all?

"Yeah, that's the one. What's the deal?"

"It's just a diner down by the beach, but they have pool tables and some arcade games. And they have a surf rental shop. A lot of the kids from school hang out down there."

"But not you?" He cuts the engine and twists around to face me.

"It's not really my scene," I say, grabbing the door handle. "Thanks for the ride. I'll catch you later."

"Don't be a stranger, Princess," he says as I climb out. I hate the nickname, but it sounds nowhere near as dirty on his tongue.

I swing my bag over my shoulder and hurry toward the building. The rain is lifting, thank god, so hopefully I can walk home later without getting soaked.

I'm almost across the parking lot when a car skids into a bay, sending a gigantic spray of water into the air and right. Over. Me.

"Fuck," I hiss, my uniform sticking to my body like a second skin. Fat droplets of water drip from my hair and down my face.

"Oh my god, Remi," a familiar voice says. "I totally didn't see you there."

I turn slowly to meet Michaela's wicked smirk. "You didn't...." I stop myself. "Of course you didn't."

"You really should go get dried off. Poor drowned rat is *so* last season."

Anger wells inside me, making tears burn the backs of my eyes. I smash my lips together, biting the inside of my cheek to stop myself from screaming... or trying to rip her pretty, vicious head off her shoulders.

Michaela and her friends step around me, their laughter lingering long after they've reached the building.

"What the fuck, Princess?" Conner jogs over to me, barely able to contain his amusement.

"Just go away," I snap.

"Come on, Remi, I think—"

"Just go!" My eyes widen. "Please."

I hate that he sees me like this, but when I turn around and start toward the building, I realize he isn't the only one watching.

Everyone is.

CHAPTER NINE

Ace

Remi's eyes are wide and full of unshed tears as she looks around the parking lot. Water drips from her hair and uniform. Her shirt is wet through and clings to her body in the most incredible way, showing off her pink bra beneath.

Wrapping her blazer around herself, she sets off to the sound of catcalls and wolf whistles. Anger burns within me that anyone else has the audacity to hurt her.

I glance around the crowd before my eyes land on the cheerleaders. And who should be front and center but the blonde she was with last night. My eyes narrow in her direction, but she's too busy mocking Remi and gesturing to the giant ass puddle she drove through in order to drench her.

That bitch needs to be taught a fucking lesson.

With everyone distracted, I take off running in the

direction Remi disappeared in. I step into the hallway just as the door to the girls' locker room shuts.

Bingo.

As I slam the door back against the wall, every set of eyes turns on me.

"Out," I bark.

Girls in varying arrays of dress scream, all running for the door once they've covered themselves up.

Good.

At least some got the message that I'm not to be messed with.

Stalking through the now empty space, I look for evidence of where she's hiding. A hand dryer starts up and I follow the sound. I come to a stop in the doorway and find a crying Remi standing in her pink bra, holding her shirt under the hand dryer.

I lean my hip against the doorframe and watch her for a few moments. Her hair has been pulled over one shoulder, the milky skin of her back on full display until it's cut off at the smallest part of her waist by her skirt. Unlike most of the other girls here, it's not rolled up to expose as much skin as possible, and while I'm happy that she's not showing every other guy more of her body, right now I can't help wishing that it was.

I've had a taste of her now, and I only want more.

I remember how compliant, how eager she was beneath my hands last night. Fuck, my cock stirs just remembering the little moans that rumbled at the back of her throat as I kissed her. I can only imagine the noises she might make when I push her over the edge.

Remi still has no idea that I'm here—she's too lost in her misery. As much as I want to stand here and just watch, my need to touch her gets the better of me.

She startles the second I press the length of my body against her back, her scream filling the room. But it soon falters when she registers that it's me.

"It's okay, Princess. It's just me." I'm sure to most people, having me sneak up behind them and whisper in their ear would be anything but okay. I take pride in my ability to strike when people least expect it. It earned me somewhat of a reputation back in the Heights.

My hands land on her waist and she trembles beneath them. "They're going to pay for that, Princess."

She sniffles. "It-it's okay. I'm used to it."

Every muscle in my body tenses.

"Bullshit. You shouldn't have to get used to that kind of treatment."

She tries to move away, but my fingers grip her waist tighter to keep her in place.

"It's just Michaela trying to be the Queen Bee, trying to impress her pathetic friends." She shrugs like it's no big deal.

She's wrong.

It's a really big fucking deal.

Reaching out, I take her shirt from her hands and place it on the basins beside us.

"Ace, what are you—?"

A gasp falls from her lips as I spin her and press her back up against the cold tiles.

Her tears have stopped, thank fuck. I'm not sure I could cope with seeing her crying again because of someone else.

If I make her cry, then that's a whole other ballgame.

I close the space between us. My eyes drop from hers in favor of the bite mark I left behind last night. My semi hard cock goes full mast at the sight of my brand on her pale skin.

"Ace?" she whispers, her voice unsure and weak.

Those motherfuckers shouldn't have the power to make her feel less than she is.

Reaching out, I run my fingertip over the bruise. Her skin breaks out in goosebumps as she whimpers.

Fuck.

Flattening my hand against her chest, I run it up to her neck and wrap my fingers around gently.

I'm the only one who holds the power to break her, and she needs to learn that.

Those cunts out there are nothing. Fucking nothing compared to me.

To what I'm capable of.

"You don't need to worry about Michaela. I'll take care of her."

"N-no. I don't want you fighting my battles for me."

"That's the thing though, Princess." My eyes bounce between hers, trying to figure out if she understands the strength behind what I'm about to say. "It's not just your battle now. They hurt you, then they hurt me. And no motherfucker hurts me."

Her lips part as if she's going to argue, and I use it to my advantage.

I crash my lips to hers and plunge my tongue into her mouth, searching hers out and encouraging her to join me.

It takes her all of two seconds before she sags against me and her tongue tangles with mine. My left hand squeezes her throat gently, and it's the final push she needs to lose control. She sucks my tongue into her mouth before gently biting down and making me groan.

So that's how it's going to be between us, is it?

My other hand skims up her waist until I take her breast in my palm. She moans, thrusting them forward, and I'm powerless but to give in to her silent demands. Slipping the cup down, I pinch her already hard nipple between my thumb and forefinger.

Her entire body tenses as the sensation races through her.

"Good?" I mumble against her jaw as I kiss across her soft skin. Her scent drives me fucking crazy to the point that I'm not sure I'm ever going to get what I need from her.

Sucking on the sensitive skin beneath her ear, I bite down gently.

"Ace," she cries, her head falling back against the wall with a thud.

The bell rings out, signaling the start of school.

"Fuck. Ace. We can't do this."

She attempts to push my hands from her body, but I'm having none of it. I've only just fucking started.

"Says who? We've got twenty minutes before our first class. Live on the wild side."

"I don't know what that is," she admits so quietly that I'm not sure if I'm meant to hear it or not.

"Let me show you."

I kiss down her neck before grazing her collarbone with my teeth.

"Fuck," she moans, spurring me on.

Slipping down her other bra cup, I stare down at her almost bare breasts. My mouth waters, and, before I even have a chance to think about it, my lips wrap around one perfectly pink nipple and I suck. Hard.

"Oh fuck. Fuck. Fuck. *Fuck.*" Her head bangs with

each word and I smile around the dusky bud, knowing exactly how much power I have right now.

I could take anything, and I've no doubt she'd allow it to happen. She's like fucking putty in my hands. Just like I knew she would be. I saw that glint in her eye that first night at James', and it seems I wasn't wrong.

She might think she's weak, running away from Michaela and her bunch of bitches, but she's wrong. This girl has the power to get whatever it is she wants. She just needs to learn to stand up for herself.

I kiss across to the other side as her fingers slide into my hair and grip tightly. The pinch of pain is exactly what I need. For someone who wanted me to stop only a few moments ago, she sure seems keen to continue all of a sudden.

Finding the bare skin of her thigh, I run my hand up the inside. "Oh god," she whimpers as I draw closer to where she needs me.

Her heat is incredible, and the desire to find out just how tight she might be as I slide into her has my cock weeping.

It's been too fucking long since I saw some action. I've had offers—more than I can count from the rich sluts who attend this school. But one look at Remi the day we moved here, and I knew no one else could come close to giving me what I needed.

"Are you wet for me, Princess?"

A groan is all I get in response.

"Answer me, or I'll stop." I'm pretty sure it's an empty threat, because I'm not sure I could stop right now even if Principal Vager walked in and caught us. I'd have to kill the motherfucker after for watching my girl fall apart, mind you.

My girl.

What the fuck, Jagger?

"Yes. Yes," she cries. "Yes, Ace. Please."

Her words are my undoing. Reaching up, I rip her panties from her body, the sound of the fabric tearing filling the room. I let them fall to the floor, and Remi gasps, But to my surprise, she doesn't say anything. Instead, she shocks the fuck out of me by parting her feet a little.

Standing to full height once again, I rest my forearm against the wall beside her head and look into her eyes. I want to see them dark with lust, full of hunger for me as I make her fall apart. As I show her exactly who she belongs to. Who owns her body.

Her lips are parted as her increased breaths race past. Her eyes are almost black with desire and her cheeks rosy red.

She looks fucking incredible.

And all mine for the taking.

"I need you to do something for me."

"Y-yes, anything."

A wicked smile plays on my lips.

"Make sure you scream my name when you come all over my fingers."

Her cheeks only get redder at my words, and I love that I can make her blush.

My innocent little princess. The things I have to teach you.

Before she gets a chance to think, I part her lips. "Fuck me," I groan, finding her soaking wet for me. "You weren't fucking lying, were you?"

She shakes her head.

Finding her clit, I rub circles around it before pinching down hard. Her lips form an *O* in shock and her eyes flutter closed. "Eyes on me," I demand. "You watch me as I do this to you."

She nods ever so slightly, and one side of my lips tilts up at her compliance.

Slipping my fingers lower, I find her entrance and circle a few times.

"Oh god. Fuck. Ace," she chants. I can tell she's desperate to close her eyes, but she follows orders like a good little princess.

Pushing one digit inside her, I bite down on my cheek when I find her incredibly tight. Fuck, how she'll feel around my cock.

Her body trembles before me as I slide deeper inside her. Mewls and moans of pleasure fall from her lips as her eyelids get heavier, but at no point does she close them.

With my thumb against her clit and two fingers deep inside her, her walls start to ripple as she drips down my hand. "Do you have any idea how wet you are for me right now?"

She shakes her head. She's so lost to what I'm doing to her, I doubt she even registers my words.

"Your juices are running down my hand."

"Oh god."

"It's. So. Fucking. Hot."

Bending my fingers, I find the spot that will have her screaming and rub at her relentlessly. A sheen of sweat begins to cover her skin, and unintelligible words and pleas fall from her lips as she races towards orgasm.

It's fucking hypnotic, watching her fall.

Then, all of a sudden her body quakes and she does exactly as she was told.

"Acccce." Her scream fills the silent space around us

and ensures that anyone who might be in hearing distance knows exactly who's doing this to her.

Exactly as I want it.

Every motherfucker in this place needs to know she's mine, because no one dares put their hands on anything that belongs to me.

Her pussy clamps down so hard on my fingers that I swear I'm only a second away from coming in my own pants like a fucking twelve-year-old at a wet t-shirt competition.

"Fucking hell, Princess. You're fucking killing me."

After a few seconds, her body stops convulsing and she comes down from her high. I know the moment that reality comes crashing down on her, because her eyes widen and she lifts her hands to cover her exposed tits. It's a damn fucking shame.

"What the fuck, Ace?"

"You're welcome."

Lifting my hand, I suck the two fingers that were just inside her into my mouth. My eyes hold hers as I do so, and hers go so wide I'm worried they might pop out.

"Mmmm... you taste like fucking heaven, Princess."

"Oh my god. I cannot believe you just did that."

She makes quick work of pulling the lace back over her tits before dropping her face into her hands and hiding from me.

"One," I say, wrapping my fingers around her wrists and pulling them from her face. "That totally happened. And two, never hide from me. Ever."

Her lips part like she wants to rip me a new one, but she doesn't say anything. Stepping away from the wall, she stares at the floor in disbelief.

Following her gaze, I find her ruined panties beside

her foot. "You," she seethes, stepping up to me, her face red with anger. "You expect me to spend the rest of the day at school with no panties on?"

I can't help the wicked smile that curls my lips.

I want to tell her that it's my way of ensuring she doesn't forget who has them as I bend down to collect them and shove them in my pocket, but the words that fall from my lips are very different.

"Spend the day with me."

CHAPTER TEN

Remi

S*pend the day with me.*

The words echo through my blissed-out state of mind.

That was not supposed to happen. But the ache deep inside me is a delicious reminder that it did.

Jesus. Ace isn't just a dangerous guy... he's a danger to my sanity.

I press my legs together and smooth out my skirt.

"What's it gonna be, Princess?" he asks.

"Where will we go?" I can't believe I ask the question, but it's not like I can stay in school in a puddle-soaked uniform wearing no panties.

A smirk tips the corner of Ace's mouth. "I have a few ideas." His eyes drift down my body, lingering on the hem of my skirt. My stomach clenches.

"I'm not going to have sex with you," I say, lifting my chin in defiance.

His deep chuckle reverberates around the locker room. "Getting ahead of yourself a bit, aren't you?"

"So you don't want me?" I'd felt the outline of his cock pressed up against me as he tortured me with his fingers.

Because it was torture.

Sweet, delicious torture that made me float away to some higher place. A place where there was no Michaela and Lylah and their merry band of cheer bitches, no cheating asshole father, or vile men who had a penchant for young girls.

But I couldn't help but think I was replacing one version of hell for another.

"Promise I won't end up dead, maimed, or drugged?"

His chuckle deepens as he stalks toward me. Curving a hand around the back of my neck, he drops his face level to mine. "I promise I won't ever make you do anything you don't want to."

"You sound awfully sure of yourself."

"Trust me when I say, Princess, that when I'm through with you, you'll be begging for me to give it to you."

Swatting his chest, I shoulder past him, fighting my own smile. He doesn't say a word as I reach for the door. Glancing over my shoulder, I try my best to look demure. "Come on then, bad boy, show me a good time."

"Shit, for real?" His eyes darken with lust.

"Yeah. It's not like I can stay in school," my gaze drops to my skirt, slowly lifting back up to meet his intense stare, "and to be honest, I like the idea of rebelling a little."

"Then what are we waiting for?" Ace strides toward me. "Let's get out of here."

I've always wondered what it would be like to ride a motorcycle. I just never imagined I'd have my maiden voyage on the back of Ace Jagger's bike, wearing nothing but my Sterling Prep uniform and no fucking panties.

I'm sure there's probably a law against this kind of thing, but from how fast Ace is riding, I know he doesn't care.

I'm starting to wonder what, if anything, Ace *does* care about.

He acted so protective back in the locker room, as if the fact that I was upset over Michaela's little stunt genuinely affected him, but I don't want to raise my hopes. Ace carries a darkness inside him, and I don't doubt he has secrets. They lurk behind his frosty gaze, taunting me.

I know, because so do I.

He pulls up alongside my house and I climb off, careful to hold my skirt in place. Ace chuckles, watching me grapple with the helmet he insisted I wear.

"Here." He leans forward to help me get the damn thing off.

"I'll just..." I thumb over my shoulder to my house.

"I'll be waiting." That trademark smirk of his slides into place, and I wonder what he's thinking. Part of me half expects him to follow me inside, but he doesn't, and in less than five minutes, I'm back at the bike in a pair of jeans and a fitted black t-shirt.

"You shoulda kept the skirt," he says as I climb on behind him, fitting my thighs around his hips. Ace slides his hand along my knee, sending shivers skating through me. His touch is like kryptonite, making me weak for him.

And I know I'm in deep trouble.

"So where are we going?"

"It's a surprise," he says.

A thrill shoots through me. I've cut the odd class before, but I've never skipped out on the whole day. My mom will lose her shit when she finds out, but I can't find it in myself to care. All I can think about is Michaela standing there, laughing at me. They were all laughing. Kids who used to be my friends. Kids that turned against me all because Queen Michaela snapped her fingers and said so.

"Easy, tiger," Ace says over his shoulder as he hands me the helmet.

"Sorry." I curl my fingers from my stomach, but he catches one of my hands.

"Don't let that bitch inside your head."

"Easy for you to say," I grumble, but he's already kicked the starter. The bike rumbles to life beneath us, drowning out my words.

It suits Ace. Sleek and powerful, and emanating danger.

He takes the coastal road out of the Bay towards the Heights. Nervous energy vibrates inside me as I hold him tighter. It's like the closer we get, the faster he goes, and I wonder if I'm going to meet the real Ace.

The Sterling Heights version.

I've only ever passed the Heights. It isn't somewhere people from Sterling Bay make a habit of going. The changes start slow at first. The big houses with immaculate yards become few and far between, replaced with derelict buildings covered in graffiti and small, dilapidated houses.

I'm suddenly relieved I traded my prep school uniform for jeans and a T-shirt.

Ace eases off the gas as he twists and turns down a network of streets. He clearly knows his way around this neighborhood, so when he pulls up outside a store marked 'Sinners,' I wonder where the hell he's brought me.

He waits for me to climb off before doing the same. This time, I manage to get the helmet off myself.

"Here," Ace says, taking it from me and hanging it over the handlebars.

"What is this place?"

"Scared, Princess?"

"You'll have to do something a little worse than bring me to the Heights to intimidate me, Ace." I level him with a serious look.

"Oh, is that right?" He flashes me a wolfish grin. "Come on." Without warning, Ace grabs my hand and pulls me toward the store. A bell jangles as we step inside, and I scan the place. The walls are covered in rattle can art and there's a distinctive hum in the air.

"You're getting a tattoo?" I ask.

"Yeah." Ace is distracted, reading his cell phone.

"Problem?" I ask, and a dark expression crosses his face.

"Nothing that can't wait. Yo, Cruz, you back there?"

There's commotion beyond the chain curtain, and a guy as scary looking as Ace appears. "Jag, my man, how's it going?"

"You know how it is."

"Who's the chick?" His eyes take a leisurely sweep down my body, and I half expect Ace to go into full alpha asshole mode.

But he doesn't.

"I'm Ace's—"

"No one. She's no one."

My stomach drops, but I bury the hurt. So what? It's not like we're together.

It's not like we're anything at all.

I avert my eyes, pretending to look at one of the design folders out on a counter pushed up against the wall.

"Kelsey know you're in the neighborhood with a..." Cruz lowers his voice so I can't hear the rest, and I'm not sure I want to.

Suddenly, coming here with Ace feels like a giant mistake. He makes me reckless and impulsive, completely disarming me.

It never occurred to me before now that maybe that's how he wants me.

I peek over at them, and I'm surprised to find them both looking at me. "You want to see a real artist at work?" Ace asks.

"You're getting a tattoo? *Now*?"

"Well I didn't come here to get my hair braided."

Cruz snorts at that. "What do you say, Ace's girl?" His eyes slide to Ace, but he doesn't flinch.

I frown, wondering what game Cruz is playing. "After you," he says, motioning to the curtain. I slip around them and part the chain ropes, but at the last second, I glance back and say, "My name is Remi, and I'm no one's property."

Cruz explodes with laughter, and I swear I hear Ace grumble at him to fuck off. I fight a smile.

I might be treated as a worthless no one at Sterling Prep, but I refuse to be that girl here.

The back room is divided into two workstations separated by a thin medical-grade curtain. Someone's boots are poking out the end as the quiet mumble of pained sighs fills the room.

"Yo, D, Jag is in the building." Another guy rolls out on a stool from behind the curtain.

"Decided to get your ass in the chair and get that sleeve finished?"

"You know it." Ace flexes his arm, the inked patterns coming to life on his skin.

"Let's get started." Cruz begins laying out his tattoo gun. "Ace's girl... I mean Remi, you can take a seat right here." He pats a stool near the chair Ace is getting comfortable in.

"Don't you have to trace the design onto his skin first?" I ask, seeing no sign of any paper.

"Nah, I let Cruz do his thing."

"Wow, you must really trust him." I glance at Cruz. "Have you ever been tempted to tattoo something really inappropriate on him?"

"Who says I haven't?" He shoots me a wicked grin. "Now watch and learn."

Tensing his arm, Ace barely flinches as Cruz gets to work on his skin. There's already a myriad of patterns, but they all seem to flow into one another effortlessly.

"You got any ink, Remi?" the other guy calls from behind the curtain.

"No," I reply, "but I've always wanted one."

"Virgin skin," he chuckles. "You know we're going to have to rectify that, Cruz, man."

"I just don't know what I'd get." I shrug. "It's a big commitment."

The guys all howl with laughter at my comment, but I let them have their fun. I'm too entranced by the way Cruz paints Ace's skin to care.

"You're really talented," I say.

"Thanks, being a tattoo artist is fifty-percent artist, thirty-percent technical ability, and twenty-percent therapist. Am I right, D?"

"Hell yeah."

"People like to talk when they're in the chair, huh?" I ask.

"Some people, like your guy here, don't utter a word. Others talk and talk—"

"And talk," D calls.

"I guess pain affects everyone differently." My eyes lift to Ace as I say the words, but he's already watching me, his gaze clouded with something I can't quite decipher.

I smile, itching to reach out and trace the patterns decorating his hard muscles.

"So Jag," Cruz says as he outlines what looks like a skull on Ace's lower bicep, "have you heard from Donny? Rumor has it he's pissed you haven't—"

Ace's eyes snap to his friend's, and he shakes his head discreetly.

"Shit, man. My bad." Cruz's eye flick to mine. "Hey Remi, you thirsty? We got a vending machine out front. You have to kick the fucking thing to get it to drop though. Or there's a water cooler."

"I could do with a soda," Ace says, his hard gaze back on me.

"Anyone else want anything while I'm up?" Sarcasm clings to my words. Cruz must hear it, because he laughs.

"I'll take a water," the guy from behind the curtain says.

I get up and go back out front, locating the vending machine and water cooler.

"So what's that all about, man?" Cruz's words give me pause. "You know if Kelsey hears..." I can't make out what he's saying, but he mentioned her name again.

Kelsey.

I want to believe it's no one, that Ace wouldn't be fooling around with me if he had a girl in the Heights. But I've been burned too many times to trust people—especially people I barely know.

When I re-enter the back room, Cruz and Ace fall silent, and it's obvious they were talking about me. I raise a brow. "Did I interrupt something?" Handing Ace his soda, I peek around the curtain and put the cup of water down on a steel tray. The guy in the chair doesn't look so good, and I quickly slip away.

"I like you, Ace's girl," Cruz says when I sit back down. "You should come back here soon and let me ink you. On the house."

"Maybe I will. It's my birthday soon." The words spill out, and I instantly regret them.

"You hear that Jag? It's your girl's birthday. You'd better get her something real nice and pretty."

Ace flips him off, grumbling some inaudible reply. Something has changed since we first got here. Ace is distant, and I can't help but wonder if it has anything to do with Kelsey.

For the next thirty minutes, I sit watching Cruz shade in the skull. It's a dark and twisted piece of art, but the way his hand moves slow and steady with complete precision fascinates me. When he's done, he wipes away the remnant ink and blood, wraps the tattoo, and snaps off his gloves.

"You know the deal," he says to Ace, who nods.

"Thanks, man." Ace stands and walks over to a mirror to check out his new addition.

"What do you think, Princess?"

"I love it."

"Yeah." His eyes darken in the mirror, fixed right on my face. "Me too."

Just then, his cell phone starts vibrating. Ace digs it out his pocket and cusses. "I need to take this." He stalks out of the room, leaving me with Cruz.

"So you're from the Bay?" he asks.

"Yeah. Born and raised."

"We don't get a lot of your kind around here." There's no malice in his words, just mild curiosity. "You sure don't look like most of those stuck-up rich bitches."

"Nice." My lips flatten, and he chuckles.

"Hey, no offence intended." Cruz holds up his hands.

"None taken. I'm a bit of a black sheep at Sterling Prep." I don't know why I'm telling him this, but he seems to get it, understanding washing over him.

"That explains a lot then."

"What does?"

"Why Ace sought you out. He likes to play with broken things."

I'm about to ask what the hell he means when Ace bursts through the curtain, his expression cold. "We're leaving."

"Something up?" Cruz asks, his expression falling.

"Yeah, one of Donny's guys is outside..."

"Shit, man. What will you do?"

"Don't really have a choice, do I?" Ace glances to me and then back to Cruz, the two of them locked in silent conversation.

"Ace, what is it?" I ask.

"We need to go," he says coolly.

"Back to the Bay?" I reply, unsure whether I'm relieved or disappointed.

He barely looks at me as the words fall from his lips. "Yeah, but I need to make a stop first."

CHAPTER ELEVEN

Ace

Killian is waiting for us outside the studio. "Boss man wants to see you," he says.

"I'm kind of indisposed right now." I flick my head to Remi, who stands quietly at my side.

"Not my problem, Jagger. You know the deal. Boss man calls, you come running."

Anger skates up my spine. But he's right, resisting will only start something I can't finish—not with Remi here.

"Come on," I say to her, ignoring Donny's goon. "We need to make a stop and then I'll take you home, okay?"

She gives me a tight nod. *Yeah, I don't like it either, Princess.*

I throw my leg over the bike, and Remi quickly follows, getting herself comfortable behind me. Her thighs clamp around my hips as she shuffles closer, pressing her soft breasts against my back. Snaking her arms around my sides, her hands land on my stomach, and I somehow manage to catch the growl that threatens to crawl up my throat.

She feels too fucking good, and now I know how she sounds when she's falling apart, I'm desperate to do it again.

The way Cruz looked at her inside his studio... I wanted to rip his fucking eyes out of his head for even talking to her. She deserves better than to have the likes of him eye-fucking her.

Hell, she deserves a lot better than me right now, but like fuck am I about to stop whatever this is.

I suck in a breath. I really don't want to take her where I need to go next, but Donny's been on my ass for days to do a drop for him, and the fucker knows I'm here.

Seems he wasn't lying when he says he has eyes everywhere.

Donny runs the Height's most exclusive club—and by exclusive I mean you need to own a gun and be able to hold your own to be allowed inside. The shit that goes down in that place doesn't even need mentioning.

His offices are on the top floor with a club below and a dungeon beneath that. I've heard the stories about that place, but I haven't ventured down there. I'd rather not know, if I'm honest.

Everything about Donny is illegal and corrupt, so while I might do the odd drop for him, that's as far as it'll go.

We have an understanding. He keeps me employed to support my brothers, and I stay on the sidelines of his business. I don't want to be someone's fucking runner, someone's pussy. If I end up staying on this path I've set for myself, I want to be the guy calling the shots. Not the one taking orders like a little bitch. I've made no secret of that fact. It's just one of the reasons he's happy for me not to dive too deep into his business.

"What the hell is this place?" Remi asks when I pull up outside the black building.

It's surrounded by fencing with vicious barbed wire on the top that's been known to take a limb or two in the past. There are a couple of guys hanging around whose eyes bore into us as we pull up.

Anyone with an ounce of fear does not belong here.

"You need to come with me," I demand once we're both off the bike.

She looks around and purses her lips as if she's going to argue, but when she notices the guys staring right at her, she moves herself into my side.

Wrapping my arm around her waist, I walk her over to the back entrance. I press my finger down on the buzzer before the click alerts me that someone's listening on the other side.

"It's Jag," I bark seconds before the door opens, revealing a dark corridor and staircase beyond.

"What is this place?" Remi asks hesitantly as we begin climbing.

"Nowhere you ever need to come again."

"Riiight."

We're buzzed through the next set of doors, and, as expected, we're met by two of Donny's henchmen.

"Smith. Black." I nod at each of them and they do the same to me before their eyes land on the girl hiding behind me.

I understand why. These guys aren't exactly

welcoming with their guns on display and constant scowls on their faces.

"I need to see the boss. Can you...?" I gesture to Remi.

"Like she's our own flesh and blood." Smith winks at me.

I'd trust these two with my life, I know they'll keep her safe. But the look on her face tells me she's anything but in agreement.

"No, no. I can just come with you."

"No," I bark a little too forcefully. "You shouldn't even be here. Do not move. Do not do anything. I will be back in a few minutes."

She wants to argue, that much is obvious as I back away from her. She looks tiny next to Donny's guys, and I get this urge to wrap her in my arms and never let go. It's weird as fuck.

Needing to break our connection, I spin on my heels and continue down to Donny's office. I knock three times and enter when he says to do so.

"Ah look, if it isn't the Bay's newest resident alive and well, and willing to come back for the right price."

"What do you want, Don?"

He throws a bag down on his desk, followed by a scrap of paper with a familiar scrawled address on it.

"Take this," he points at the bag, "to that address. The usual stands. No questions asked, and don't look any further than your payment sitting on the top."

"You got it. When does delivery need to happen?"

"Thirty minutes ago."

I think of Remi, who's hopefully still waiting outside for me. I shouldn't have brought her here. I *really* shouldn't take her to the drop. There could be anything inside that bag, and the last thing I need is to get her tangled up with Donny's dealings.

"Can I—"

"Take your bitch back to the Bay first?" he asks, proving that he really does know what's going on. "No. No you fucking can't. Either take her or dump her, I don't give a fuck. But this needs delivering now, or you're fucking done here."

Anger stirs within me, making my fists curl in my need to make him forget everything about Remi. He has no right knowing she exists or what she looks like. I might be reckless, but I'm not fucking stupid enough to start something with Donny fucking Lopez. Not unless I wanted to dig my own grave first.

"Fine. But this had better be worth my while."

"When isn't it?"

Grabbing the bag, I pull it from the desk and turn back to the door.

"I'll call you," Donny says before I reach for the handle.

"I'm sure you will," I mutter before disappearing and allowing the door to slam behind me.

"Let's go," I bark at Remi long before I get to her.

She startles at my booming voice but soon jumps into place behind me as I stride past her bodyguards and down the stairs without so much as a thank you.

After throwing Donny's bag over my shoulder so it rests over my front, we silently climb back onto the bike. I'm not sure if Remi's too terrified to ask or if she just knows that I won't give her any answers. Either way, I'm glad she's keeping it zipped.

She really doesn't need to know any details of what we're about to do.

I try my best not to know any details, which is why I always follow orders and never look inside the bag after taking my fee.

Gunning the engine, we speed out from the parking lot, leaving a cloud of dust and gravel behind us. Having her wrapped around me helps dissipate the anger that this whole situation has kickstarted within me.

When I suggested she spend the day with me, I was not expecting to make her my fucking accomplice. Seems Donny had other ideas.

The drive to the other side of town is quick, and before long we're pulling up in another questionable parking lot. Thankfully, there's no one loitering in this one.

"I need you to stay here."

"Are you fucking kidding me?" She looks around, her eyes wide with fear. "I'm not staying out here alone."

"And I'm not taking you in there." I nod my head over to the black door I need to go through. This isn't my first time here, so I know I'll be in and out.

Her hands land on her lips and her lips purse.

Fuck. I really want to kiss that defiance out of her.

"You really need to do as you're fucking told."

"Do I?"

Reaching behind me, I pull my gun from the waistband of my pants. "Take this and shoot any motherfucker who comes near you."

She lifts her hands away and stares down at it like I'm handing her some maimed animal.

"It's a fucking gun, not a grenade, Princess. Take it."

"No."

"For fuck's sake." Lifting her shirt, I pull her waistband away from her body and shove my gun inside.

"Ace," she squeals. But I'm already halfway to the door.

"Just stay put. I'll be two minutes, max."

She mutters something, but I'm too far away to make out what it is. It's probably a good thing.

I unzip the bag the second I'm in the building, pull the cash from the top, and shove it in my pocket. A guy who looks familiar greets me at the next door and takes the bag without saying a word. Just how I like it.

In less than a minute, I'm jogging back to where I left Remi. She's standing in the exact same spot with a scowl.

"You might want to wipe that look off your face," I say when I get to her.

"Oh yeah. Why's that?"

"Because it makes me want to fuck you over the side of my bike."

Her lips part and form an *O*.

I chuckle at her shock as I lift her shirt once again and retrieve my gun.

"Y-you take that thing to school?" she asks in utter disbelief.

"Nah, usually I take my knife. Just depends on how I feel."

"Fucking hell," she mutters, spinning away from me and running her hands through her hair. "Please tell me that bag wasn't full of drugs."

I shrug. "I've no idea. Maybe."

"Maybe? You don't know what you're carrying?"

"It's not my job to ask questions, Princess. You hungry?"

"Just like that?"

"Just like what?"

"You forget about what you just did—what you just delivered—and think about food."

"I know this is all new to you, Princess. But you're forgetting something."

"Oh yeah. Care to enlighten me?"

"This is my life. This is how I make my money. This is what I do. Don't like it, then you know what to do." I say the words, but I'm pretty sure she knows just as well as I do that I'll never let her walk away from me. Not until I get what I need from her.

Her mouth opens and closes like a goldfish.

"So, food. Shall we?"

Without giving her a chance to argue, I climb on to my bike and wait for her to join me. She mutters something under her breath, but I allow her to vent before she eventually climbs on and wraps her arms around me.

I take off, but I'm not ready to leave my home yet. I drive to the nicest end of town. I mean, it's still a shithole, especially compared to anything she's used to, but I'm confident my gun won't need to come out here, put it that way.

"Pizza?" I ask over my shoulder after killing the engine.

"Sure." I'm fascinated as she pulls the helmet from her head like a pro. I watch as her long curls settle around her shoulders.

She's really fucking beautiful.

As I hold my hand out, she slips hers into it and together we walk toward the pizza place in which I've spent hours of my life.

I'm greeted like a long lost family member when we step inside Lucio's.

"Is there anyone in this town who doesn't know you?" Remi whispers as we're shown to my usual table.

"Nah. Anyone who is anyone knows who Ace Jagger is."

"Whoa, your ego really knows no bounds, does it?"

"Nope. Two of the usual, please," I ask Lucio before he runs off to place our order.

"I can order for myself, you know," she seethes, sitting back in her seat and looking around the place.

"I'm aware, but I wouldn't want you ordering anything but the best this place has to offer."

"And what if I don't like it?"

"Not possible."

"Really? What if you've just ordered me meat and I'm a vegetarian."

"You're not."

She narrows her eyes at me in frustration. "What if I'm allergic to something?"

"Are you?"

"Well... no, but that's not the point."

"So what is the point, Princess?"

"I have my own mind, and I appreciate being able to use it."

"You can choose dessert," I smirk. "How's that?"

"Fine. I hope you're allergic to chocolate and ice cream."

I can't help but laugh at her as she crosses her arms over her chest and pouts. "Please don't sulk. It makes you look like the cheer bitches from school."

"You noticed them, huh?"

"Hard not to when they constantly want to get on my dick."

"Why am I not surprised." Remi rolls her eyes.

"That Michaela's hot, though," I tease. "I might let her wandering hands go a little farther next time."

Her face goes bright red in the blink of an eye. "She's a slut."

"Oh, I'm fully aware of that, Princess. What I don't know is what her beef with you is."

"She stole my life," she mutters, avoiding my gaze.

"How so?"

She blows out a long breath and is silent for so long that I don't think she's going to open up. "She's... my stepsister."

"Oh?"

"My dad hooked up with her mom. They've got the perfect life while Mom and I got left behind. You still want to fuck her?"

"I never said I wanted to fuck her."

"Silly me, you just want her to feel you up."

The thought of her even touching me turns my stomach, but I don't allow Remi to see that.

I've got a game plan here, and anyone I can use to get me the result I need, I will—whether that be Remi, her best friend, or her worst enemy.

I will find out the truth about my life.

CHAPTER TWELVE

Remi

I'm grinning ear to ear when we leave the pizza place. Ace is intimidating as hell, but feed him pizza and beer and he's actually a pretty fun date.

Not that that's what this was. I doubt Ace is the kind of guy who dates. But still, it was nice. And he picked up the check, which was a bonus, although after our little trip around his old neighborhood, I really don't want to think about what he does to make money.

We almost reach his bike when my cell vibrates. "Oh, shit," I say, scanning the message from my mom.

"Problem?" Ace asks.

"We've been busted." I show him my mom's demand for us to return to the house at once.

"I'd better get the princess home, then." He stares down at me, the air growing thick around us.

"What?" I grow self-conscious under his intense scrutiny.

"I want to kiss you so fucking bad right now."

"But?" I swallow, heat flashing through me. Ace just ate a huge pizza and he still looks ravenous.

A knowing smirk tugs at his mouth. "It wouldn't be a good idea, not here. Come on." He motions toward his bike.

I try to ignore the dejection pulsing through me, but it's right there, coiled around my heart.

Ace tries to help with my helmet, but I snatch it off him. "I can do it myself."

"Whoa, what's gotten into you?"

"Nothing," I bite. "We should probably go." My mom and James are going to be pissed.

Ace rests his butt on the seat of the bike, folding his arms over his chest. "I'm not moving until you tell me what's wrong." I'm relieved the helmet shields most of my face, because I know my expression is probably betraying me right now. "Spit it out, Princess. I'm waiting."

"Ugh," I release a frustrated breath. "Fine. I can't figure out why you brought me here is all."

His brows furrow. "You didn't have fun today?"

"I... that's not what I mean," I sigh. "Do you have a girlfriend here? Is Kelsey—"

Laughter crinkles the corners of his eyes. "You think me and Kelsey... fuck, no. She's no one to me. But you've seen what I do, the kind of people I hang out with. It probably wasn't the smartest move bringing you here."

"I see."

"Listen, I want nothing more than to kiss you. To strip you bare on my bike, bury my face in your sweet pussy and eat you out." Lust floods me, making my knees weak. "You drive me in-fucking-sane, Princess."

"Oh," I breathe.

"Yeah, oh. Now get on the fucking bike before James calls the cops on me for endangering his precious Remi." He throws his leg over the bike and grabs the handlebars.

It's a strange thing to say, but I don't question it as I slide on behind him, tucking myself into his back.

"Ready?"

I nod, and Ace revs the engine. Before I can say another word, Sterling Heights is disappearing behind us in a rush of warm air and exhilaration.

All too quickly the landscape changes to the familiar postcard perfect scenery of Sterling Bay, but Ace surprises me by pulling off at a rest area before we hit town. "Off," he orders, and I slide off the bike, wondering what the hell he's playing at. Roughly grabbing me, he tugs me around to him and shifts his body to the back of the seat. Then he gently pulls the helmet off my head.

"Get on." He drops his steely gaze to the sliver of space in front of him.

"Excuse me?"

"I said," he hooks his finger into the loop on the waistband of my jeans, "get. On."

With a quick glance around to make sure we're not being watched, I maneuver myself back onto the bike. Ace tracks my every move, using his big hands to fit my legs around his hips until we're impossibly close.

"We need to—"

"Just shut the fuck up a second," he growls, sliding one of his hands around my throat. "You look so fucking hot like this. Got all kinds of bad things running through my head right now." He leans forward, dragging his tongue up the side of my neck. "One day," he murmurs against my skin.

I want to ask him what he means, but I'm too blissed out. He's barely touched me and I'm already losing control.

"Ace," I murmur, pressing myself closer. He pushes gently, making my back bow against the handlebars.

"Fuck, Remi, the things I want to do to you."

Delicious sparks of anticipation zip through me. And the thought hits me square in the chest.

I want him.

I want Ace Jagger.

But there are things he doesn't know about me. Things that could get in the way of whatever this is growing between us.

He continues his exploration of my skin, licking and nipping until I'm a writhing, pent-up ball of nerves. I'm about to ask him to touch me, to make it all go away, but then he's there. Kissing me. Devouring me. His tongue delves into my mouth, so deep it's like he's trying to crawl inside me. I kiss him back just as forcefully, sucking and biting his tongue.

"Fuck, yeah," he hisses.

I can feel him rock hard beneath me, and I can't resist dipping my hand between us, feeling the outline of his cock. My fingers creep to the zipper of his pants but a car flies past us, honking their horn. "Get a fucking room," someone yells, and I bury my face in his shoulder. The sudden disruption is like a bucket of ice cold water, dousing what seems to ignite between us every time Ace touches me.

"Oh my god," I breathe, soft laughter spilling from my lips.

Ace curves a hand around the back of my neck and coaxes me out of his chest. "You're right, we should probably go before we get arrested for indecent exposure." Hunger burns in his eyes, and there's something so heady, knowing that Ace wants me as bad as I want him.

He leans in, kissing me again. But this time, it's a soft brush of his lips against mine. "You'd better move, Princess. My restraint won't last forever."

Fighting a smirk, I scramble off the bike and pull the helmet back on. It's less that a ten-minute ride to his uncle's house. Anyone from town could drive past and see us. But as I curl myself around Ace's body, I can't find it in myself to care. Because for the first time in a really long time, it's like someone gets me.

He *sees* me.

And I don't want to give that up for anything.

Sure enough, when Ace pulls into his uncle's driveway, James' town car is sitting there, like a warning sign, and next to it is my mother's second-hand Corolla.

"What do you think they're going to say?" I ask Ace as we climb off his bike.

"Don't really care," he grumbles, raking a hand through his hair. "Do you think your mom will flip?"

"I don't think she'll be too happy, no."

"Well, you're almost eighteen, right?"

I nod. "My birthday is in a couple of weeks."

"So you're almost an adult." He shrugs as if it's nothing. But then, I know Ace has probably been used to a lack of parental figures in his life.

As we approach the house, I want to believe nothing has changed between us, but I can already feel Ace's walls coming back up. Whatever there is between him and his uncle it isn't good, and part of me wonders what we're about to walk into.

The house is quiet as we step inside, but then a deep voice shouts, "Ace, kitchen. Now."

Without thinking, I reach for Ace's hand but catch myself at the last second. Anger rolls off him in waves, and I'm not sure the Ace I just spent the day with is here anymore.

"Remi, thank god," Mom says the second I step into the kitchen. But the relief in her eyes is short lived, turning to disappointment. "You have some explaining to do, young lady."

"I'd like to hear Ace's side of the story first, Sarah." James looks murderous. "Imagine my surprise when I received a call from Principal Vager saying you had skipped out of school—two days in a row. Really, Ace, I expected you to rebel, but pulling Remi into your games is not—"

"It wasn't his fault," I blurt out, and my mom's brows pinch with disbelief.

"Remi?"

"Look, something happened this morning... with Michaela." I take a deep breath, anger licking the inside of my stomach. "I couldn't stay in school. My uniform was ruined and I just needed to get away, so I asked Ace if he'd give me a ride."

"You asked Ace if he'd give you a ride... on his motorcycle?" she splutters.

"I wore his helmet," I say, as if it makes a difference.

"Is Remi telling the truth?" James asks Ace.

A beat passes, and I think Ace is going to admit everything. But then he surprises me by releasing a long breath. "Yeah, some girls pulled a cheap stunt on Remi and soaked her through. She asked me to give her a ride home to get changed, and I guess time just ran away with us."

"I bet it did," James says coolly. He's not buying it, and I'd pay to be a fly on the wall to the conversation I know they'll be having later.

"Well, I'm just glad you're both safe." Mom levels Ace with a classic mom-look. "And I'd like your reassurance that, next time, you'll encourage Remi to do the right thing."

I smother the laughter building in my chest. She's so far off the mark it's ridiculous.

"Off course, Ms Tanner. I'll be sure to keep Remi on the straight and narrow." His eyes flick to mine, full of dirty thoughts and reckless decisions.

"I suppose we'll leave you boys to it." Mom curls her hand around James' arm and leans up to kiss his cheek. "I'll call you later."

He gives her a dismissive nod, too busy glaring at Ace to really notice.

"I guess I'll see you tomorrow," I say to Ace. "Thank you... for today." My eyes lock on his as I pass him, and I see the faintest of smiles crack over his face.

The second we leave their house, I turn to Mom and say, "I'm sorry, okay? I made a bad choice."

"Don't, Remi," she says, jabbing her finger in the air.

"It's the second day of semester and you didn't just cut class, you skipped out the entire day. Do you have any idea how embarrassing it was, taking that call from Principal Vager?"

"Do you have any idea how embarrassing it was, standing there, in front of the entire class, while Michaela deliberately sprayed that puddle all over me? Even my underwear was wet, Mom."

"Remi," she exhales a shaky breath, "this war with your step-sister has got to stop. I know she's difficult—"

"Difficult?" I grab the handle and yank it open, climbing inside the car. "She's not difficult, Mom. She's a bitch."

"*Language*!"

"Sorry." I sink back in the seat, letting out a small huff. "She just drives me crazy."

"You need to let it go, sweetheart. She can only hurt you if you give her the power." Mom turns the key in the ignition and starts backing out of the driveway.

"Right, because if I just ignore her, she'll disappear."

"Not what I'm saying, Remi, but all this hatred isn't good for you. I know she hurt you..."

I tune her out. Mom doesn't get it. She never has. After her ex-boyfriend left and she got sober, Mom changed. She became all about good vibes and positive thoughts. But she doesn't know what it's like to be the social pariah. I can't just forget about that.

I won't.

She's toxic. An insidious creature that gets under your skin and poisons you from the inside out.

Michaela Fulton ruined my life.

One day, I'll figure out a way to ruin hers.

The next day at school, I'm hardly surprised by the whispers and wagging fingers as I navigate from class to class. Principal Vager hauled me and Ace into his office separately. He was more than shocked to hear my version of events, but I refused to let Ace take the fall for saving me in my hour of need.

I have detention for the next three afternoons, and I have to write a paper on the school codes of ethics and why skipping class is an unacceptable way to deal with 'student disagreements'.

What a fucking joke.

But I guess that's what you get when the student you were *disagreeing* with is head cheerleader, student council president, and has one of the most prominent names in Sterling Bay.

"Hey." Hadley flounces down beside me on the bench hidden around the side of the building. It isn't really in bounds at recess, but I like to avoid eating in the cafeteria whenever I can, and no one usually bothers me back here.

"What's up?"

"No way." She shakes her head. She's gone for cheer-issue braids today that sit tight to her head. "I want to hear all about what happened yesterday. A little birdie told me you skipped out with Ace Jagger?"

Just the mention of Ace has my stomach flipping. I hoped to see him this morning and find out what his uncle said, but our paths haven't crossed yet. That, or he's avoiding me.

I frown at the thought.

"What's wrong?"

"Nothing." I snap myself out of it. Ace has no reason to avoid me. Especially not when I took the fall for him.

"So... yesterday..." Curiosity glitters in Hadley's eyes.

"He gave me a ride home and then we hung out."

"You hung out with Ace Jagger?"

"Yeah." I shrug. "Is it that hard to believe?"

"Well, I guess not. But he's so... and you're so..."

"Nice, Hads." My lips mash together as I pick at the bag of chips in my lap.

"Oh, come on." She nudges my shoulder. "You know I don't mean it the way it sounds. But I've heard the rumors. He's bad news, Remi."

I can't disagree with her there, but a person isn't always defined by the choices they make. Sometimes life molds you into who you become.

I should know.

"I didn't see anyone else chasing after me yesterday to make sure I was okay."

Guilt creeps into her expression. "I'm sorry. But you know I can't—"

"Yeah, I know." Hadley has her own secrets, and she needs to keep her place on the team, which means keeping the peace with Michaela.

"I'm sorry she did that to you."

"It's nothing new. I constantly try to rise above it, but one day, she's going to push me too far..."

"Just don't do anything stupid, okay?" She cuts me with a concerned look. "Michaela is next-level crazy."

Don't I know it.

"So you and Ace, is it a friend thing or is there something there? Because I've got to admit, the guy kinda terrifies me."

"He's really annoying," I say. "And so bossy. But he

gets me, I think. It's all very confusing." I avert my gaze, remembering what it was like when Ace touched me yesterday. How he gave me exactly what I didn't know I needed. A slow tingle starts in my belly.

"You like him, don't you?"

Reluctantly, I lift my eyes to hers and smile weakly. "Yeah, I think I do."

CHAPTER THIRTEEN

Ace

My head pounds like a fucking bass drum when I climb the steps to James' house the next morning. I probably shouldn't have done it, but the second Remi and Sarah left last night, I wasn't far behind them.

He was three words into his 'rip Ace a new one' speech when I turned and walked away. I don't need him laying down the law. I'm an adult, for fuck's sake. I don't need to fucking be here. I can make my own choices in life.

I jumped on my bike and headed straight back to the Heights. Thankfully, Cruz was still at Sinners and took me up on my offer of getting shit-faced. I ended up spending the night with him, drinking scotch and smoking. It was exactly what I needed. Actually, no, that's not true. What I really needed was to be balls deep in Remi, but I didn't think climbing the trellis to her room was a particularly good idea. Sarah already looked on the edge of losing her shit when they left; I didn't want to make it worse for Remi than I already had.

She took the fall for me.

I was not fucking expecting that. Not that I really think it matters what she says to James, because to him everything will be my fault. That's just the way he sees me.

"Ace Jagger, get your ass in the kitchen right this fucking second." His voice is murderous. I don't need to look at his face to know it's bright red and that his eyes are bulging, ready to burst.

Rolling my eyes, I stagger towards him, more than ready to have it out with him. This fight has been brewing. I'm actually looking forward to it.

"Uncle," I slur when I get to him. "How wonderful to see you."

His eyes are murderous, but his anger has little effect on me. If he wants to scare me then he's going to need to do a little more than give me a look. At least do it while holding a gun for half a chance.

"Where the hell have you been?" He looks me up and down, disapproval written all over his face.

"Out," I seethe.

Pushing from where he was leaning against the counter, he steps towards me. He's trying to make me feel small, like I'm the child in this situation. It's not working.

"This is not how you act under this roof, boy."

"I think it is, *Uncle.*" I narrow my eyes at him, warning him about getting any closer. I'm more than happy to settle this thing with my fists if he'd like to lose.

"Do you have any ideas how many strings I had to pull, how much money I had to spend to get you into that school?"

"I didn't ask to go there, to even be here. You instigated this."

"Because it was the right thing to do." He lets out a weary sigh. "The three of you deserve a chance at a future, a real future, after the childhood you've had."

Memories flash through my mind like a fucking movie. Mom strung out on the couch while I attempted to cook dinner so my brothers wouldn't go to bed hungry. Mom having her special friends visit and me having to take my brothers out in the rain just to get them away from what was about to happen, the noises that she would happily allow them to listen to in the other room.

Then there's the most pressing issue. Our dad. The man who *died* all those years ago, leaving us with that fucking disaster of a mother while our dear old uncle turned his back on us.

He knew what our life was like, and he just walked away.

"Guilt," is the only thing I say, and his eyes widen in shock.

"What? No. I'm doing this because you're my family. Because it's what you deserve."

"Bull. Shit. I know, James. *I know* what you did. I know the hand you had in how our lives turned out. So if you think you're ever going to get me on board with this little perfect life you've attempted to drop us into, then you need to think again. All this is you trying to rid your guilt. Trying to wash your hands of the blood you think is staining them. Well, newsflash, *Uncle.* I know everything. And rest assured. Revenge is the first thing on my list."

The blood drains from his face as he swallows nervously.

"Yeah, you should look worried, Uncle. I'm coming for you."

He's silent as I back out of the room, our eyes locked in our silent exchange.

"It's not what you think, Ace," he cries as I disappear from his sight. "And stay away from Remi."

Shaking my head, I make my way up to my room to put on that lame ass uniform so I can get to school. This whole situation might be fucked-up beyond belief, but he's right about something: my brothers deserve a chance at a future, and I'll be damned if I'm going to ruin that for them.

Thankfully, by the time I'm hauled into the principal's office for my dressing down for skipping the last two days, my hangover has almost subsided and I can see straight again. He either ignores the stench of alcohol I'm sure is clinging to me, or this place drives him to drink so much that he barely notices.

For the first time, I actually make it until lunch. Although it's not because I want to be here but more that it's easier to sit in class and stare at whatever I'm meant to be doing than it is to leave. I probably had two hours' sleep last night on Cruz's couch. Even without the hangover, I'm like a zombie.

I grab some food from the cafeteria before leaving as fast as I entered. Eyes drill into the back of my head the entire time I'm there. I can't think of anything worse than being forced to eat in here.

With my lunch in hand, I walk around the building to find a quiet spot so I can be alone. Cole should be hanging out with the team as I made him promise me he'd do in an attempt to fit in, and I've no idea where Conner is. He's probably trying to bag some poor unsuspecting girl with his bad jokes and even worse banter.

I shake my head at the thought of both of them. With my own drama and the distraction of Remi, I've not really checked in with them about how it's going. Guilt floods me. They should be my priority right now, not how soon I can get back inside Remi's panties.

I come to a stop around the side of one of the buildings when a familiar voice hits my ears.

"He's really annoying," Remi says, and I can't help but smile. I don't need to hear any more to know she's talking about me, but, helpfully, she continues anyway. "And so bossy. But he gets me, I think. It's all very confusing."

I think back to yesterday and the connection that was between us. I'm about to keep walking to give them some privacy when her friend asks a question that freezes my body in place. "You like him, don't you?"

My heart pounds wildly in my chest, although I'm not sure if it's with panic or fear. Fucking hell, do I want her to say yes?

"Yeah, I think I do."

All the air comes rushing out of my lungs, and I stagger back a little. There might have been a part of me that wanted her to say yes but fuck, I was not ready to hear it.

My feet take me away from the scene, and, before I realize it, I'm at my bike. I glance back over my shoulder to see kids laughing and joking with their friends, enjoying their stress free bullshit privileged lives, and I cave. Throwing my lunch into the nearest bin, I throw my leg over my bike and get the fuck out of here.

The house is in silence when I enter. I'm really fucking grateful, because I really don't need to go for a second round with James right now.

"James, is that you back?" Ellen calls from the kitchen before her head pokes around the kitchen doorway. "Oh, Ace. Finished school already?" she asks with a knowing wink.

"Something like that."

"Have you eaten, or would you like me to make you some lunch?" I want to say no, but my stomach rumbles loudly, making her chuckle. "Come on, what's your favorite?"

"I... um... whatever you've got. I'm not fussy." I drop down onto one of the chairs around the table in the center of the huge kitchen.

"I really don't mind, Ace. James pays me to ensure the four of you are well looked after."

I scoff. "That's really not necessary. I'm more than cap—"

"I know, Ace." She rests her hand on my shoulder and squeezes slightly. "I know. But you don't have to now. So just enjoy the rest, eh?"

"I'm just not used to it."

"Just give it a few weeks. This place will feel like home in no time."

"We'll see."

"So tell me about school," she starts. "Made any

friends yet?"

I can't help but laugh at her positivity. "Do I look like the kind of guy who's going to make friends with anyone in this town?"

She shakes her head but doesn't comment. "James said you'd been hanging out with Remi."

"Yeah, he's real happy about it too."

"Things haven't been easy for her and Sarah since Remi's dad left. He's just looking out for them. I know they've not been together long, but he cares about her as if she's his own. He only wants the best for her."

"Yeah, and that isn't me apparently."

Ellen glances over her shoulder at me, an amused smile playing on her lips and a twinkle in her eye.

"What?" I ask, not knowing what she's getting at.

"Oh, nothing, Ace. Nothing at all."

She falls silent as she continues with whatever she's making me, and my mind wanders back to Remi.

I knew the moment I saw her, saw how James looked at her with pride and love in his eyes, that she was going to be the perfect target. But it's only been a few days and she's already admitting to her friend that she likes me.

Even though the plan is to make her fall for me and force James to watch as I break her, proving that he doesn't have the control he thinks he does... I need to stay away from her. For a while at least.

I can't lose my head.

Not now.

Not when I'm so close to the answers I need.

So what if she's a hot girl who's clearly interested? I need to focus on my end game here. And it's not for her to fall for me.

Or worse.

Nothing good can come from that.

I don't leave my room for the rest of the day, and when the sun rises the next morning, I reluctantly pull my uniform on and get ready for another day in Hell.

My down time yesterday gave me chance to sort out what I'm going to do where Remi is concerned. I have a plan. Now I just need to put it into practice.

She makes avoiding her at school easy, and throughout the day I don't even get a flash of her dark curls in the hallway. I actually start to think she's not in school until our last class of the day.

I ensure I turn up first.

The teacher gives me a double take when I'm through the door before the bell. "Well, well, well. This is a nice surprise, Mr Jagger."

"Don't get used to it," I grunt. "I didn't have anywhere better to be."

"I'll take that as a compliment."

I mumble something at her before finding a seat.

It's only a few moments later that the bell rings and students start filing into the room. They all take a seat, but the one beside me remains empty. It's like they're too scared to sit beside me or something.

That is, until she walks in.

My eyes lock onto her immediately and I have to fight to pull my gaze away so I don't look more interested than I want to. I know the moment she finds me because my skin tingles with awareness. I watch her move through the room out of the corner of my eye before she comes to a stop at the table beside me.

"Sorry, that's taken." I don't look up at her, but that doesn't mean I miss her gasp of surprise.

"O-oh... okay. Sorry." She stares at me for a beat, but when I don't so much as look up at her she spins and walks away.

I have no idea who I'm reserving it for, but I soon get my answer when a familiar blonde walks through the door. She scans the room before her eyes lock on mine.

A smile twitches at my lips and I gesture to the spare seat. She beams at me, delight filling her eyes as she drops down in the chair beside me, but not before she slides her table a little closer.

"I thought it was about time you and I got to know each other a little better." Her voice turns me off immediately, but I smile at her like I'm interested in doing just that.

All the while, Remi's death stare burns into the side of my head.

I'm getting to her.

Good.

"You're coming to the pep rally tonight, right?" Cole asks, poking his head into my bedroom Friday morning before school.

"Uh..."

"Come on, man. They're going to announce the starting line-up. I need you there." He knows exactly what he's doing. I can't say no to something like that. He barely asks me for anything, so I know this is a big deal for him.

"You'd better get that fucking spot," I mutter, pulling on my shirt. I don't do pep fucking anything, but for my brother, I'll make an exception.

The last thing I want to do is spend the night with Bexley and his bunch of assholes, but seeing as I helped force Cole into it, I guess the least I can do is support him.

"It's in the bag, man. I'm the best fucking running back the Seahawks have ever seen."

"You'd fucking better be."

"I'm sure it won't be a total loss for you. No doubt Remi will be there."

My head snaps up in his direction and my eyes narrow.

"I see everything, Ace." Of course he fucking does. He's always fucking watching.

"I'm not interested in Remi."

His eyebrow quirks. He's obviously used his quota of words for the day. After shrugging one shoulder, he backs out of my room.

"I'm serious. I don't want her," I call after him.

It's Friday night, a pep rally is the last thing I want to do.

But he's right. There's a good chance that Remi will be there...

CHAPTER FOURTEEN

Remi

"Come on, you have to come," Hadley whines down the phone.

"No way. I'd rather douse myself in gasoline and set myself alight than spend the night pretending to cheer on the team."

"You could always come and cheer on your friend. You know, the girl who has to pretend she actually wants to be a Seahawk cheerleader." Her voice is full of sadness, and I feel like a total bitch.

"I'm sorry, Hads, but I can't—"

"Cole Jagger is going to be there, which means there's every chance Ace will be too."

Just hearing his name makes my stomach dip.

We spent an amazing day together, and then he completely ghosted me. No, that doesn't accurately describe what he did to me. He hit me right where it hurt most.

Michaela.

I still can't quite believe he did that, especially after what I told him about her.

Foolish girl.

I let myself fall for the bad boy's charm, ignoring all the warning signs. Ace Jagger is everything people whisper about him.

Cold.

Cruel.

And a complete asshole.

"He is the last person I want to see at the pep rally."

"I'm not saying you have to try and talk to the guy, but you could use the opportunity to show him that you don't care."

The problem, though, is that I do care.

I thought we were the same. I thought he saw me.

Turns out, he just saw me as a bit of fun. Something to pass the time. Hell, he was probably just using me to say a giant 'fuck you' to his uncle.

Dejection burns through me.

"Bexley will be there," Hadley continues. "I bet he'll be more than willing to lift your spirits." I can practically hear her smirk down the phone. "And you know it'll drive Michaela crazy if you show up and steal his attention."

"I doubt that," I say, knowing that my step-sister has her eyes on another guy.

A plan unfolds in my head. It's not the best idea I've ever had, but what was it Ace said? *Live a little.*

Maybe it's time I start doing just that. Screw

Michaela and her stuck-up cheer friends. Screw Bexley and his entitled ways.

Screw Ace and his games.

"I'm in," I say, feeling a sliver of excitement snake through me.

"Oh no," Hadley sounds concerned. "What are you planning?"

"Who, me?" I reply sweetly. "Nothing."

"Remi, I didn't mean..." She stops herself, letting out a resigned sigh. Hadley knows me well enough than to try and talk me out of anything. Only, before now, it's always been her trying to talk me out of hiding out at lunch or avoiding extra-curricular activities.

But she's right. It's senior year. I don't want to graduate and regret being the girl who let everyone walk right over her.

"Just don't do anything too crazy tonight, okay?"

"I can't make any promises," I reply, and she chuckles.

"I'm going to regret ever saying anything, aren't I?"

My lips curve into a devious smile as I whisper, "We'll see."

The football field is a sea of blue and white as I weave through the crowd. Kids stare at me; girls sneering and guys checking me out. I'm not usually on the end of their appraisal, but tonight I came dressed to impress. The black denim mini skirt hugs my hips and skims my ass, and the Seahawk tank I dug out of the bottom of the wardrobe is two sizes too small, but it makes my boobs look great and shows off a sliver of my toned stomach. I've gathered my long curls into two bunches that flow down my shoulders, and the pristine white sneakers I'm wearing give me that prep school look the boys of Sterling Bay seem to love so much.

Someone wolf whistles, and I glance over my shoulder. "Looking good, Tanner," a guy from class calls, his eyes roaming down my body.

Fickle jerk.

I flash him the fakest smile I can muster and continue moving deeper into the crowd. The cheer team is already on the field, whipping up a frenzy, but there's no sign of the football team yet. I've just found a seat in the bleachers when Hadley spots me. Her eyes widen as she approaches me. "Holy shit, girl, you look..."

"Thanks," I smirk. "Thought I'd better make the effort, you know? Go Seahawks." I punch the air.

She chuckles, but her smile quickly melts away. Hadley leans in, whispering, "Are you drunk?"

"What, no!" She gives me a pointed look. "Okay, so I may have had one or two of Mom's wine coolers before I left the house."

"Remi." Disappointment etches into her expression.

"I needed some Dutch courage to leave the house dressed like this."

Her brows crinkle. "Are you sure you're going to be okay? I have to go do my thing." She flicks her head to the field, and, surprise surprise, Michaela is glaring right at us.

"You should go. I'll see you after. Besides," I slide my arm through the guy's sitting next to me, "my new friend here will keep me company."

"I will?" he chokes out.

"Is that going to be a problem?" I flash him a smile. I recognize him from a couple of my classes last year but can't remember his name. It's clear he's the booksmart type. He's wearing a button down shirt, dress pants and a sweater vest. The poor guy looks as out of place here as I feel.

"I… uh, no… sure, whatever." His friends all snicker, teasing him, but then the music booms over the PA system, drowning them out. The cheer team breaks formation and starts tumbling and flipping across the field. I scan the crowd, wondering whether Hadley is right about Ace coming to support his brother. I can't imagine him being here, with the prep school masses.

But then I spot him, standing over by the edge of the bleachers, in the cover of the shadows. He notices me and his eyes narrow dangerously, sending a violent shiver rolling through me. He looks pissed.

Good, that makes two of us.

Inhaling a long drag on his cigarette, he exhales a tendril of smoke, never once taking his eyes off me. I break the spell, forcing myself to look at the cheer team. I don't know what game Ace is playing, or what changed after the day we spent together, but I'm done being his toy.

Tonight, I'll give him a taste of his own medicine.

Hadley blows off the cheer team after the pep rally and we ride together to the party… with none other than Cole and Conner.

"I can't believe my little brother is a fucking Seahawk." Conner leans over and grabs Cole's shoulder.

"I thought you were twins," Hadley says.

"We are, but I'm the eldest."

"By two fucking minutes," Cole grumbles. He doesn't seem very pleased to have made the team. I thought Hayden was going to combust when Coach Miller announced Cole as first string running back. He's held that spot for the last two years, and it's a definite blow to his cred.

"You need to take the next right," Hadley says. "Lylah lives in that house over there." She points to the house in the distance. There are already kids everywhere, cars lining the street and a bonfire flickering high into the sky.

"Holy shit, she lives here," Conner breathes as he tries to find a parking spot.

"It's probably the best house in the whole town." Hadley isn't wrong. The Donovans own a premium piece of Sterling Bay real estate, a big Art Deco style house overlooking the ocean, complete with indoor *and* outdoor swimming pools, tennis courts, and its own private access to the beach.

But tonight, it's party central.

Conner pulls out a blunt and lights it up. "You girls want in?"

I decline, but my jaw falls open when Hadley takes it. "What?" she says with a dismissive shrug. "It helps to relax me."

"Hell yeah." Conner winks at her.

"Cole, you in?"

"I can't, Coach makes us take drug tests."

"Fuck, for real?" Cole nods and Conner howls with laughter. "More for me then."

Cole flips him off, pulling out a bottle of vodka from

somewhere. "Doesn't mean I can't get shitfaced though."

They pass the bottle back and forth, until eventually Cole twists his body around and offers it to Hadley. "I'm good." she says, taking another drag of the blunt.

"Remi?"

I stare at the bottle. The buzz I felt earlier is long gone, and now I'm about to venture into enemy territory. Snagging the bottle from him, I down the rest of the contents.

"Holy shit, Princess," Conner says. "You're supposed to savor it."

"Whatever." I shoulder the car door and climb out. Hadley and the guys follow suit, and before I can change my mind, we take off toward the party.

"Hey," Hadley loops her arm through mine, "are you sure this is a good idea?"

"I have no idea what you're talking about."

She pulls my arm, letting the guys go on ahead. "Remi, it's me. You don't need to put up those walls of yours. Talk to me."

"I don't want to talk. I want to live." *I want to forget.*

"So this isn't about getting back at Michaela and making Ace jealous?"

"It was your idea," I hiss.

"Yeah, but I didn't think you'd actually go through with it. I just wanted you to come tonight."

"I guess you should have thought of that before you planted the seed."

She lets out an exasperated breath, defeat clouding her eyes. "Just be careful, okay? I don't want to see you get hurt."

Too late for that.

The party is already in full swing when we reach the

house. People file in and out, carrying red Solo cups, their bodies swaying to the mellow beat. We've already lost Conner and Cole, but it hardly surprises me.

"Holy shit." Hadley grabs my arm and I glance back at her, frowning.

"What's wrong?"

"I feel so buzzed." She laughs, her eyes cloudy and hooded. "You don't think Conner laced the blunt?"

"You need some water."

"Nah, I need some snaaaacks."

Jesus. I roll my eyes, grabbing her hand and pulling her further into the house. We're bumped and jostled as we make it inside. I've been here before, but not since we were all middle graders. The kitchen is a big open space with a huge island in the middle. It's been set up as the bar for the night, chock full of liquor bottles, ice buckets, and trays of snacks.

"Eat," I instruct Hadley as she dives for the bowl of chips. Leaving her to it, I make myself a mixer drink. The vodka is already burning through my veins, taking the edge off. But when I spot Ace through the open patio doors, Michaela hanging off him like a cheap throw, my body tingles with jealousy. He sees me, his piercing eyes locking right on mine as he takes a long pull on the beer bottle in his hand.

I want to know what he's thinking, because if the way his hard gaze moves over my body is anything to go by, he wants me.

So why did you push me away?

Michaela spots me and sneers, making a scene of standing up and grinding herself all over Ace. He lets his hand run up her thigh and disappear underneath her ridiculously short cheer skirt. I suck in a harsh breath.

She barely takes the thing off, preferring to spend her life dressed like Cheer Barbie. It brings her too much power and status.

I want to rip the thing off and tear it to shreds, but first, I want Ace's hands off her body.

Fuck.

Why is he doing this?

Downing my drink, I pour another. I shouldn't have come tonight. I'm playing right into his hands. For some reason, he wants me to be jealous. It's right there in his icy gaze as he watches me while I watch Michaela writhe above him.

"She might as well piss all over him," Hadley says over my shoulder.

"Feeling better?" I ask her, and she nods around a lazy smile.

"Much. Let's dance." Before I can protest, she drags me outside to where the girls are dancing. There's a DJ set up in the corner, lights bouncing off the surface of the pool and disappearing into the night sky.

Oh, how rich kids party.

I'm about to tell Hadley this is a bad idea when a hand hooks me around the waist, dragging me against a hard chest. "I hoped you'd come," Bexley slurs in my ear. He's buzzed, the faint scent of scotch on his breath. *Like father, like son*, I think to myself.

"You're drunk," I reply, twisting my face to his. He grins down at me.

"Maybe, a little. Me and the guys did shots after the pep rally. It's a team thing."

I roll my eyes. I couldn't care less about the team.

"Don't be that way, Remi Bear." The use of his childhood nickname for me has my chest constricting.

"Don't call me that."

His hand curves up my stomach, anchoring my body to his. "You used to love it when I called you that."

"We were twelve," I whisper.

"Yeah, and I thought I was going to grow up and marry you."

Tears prick my eyes, but I won't cry. I'll never shed another tear over Bexley Danforth and his sweet lies.

"We're not those people anymore, Bex." I don't bother to disguise my sadness.

"You're right, we're not." His hand moves up, hovering precariously near the curve of my breast. People are watching. I can feel the weight of their stares. Bexley Danforth is the most popular guy in school... and I'm the girl who no longer belongs here.

A wave of emotion hits me, and I know I'm two seconds away from crying or making a break for it. But the buzz of the liquor gives me the strength to start swaying in Bexley's arms. I look away from him, landing my glassy gaze on Ace and Michaela. Her lips part, betrayal burning in her heavily made up eyes. She's wanted Bexley for as long as I can remember. But he's never wanted her for anything more than a casual hook-up.

I keep my eyes fixed on the two of them as I roll and pop my hips against Bexley's crotch. He's rock hard, making no effort to hide how much he wants me as he grinds his cock against my ass. Desire snakes through me. I don't want Bexley, but he's holding me with such possession it reminds me of a certain tattooed asshole who is now watching me with pure hatred in his eyes.

Good, I hope it hurts as much as you hurt me.

Bexley lips land on my neck, but I don't stop him. I

can't. I want Ace to feel every bit of jealousy, hurt, and dejection I felt. He sucks and licks my skin, making my traitorous body shiver.

"Fuck, Rem, do you have any idea how long I've waited for this? I want you so fucking much." His hands grip my hips a little.

"Okay, ease up," I say.

"No way, baby. I've waited too damn long." He starts moving, pulling me away from the crowd until we're secreted away in the shadows. Spinning me around, he pushes me up against the wall and cages me, his hands either side of my head.

"What the fuck, Bexley?" I hiss. "We were just dancing." My heart crashes violently behind my ribcage. I wanted to make Ace jealous. I didn't want... *this*.

"Nah, baby. You want me, I know you do." My eyes dart around him wildly. The liquor in my blood is in full effect now, making me feel a little unsteady, and everything starts spinning.

"Let's go back and dance," I say, forcing a smile.

"So I'm supposed to believe you don't want this?" He grabs my hand and shoves it to his cock. "Because I sure as fuck want you. I can't wait to be deep inside you. It's all I've ever wanted."

Fear takes hold as I realize what a stupid mistake I made, thinking I could play with fire. Bexley Danforth doesn't take no for an answer. Eventually he always collects what he thinks he's owed.

And right now, his sights are set firmly on me.

Fuck.

"Bexley, you're drunk, and so am I." I press my hands against his chest, trying to leverage enough space to slip around him. "Let's go back to the party."

His hand clamps around my arm and he lowers his face to mine, forcing me flat against the wall. "I don't think so, Rem," he says in a low voice. "We have unfinished business."

CHAPTER FIFTEEN

Ace

Michaela's fingernails run over my abs and scratch down the skin to my waistband. Her lame ass attempt at seduction makes my skin crawl, and I wish she'd just claw my cock off so there is nothing of me left to rub herself up against. How any of the guys around here find her attractive, I have no fucking clue.

"We're done," I say, taking her shoulders in my hands and pushing her away.

She clings to me like a koala would a tree.

It's not cute.

"I said we're done here."

"But, Ace," she whines in her high-pitched, annoying voice.

"But nothing." I'm a little more forceful this time and successfully shove her from my body.

I have just watched Bexley pull Remi into the shadows of the pool house, and like fuck am I allowing him any more time with her than he's already had. He touched something that belongs to me. He kissed what's mine. For that, he's going to pay. But it won't be tonight. I'll let him stew for a bit.

Her scream rings out in the air, and I take off running. Only when I turn the corner to where they disappeared, what I find has my eyes bulging.

Remi is standing over a curled up and moaning Bexley. I'm a guy, I know the pain he's going through right now thanks to her knee, and I can't help but smile. There's also a little trickle of blood coming from his lip.

Fucking hell, did she punch him?

Pride swells within me for my girl.

My girl? No. She's just my plaything. My pawn.

"Looks like you don't need me."

"When did I ever say I did?" she spits, looking me up and down, the same disgust in her eyes that most of her classmates look at me with on a daily basis.

I put my hands up in surrender. Some movement over her shoulder catches my eye, but it's too dark to see who it is lurking in the shadows.

"Excuse me," she spits, shouldering past me and attempting to go back to the party.

"No." Reaching out, I wrap my fingers around her wrist and stop her when she's beside me.

"Get your fucking hands off me. You're no better than him."

Images of him touching her around here flicker through my mind, and my blood boils.

"Just go back to your cheer slut and continue ignoring me. It was much easier then."

She refuses to look at me as she says this, and it only angers me further. With her chin grasped in my hand, I push her back against the wall. Staring down into her large, dark eyes, I almost fucking drown in them.

They're mesmerizing.

She's fucking mesmerizing.

"She," I spit, "is not my anything."

"You might want to tell her that, she was climbing you like a fucking tree."

A smile twitches at my lips. "Jealous, Princess?"

"Never."

Our stare holds, chemistry cracking between us, but neither of us takes action.

Her chest heaves and her pupils dilate. I'm just about as sure as I can be that she'll accept my kiss when Cole stumbles around the corner, a few leaves stuck to his Seahawks jersey.

"Hey," he grunts as if this is totally fucking normal. "I need a drink."

He disappears as fast as he appeared, leaving my head spinning, but Remi spots my moment of weakness and slips from my hold.

"I'm going to get a drink. Stay away from me."

"Motherfucker," I mutter to myself.

I watch her ass sway in that short as fuck skirt, and my fists clench.

A moan comes from behind me. I'd forgotten that piece of shit was still there.

I drop down to my haunches and look at him. His lip is really starting to swell. It seems she's got a fine right hook. Something I should probably remember. I'm sure I already deserve a couple.

His eyes widen when he drags them open and finds

me staring back at him. Fisting my fingers in his jersey, I drag him closer, so we're almost nose to nose. "Don't fucking touch her ever again. You hear me?"

"Fuck off, man. She was mine long before you showed up." I pull the fabric tighter.

"She's. Not. Yours."

"She fucking will be. I've waited years for her. It seems like she's softening at last."

"You fucking touch her, and I'll make sure you're unable to do anything with a woman ever again."

"Fuck off, Heights scum. You don't scare me."

I laugh. It's calculating and evil. "Oh, I really, really should." He swallows nervously, proving that he's all talk, and I stand.

Towering over at him, I cast my eyes over his curled up body. "Worthless piece of shit." I spit at him as if he's a piece of trash and walk away.

Cole and Remi were right about one thing. I need a fucking drink.

The party is exactly as I was expecting: rich kids drinking their fucking rich drinks and attempting to go crazy. I guess it's okay enough, company aside, but it's not exactly my idea of a great night. There's not enough weed or decent pussy for that.

"I drop down onto a lounger beside Cole, who's enjoying watching the girls in bikinis jumping about in the pool.

"If I watch long enough, I'll get to see some nip, right?" he slurs when he sees it's me. Cole might be a quiet motherfucker most of the time, but give him enough alcohol and he soon starts talking.

"Just go chat one up, you're a Seahawk now. They'll be fighting over which one gets to suck you off."

"You reckon they could do the job right?" he asks, not removing his eyes from them. "I mean, they might have been skanks back at home, but they had mad skills, man. I'm not sure these rich chicks could compete."

"Maybe you should find out."

He looks at me, a plan formulating in his drunken head, and he smiles.

"Where's your girl? I thought she'd be all over you after you rescued her from the douchebag."

"She rescued herself, it seems," I say, tipping my beer bottle to my mouth.

"Man, if you saw what I saw then—" Suddenly his loitering in the bushes makes sense. He was about to jump out and protect her.

"He'll get what's coming to him," I mutter. My muscles ache to feel myself laying into him for thinking he had a right to Remi.

"Oh yeah?"

"Yeah. Just not here, not tonight. When he least expects it."

"Good. No motherfucker should touch a woman like that." His words stir something ugly inside me.

Glancing over my shoulder, I check to see if Remi is still standing with her friend where she was only a few moments ago. She might think I've allowed her to enjoy the party, but she'd be very much mistaken. I'm watching her every move. Or at least, I was until I was distracted by plotting my revenge on that motherfucker.

"Fuck." Getting up, I leave Cole behind on his mission to see some tit and march up to Remi's friend.

"Where is she?"

"Uh..." She pales as she looks up at me.

"I said, where the fuck is she?"

"S- she just went to the b-bathroom."

"Fucking hell. Why didn't you go with her?"

"I'm not her fucking minder." Her friend's eyes are blown and she sways on the spot. Great.

Running into the house, I locate the downstairs bathroom easily with the huge line formed in front of it. But Remi isn't in it. Storming to the front of it, I twist the handle, much to the girl's annoyance who's next in line.

"Hey, wait in the queue," she whines.

"Whatever," I mutter. Standing back slightly, I ram my shoulder into the door. It flies open on the first attempt, but she's not inside, just a girl who screams bloody murder and tries to hide from all the prying eyes as she takes a piss.

Stalking away, I ignore the abuse being hurled at me as I take the stairs three at a time. I swing open every door I pass as I make my way down the hallway. Couples fill most of them in varying states of dress. Some of them look horrified that they have an audience and race to close the doors, others don't give a shit. One of them even asks if I want to join their little party for two.

Shaking my head, I make my way to the end and the final few doors. I swear to god that if I find her in one of these with a guy, I'm going to lose my shit. If I find her with him, then I know things are going to get messy.

I reach behind me to ensure my switchblade is in place should I need it and run my fingers over the handle. The final door taunts me. Rushing over, I swing it open and stare at the empty room beyond. There's Seahawk shit everywhere, but there's no sign of Remi or the guy whose room this clearly is.

I'm about to turn and keep searching when a noise hits my ears. A groan. Running inside the room, I find the connecting bathroom and dart through it.

"Fuck."

I discover Remi curled up on the floor. The room stinks of puke, and when I look closer I find she's covered the floor in her attempt to get to the toilet.

"Hey, Princess," I say, dropping down to my haunches in front of her and moving a lock of hair from her face.

Her skirt has risen up, showing me the swell of her ass and the scrap of black lace that's covering it, her hitched top displaying her tanned and toned stomach.

Even passed out she's fucking hot.

Sliding my hands under her arms, I lift her until she's sitting against the wall. "Ace?" she moans. Her eyes flicker open, but they don't focus on anything, so I'm pretty sure she has no idea my name just fell from her lips.

"Let's get you out of here, Princess."

I sweep her into my arms and hold her close as I make my way out of his fucking room. When she wakes, she's probably not going to want to know I helped her, but fuck, it could be a hell of a lot worse if I didn't. That motherfucker knew what he wanted earlier, and I doubt he'd have stopped, especially if he found her in this state in his bedroom.

"Conner," I shout when I get to the bottom of the stairs. He's dancing with some redhead, but the second he hears my voice he drops her like a stone.

"Shit, is she okay?" he asks, coming over and running his eyes over Remi. He's more sober than I was expecting, thank fuck.

"Yeah, just drunk. Get Cole and meet us at the car."

He nods and runs off in the direction of the garden. I've just managed to maneuver the two of us into the car when they both climb into the front.

"Where to?"

"Home."

"But?"

"No buts. I'm not taking her back to Sarah like this."

"But if James—"

"James won't know. I'll take her to the pool house, clean her up, and let her sleep it off."

Conner looks at me in the mirror, concern filling his eyes. I know what he's worried about. He thinks I'm going to get fed up trying to fit in with this life and end up running back to the Heights, leaving him here. I don't know how many times I need to tell him that won't happen. Not until they've both graduated and have their futures mapped out, that is. Like fuck am I staying here after they both fuck off to college.

"Just drive," I demand, and he thankfully does as he's told, but not before grumbling, "If she pukes in here then you're cleaning it up."

The drive is short, and in only a few minutes, Cole is holding the door open so I can get out with Remi still in my arms. She snored lightly all the way here.

"You two go in. We'll be fine." They both look between Remi and me before glancing at each other. They're not happy about it, but they eventually do as they're told and disappear into the house via the side door that leads directly to our staircase.

Remi doesn't stir until I get us into the bedroom at the back of the pool house. That's when she pulls her head away from my chest, looks at me through hooded eyes for the briefest moment, and then pukes over both of us.

"Jesus fucking Christ, Princess," I groan, walking straight for the bathroom. I drop her on the floor before pulling my shirt off and leaning into the shower to turn it on.

I glance at her slumped on the tiles and something aches inside me. I'm just doing this to keep her safe, I tell myself. To keep her away from Bexley and his wandering hands.

Biting down on my lip, I think about what to do for the best. She's going to be pissed in the morning when she finds out I stripped and showered her. But what's the alternative? Allow her to sleep with her hair caked in her own puke?

Pushing my concerns aside, I reach down and pull her own shirt off before standing her up and pushing her skirt down her thighs. I unclasp her bra and tell myself that I'm not going to look, no matter how much her dusky pink nipples might call to me. I remember all too well how sweet they were as I sucked them into my mouth. The little moans of pleasure that fell from her as I ran my tongue around them.

My cock swells as I remember her in that bathroom, totally at my mercy. Fuck, I need that again.

I carry her into the shower and allow the water to soak us both. Rinsing her hair, I ensure she's puke-free before stepping out and wrapping her in a towel and attempting to squeeze the water from her long locks.

This isn't the first night I've stayed out here when

I've needed space from the house and the asshole who owns it, and thank fuck, because when I step from the bathroom, I find an old t-shirt I abandoned on the chair waiting for me.

After sitting Remi on the edge of the bed, I pull it over her head and remove the towel from her body before dragging the sheets back and laying her down. It takes me forever to tug my sodden jeans from my legs, but after I do, I have the quickest shower ever before climbing into bed with her.

I want to pull her to me. Tell her she's safe. But I don't.

I can't.

It's not my place.

CHAPTER SIXTEEN

Remi

I wake to the sound of drums. No, that isn't right.

Ugh.

My head.

What the hell happened?

I lie as still as a statue, staring up at the ceiling, trying to piece together the night before.

The pep rally.

My plan to ruin Michaela's night and make Ace jealous.

Bexley.

Oh god, Bexley.

A wave of nausea hits me, and I scramble out of bed, almost tripping over my own feet. Rushing into the unfamiliar bathroom, I drop down and dry heave into the bowl.

Bexley tried to...

Shame burns through me. If I hadn't gone there dressed like a cheer slut, rubbing myself all over him—

No.

I steel myself. Nothing I said or did or wore excuses what he did—what he tried to do.

Finally convinced nothing is going to make a reappearance, I sink back against the tiles, giving myself a second to calm down. Pulling myself up, I run the faucet and splash my face with cold water. I'm a mess. My hair is damp and matted, and I have last night's mascara still caked around my eyes. I frantically search the cabinet for supplies. Relieved when I discover toothpaste, a new toothbrush, and a packet of facial wipes, I set to work on making myself feel human.

But even when I'm done, I still want to die.

Movement from behind me startles me, and then it hits me.

I have no fucking idea where I am.

Crap.

My heart races in my chest as I tiptoe out of the small bathroom and back into the bedroom. The air is sucked clean from my lungs when I find Ace sound asleep in bed—the bed I just ran from.

Oh god... did we?

No way. I would know if Ace had touched me. I'd feel... *something*.

"Stop overthinking," he grumbles, cracking an eye open at me.

"What the hell—"

"It's early, I'm tired." His hand slides to the empty space beside him and pats the mattress. "Come back to bed."

"You're more deluded than I thought if you think I'm going to—"

"Stop making everything so fucking difficult and come back to bed, Princess." His voice is heavy with sleep. Ace shifts onto his back, throwing an arm behind his head. His eyes are closed, and the rise and fall of his chest is heavy.

I can't help but smile. He's out cold again but looks so adorable—if adorable comes gift-wrapped in ink and shredded with muscle.

But as I watch him sleep, reality crashes down around me. Why am I here, in what I finally realize is James' pool house?

Ace brought me here, that much is obvious.

But why?

Spotting my cell phone on the nightstand, I grab it and check for messages. There's one from Mom, worried that I'm not in my bed. I quickly text her back and tell her I stayed at the dorms with Hadley. Speaking of my only friend, I open the text message from her.

Hadley: What happened to you?

Remi: Not sure. I have black spots.

Hadley: Shit, girl. Are you okay?

I glance over at Ace again. The sheet is thrown over his waist, but his upper body is on full display. Even in sleep he frowns, emanating danger. But his body is a work of art, literally. He's so beautiful it hurts to look at him. And despite how he treated me, I want nothing more than to crawl back into bed with him and soak up his presence.

Remi: My head feels like it's going to explode. Are you okay?

Hadley: I had a great night. Hayden walked me back to the dorms.

Remi: Hayden? You're kidding, right?

He's almost as bad as Bexley.

Hadley: I know, I know. But it isn't like that. He's just a friend.

Remi: Whatever you say. Just be careful, okay?

Hadley: Yes, Mom. Call me later if you want to hang.

I place my cell phone back down and, without overthinking it, slip back into bed beside Ace. I lie on my side, watching him. He doesn't move, his gentle snores filling the room. It's still early, and I have no desire to go home and face Mom. Not yet.

Smiling to myself, I turn over and close my eyes. I'm teetering on the edge of sleep when a hand curves around my hip and drags me backwards. Ace's body fits against mine as if we're two pieces of a complicated puzzle. He rests his chin on my shoulder. "Sleep," he whispers, his warm breath fanning my ear.

And this time, I listen.

When I wake again, Ace is gone. If it wasn't for the trickle of the shower coming from the bathroom, I might think it was all a dream.

I find a glass of water and some Advil next to my cell phone. For someone who acts like he doesn't care, he sure is thoughtful.

There's a slight drum in my head still, but nothing compared to earlier. A different sensation is vibrating through me, knowing Ace is on the other side of the door, naked, hot water sluicing down his cut abs. Even after the shitty way he treated me, I crave his touch. I'm like an addict chasing their next high. Needy. Desperate.

A slave to the cause.

I know I'll probably regret it later, but right now, I don't care.

Throwing back the sheet, I pad out of bed and move toward the bathroom door. It's slightly ajar, tendrils of steam melting into nothing as they meet the cooler air. Without thinking, I slip inside.

Ace has his back to me as he cleans himself. The taut muscles in his back and shoulders ripple with every movement. Before I chicken out, I pull the t-shirt off my body. It's one of those big walk-in showers we used to have in the old house, so he doesn't feel me approach.

At least, I think he doesn't until he grits out, "If you're coming in here, you'd better mean it."

Feeling a lick of confidence shoot up my spine, I curve a hand around his hip, letting it trace down his V-line and fall to his cock. It's at half mast, thick and heavy in my hand. "Jesus," he groans as I close my fingers around him and start pumping.

Ace's head drops as he slams a hand against the tile. His cock swells between my fingers as I go faster, slowing at the top and running my thumb over the bead of pre-cum. He hisses, cussing into the waterfall. I don't really know what I'm doing, but he seems to like it, and I like watching this big, powerful guy at my mercy.

"Shit, Remi, yeah, just like that," he groans as I jack him harder. He begins thrusting into my hand as I press my body up against his, desperate for some friction. Anything to relieve the ache deep in my belly.

"It feels so fucking good." One of his hands covers mine, forcing me to squeeze him harder, sliding our joined fingers all the way down his shaft and back up again in a punishing rhythm.

"I knew the first time I laid eyes on you, I was going to enjoy corrupting you," he chokes out. "Fuck, Remi, I'm going to come." Ace rips away from me and grasps his cock. His large hand lands on my shoulder and forces me to lower myself before he shoots himself all over my breasts.

"Ace!" I shriek.

"Needed to dirty you up a little, Princess." He reaches out, letting his thumb trail his sticky release all over me. I let out a breathy moan when he brushes my nipple.

"Fuck, you look good like that." He advances toward me, hunger simmering in his eyes. But I stand quickly, inching back.

"Why'd you do it?"

A frown crinkles his face. "Do what?"

"Really? That's how you want to play this?"

Ace rushes toward me, pushing me up against the tiles with his body. "No," he dips his head, licking my throat. "What I really want is to brand you again. It seems that fucker Bexley didn't get the message the first time around."

He sucks my skin hard, grazing his teeth there. "You were playing a dangerous game last night, Princess." Ace sucks harder, and I know he's going to leave a mark. "You. Are. Mine."

"God, Ace," I mewl because it feels so damn good, even when I know it shouldn't. My fingers slide into his hair, pulling hard. "Tell me you don't feel this... tell me."

There's something between us.

It's dark and delicious, and I can't get enough.

Even if he is a total asshole most of the time.

"I feel this." He smirks against my neck as his hands run over my body, sliding between us and finding my sweet spot.

"God," I gasp as his finger dips inside me.

"You like that?" He gives me his eyes and I nod, barely able to hold on as his finger works in tandem with his thumb.

"I'm not a good guy, Princess. I don't do hearts and flowers and all that fucking bullshit". He adds another finger, curling them inside me in a way that makes my knees go weak. I grab his arm, steadying myself, and he chuckles darkly.

"Yeah, ride my hand, Remi. Show me how much you want it." His eyes are blown with lust.

"More," I pant, "I need...more."

Ace drops to his knees, licking my navel. I gasp at the new sensations. Water trickles down on us, making everything so much more intense.

I stare down at him. He looks so playful, grinning up at me. "I'm going to make you shatter," he promises, and then his tongue is on my clit, licking and sucking and pushing me off a cliff so high I fall and fall and fall.

"Ace, fuck," I breathe. But he doesn't let up, working me with his tongue and fingers until I'm a boneless mess. Another orgasm crests, crashing over me with such force I scream his name.

Kissing up my stomach, Ace eventually meets my gaze once more. "Better?" His pierced brow lifts.

"I think you ruined me."

Something flashes in his eyes, but it quickly melts away, replaced with a smirk. "Ever tasted yourself, Princess?"

"Wha—"

Ace captures my lips, shoving his tongue deep in my mouth and wrapping it with my own. I can taste myself on him, and it's so fucking sexy.

"Suck," he demands, easing away and slipping his finger into my mouth. I make a show of it, licking him clean.

"Good girl. Next time, if you're lucky, it'll be my cock."

Heat pulses through me. I already want him again. But this is crazy.

He's crazy.

"We need to get cleaned up," I say, pushing him away so I can slip further under the water.

I need a second.

Ace is a lot.

My feelings for him are a lot.

"Hey," he says, his hands curving my waist and holding me close against his body. "Are you—"

"I'm fine. I just don't know where I stand with you. You drive me insane."

"What do you feel when I touch you?" His finger skates down my neck between the valley of my breasts and dips inside my navel. It's so erotic, a needy moan slips from my lips.

"I feel... alive."

I feel free. I swallow the words.

"Then does it need to be anything else?"

I tilt my head back to look at him, but Ace is lying in wait. He fixes his mouth over mine and kisses me.

Slow.

Tender.

And everything I don't expect it to be.

I want to believe he feels it too. That he needs this as much as I do. But I know there's still so much I don't know about the blue-eyed boy from the Heights.

I want to, though.

If he'll only drop his walls long enough for me to burrow inside.

We hang out at the pool house for the rest of the day. I'm not sure how it happened, but Conner came out to check on us and ended up staying. Then Cole appeared a bit later, so here we are, the four of us camped out in front of the TV watching reruns of *The Walking Dead*.

James is away for business again, but I only know because Mom mentioned it yesterday.

"Refill, anyone?" Conner asks, clambering to his feet. He's on a beanbag on the floor, with Cole in the chair and me and Ace on the couch. I'm curled up on end, my feet in his lap.

"Me, please." I hold up my glass and he lets out a little huff.

"Is this how it's gonna be now? The three of us waiting on the princess?" I can't see his face, but I do catch Ace glaring at him.

"And I thought you enjoyed being the little bitch boy," Cole grumbles.

"Fuck you, man. Just because you're a Seahawk now. Hey, does that mean you'll get a letterman jacket? I can just picture it now. Our little brother, rubbing shoulders with Sterling Prep elite in his new shiny—"

"Knock it off, Con," Ace grunts. "I'm watching this."

"I did not have you down for a *TWD* fan," I snicker.

"What the fuck did you just say?"

"*The Walking Dead*," I enunciate each word. "I figured you'd be more of a *Sons of Anarchy* kind of guy, or *Good Girls*. Yeah, that's more like it." I flash him a knowing smile, but he doesn't return it.

"Isn't that the one with the gang banger who fucks the rich bitch—"

"Con!" Ace and Cole both yell.

"Yeah, yeah, no swearing in front of the princess." He returns with my soda and flops back down on the beanbag.

"Hey, Conner," I say and he looks over at me. "Go fuck yourself."

Ace howls with laughter, and even Cole cracks a smile.

"She's trouble, Ace." Conner flips me off and I poke my tongue out at him. "This is the life, huh?" He relaxes back against the bag. "No adults to tell us what to do, no leaky rotten trailer, and we have a fully stocked refrigerator. I know James is a pretentious asshole, but you can't deny we dropped lucky with this gig."

Ace's hand stiffens around my ankle, his eyes turning dark.

"It's all right," Cole says. "But I miss the Heights."

Suddenly, I feel like an outsider to their conversation. Ace is pissed. Cole looks sad. And Conner is just Conner. He's so laid back I'm surprised he can stand half the time.

"Yeah, I know," he goes on. "But prep school pussy isn't so bad."

"I am right here," I hiss.

"Good job it's not your pussy I'm talking about then. Besides, I think Ace already staked his cla—" I grab a cushion and throw it at his face. My cheeks burn with indignation.

"Conner," Ace says.

"Yeah, bro?"

"Shut the fuck up."

CHAPTER SEVENTEEN

Ace

"Did you find out where he's going to be?" I whisper to Cole in the kitchen area of the pool house while Conner and Remi are distracted.

"Yeah. Party on the beach."

"Fantastic," I mutter, thinking that half the fucking school are going to be there, which means lots of potential witnesses.

The last thing I want to do is drag Cole into my bullshit with his captain, but he saw what I didn't, and, if it's possible, he looks even hungrier for Bexley's blood than I am.

"I'll text you when we're good?"

"You got it, bro."

I nod at him and take the drinks back through that I used as an excuse to get Cole alone in the first place.

After handing out the sodas, I drop back down on the couch. Remi immediately puts her feet back in my lap, and I'm powerless but to drop one of my hands to her ankle. What I really want to do is push it higher and up under the skirt I washed and dried for her so she had no excuse to leave after our very enjoyable shower this morning. But that was just the beginning. I need so much more from her today.

The episode they were still both staring at comes to an end, and I breathe a sigh of relief. I might be a patient guy when necessary, but having her long and very bare legs in my lap all this time is pushing my limits.

"You two can fuck off now," I grunt at my brothers who both look like they're getting comfortable for the night.

"But..." Conner whines when the next episode starts.

"Now," I bark, killing the TV with the remote that's sitting on the coffee table.

"It's okay, they can stay." Remi's soft voice fills the space.

Nice try, Princess, but it's time I got you alone. And naked.

I turn to her, holding her gaze for a second before dropping it down to my shirt that she's still wearing in favor of her own skintight Seahawks one. I'm fucking grateful, because that thing had Bexley's number on the back and he doesn't deserve to even look at Remi, let alone attempt to claim any kind of ownership of her.

Her nipples pebble behind the fabric, and I'm reminded that there's nothing beneath my shirt. She squirms, her thighs rubbing together, her foot moving against my growing cock.

"Jesus fucking Christ, we're going. Just stop doing that when you've got company." Conner's words barely register as I glare at Remi's skirt as if its mere presence offends me.

"Don't break her, Ace. We need someone to deliver the drinks next time we hang."

"Fuck. Off."

The second the door shuts behind them, I dive for her. "Fucking hell, Princess. Do you have any idea how badly I need my hands on you right now?"

She shakes her head, a shy, innocent smile playing on her lips.

"Well, let me show you."

I part her thighs, exposing her lace covered mound, and settle myself between them. Dropping my lips to hers, she makes a point of keeping hers closed for a few seconds in defiance.

I growl. "Hmmm... you know how much I like it when you fight. But you forget something, Princess. I fight dirty."

My hand dives under my shirt, and I cup her naked breast in my palm. She gasps at the sensation and her lips part for me.

"Wasn't hard now, was it?" I mutter against her mouth.

Her response is a groan as I pinch her nipple, making her hips roll against me.

Fuck. Revenge shouldn't feel this fucking good.

I still for a second as the reality of why we're even here hits me full force. But I lock it down. None of that matters right now. I'll worry about that later when I step outside of this little bubble we've found ourselves in.

Right now, all that matters is hearing her scream my name as I make her lose control.

I kiss along her jaw and down her neck. "You want me to make you come again, Princess?"

"Yes," she whispers.

"How do you want me to do it?"

When she doesn't respond, I give her some suggestions.

"My fingers?" I pinch her nipple again.

"Yes."

"My tongue?" I lick up the column of her neck and she trembles.

"Yes."

"Or my teeth?" I bite down, hard enough to leave a temporary mark. I can't help it. I need everyone in this fucking town to know who she belongs to.

"God, yes."

I don't offer her my cock. Not yet, anyway. Something tells me she's not ready. The slightly hesitant way she touched me earlier leads me to believe she doesn't have all that much experience in this area, and unlike fucking Bexley, I don't take things that aren't offered to me.

I might ruin them after, but at least I get their permission first.

Pushing the fabric of my shirt up her stomach, she helps me out by lifting from the couch and allowing me to pull it from her head. I stare down at her, and my mouth waters.

"So fucking perfect," I mutter, running my fingertip over her brand.

Mine.

"Ace," she begs, thrusting her full breasts towards me.

Reaching behind me, I tug my own shirt off and drop it to the floor. Her eyes immediately drop to my ink. I know she's curious about the story behind the art, but like fuck am I tainting her with those fucked-up stories.

Dropping my head, I suck one of her nipples into my mouth and then the other. She moans and writhes beneath me, but as much as I might want to take her right here on the couch, I know that anyone could see us right now if they cared to look.

Pulling her into my arms, her legs automatically wrap around my waist and her arms around my neck. She plays with the hair at my nape before leaning forward and dropping light kisses to my neck. Unable to cope with her softness and the things it does inside my chest, I throw her down on the bed. Her eyes fly open as she bounces.

"I already told you, Princess. I don't do hearts and flowers. I do hard and rough. That okay with you?"

"Y-yes."

"Good."

I push my sweats and boxers down my legs in one go, and her eyes drop to my hard length. I'm not sure if she's aware of it or not, but she licks her lips.

"All in good time, Princess. Let me take care of you first."

I pull her skirt down her thighs without undoing it, before wrapping my fingers around the edges of her panties and tugging until the fabric rips. "Now when you walk out of here, you'll be forced to remember what happened between us."

She bites down on her bottom lip as she watches me stare at her. My cock juts out in front of me, but I ignore it. Although I fully intend on having it seen to the second I'm done with her.

I grab her ankles and she squeals as I pull her to the

end of the bed before dropping to my knees before. "Such a pretty pussy." I run my finger through her folds, smiling when I find her wet and ready for me.

"Ace," she moans, bucking from the bed.

"You want my mouth, Princess?"

"Yes, yes I need... fuuuuck."

Leaning forward, I part her and suck on her clit. The second her taste hits me, I realize that I've got a problem.

I'm fucking addicted.

Her fingers dive into my hair and she pulls me closer, needing more. I slide two fingers inside her, and with them and my tongue working together, I play her until she screams my name for the entire town to hear.

Fuck, yes.

"Jesus, Ace. I feel like I could sleep for a week," she mutters as I climb up her limp body. Her eyes follow me but they're tired and hooded. Exactly as I planned.

"Too tired to repay the favor?"

Her eyes flick to my cock and she once again licks her lips. "I've... um... never..."

Her innocence fucking slays me, and I do something I never thought I would when next beside a hot body. "It's okay." Wrapping my hand around the back of her neck, I pull her in to kiss me.

She moans as she tastes herself, and my cock weeps, knowing that it's turning her on.

I wonder how quickly I could get her off again?

I'm just about to put that thought into action when she pushes harshly at my shoulder and forces me to lie back. She throws her leg over my waist before taking charge of the kiss.

Sexy. As. Fuck.

Her heat grinds down on my length. I'm so close to grabbing her hips and thrusting up into her, but I know I can't. I've got to wait.

She shimmies down my body, kissing over my pecs before running her tongue along the indentations of my abs.

"Remi," I warn. She's getting dangerously close as she starts to make her way down my V, licking and nipping at me with her teeth. If she doesn't finish the job, then I can't be held responsible for my actions.

Her innocent dark eyes look up at me.

Fuck.

All the air rushes out of my lungs at the sight.

So fucking perfect.

"Don't worry, Ace. I got it covered."

"O-okay," I stutter like a fucking idiot when she's hovering right over me. Her breath tickles my sensitive skin. It's the ultimate tease.

"Just tell me if it's—" I cut her off.

"It'll be perfect," I grate out, beginning to lose grip on my restraint.

Thankfully, she wraps her hand around my length before staring at it like it's a fucking popsicle stick.

"Remi. Fuuuuck," I grunt when she licks the head.

My body tenses as I wait for more. Almost as soon as she pulls back does she get braver and suck the tip of me into her mouth.

Her wet heat is fucking mindblowing, and all I can do is focus on the sensation as she begins bobbing up and down.

I fight to keep my eyes on her, to try to remember what it's like, because I know the time is coming where this is going to come to an end and all I'll have is memories.

"Jesus, Princess. So fucking good."

She smiles around me at the praise and takes a little more of me.

My fingers thread into her hair, but instead of using it to guide her like I usually would, to make her gag on my length like the dirty sluts of my past, I hold gently and allow her whatever she needs.

Fuck, she can have anything she wants if she keeps fucking going.

Long before I'm ready for it to end, tingles erupt in the base of my spine and my balls begin to draw up.

I don't want to warn her. I want her to drink me down. But I can't do it to her.

She isn't them. She's different and she deserves more.

Hell, she deserves a lot more than me and how I'm going to treat her. But that's who I am, the motherfucker with no conscience from the Heights.

"Rem, I'm gonna come, baby."

I tug on her hair a little, giving her an out should she want one, but she doesn't even flinch.

Okay, don't say I didn't warn you.

"Fuuuuuck," I groan as my orgasm hits me.

And even still, she keeps fucking going.

Once I've come down, I pull her up my body and kiss her until I'm once again hard and ready for more.

Fucking hell, will it ever be enough with her?

I lose track of how many times I make her come, but by the time she passes out beside me, I've fulfilled my promise of using my fingers, tongue, and teeth. Now all I need is to sink inside her and find out just how tight she is. But I'll wait until she's begging me to take her.

After convincing her to stay, Remi texted her Mom earlier and said she was spending another night with Hadley. She wasn't all that happy about doing it until I reminded her of the benefits of staying with me—none of which she'd be able to have if she were alone in her own bed. She caved pretty fast to my way of thinking after that.

I could have let her go, but I need her here, believing I spent the whole night in bed beside her, because I've got some revenge to go and serve.

Thirty minutes after she passes out in my arms, I slip from the bed and silently pull on some dark clothes. After texting Cole, I leave the pool house and meet him at the side door, ready to go.

"What's the plan then, bro? Beat him black and blue so he misses the first game of the season?"

"We're not going to lay a hand on that cunt. Not yet, anyway. I've got something much more painful to his ego in mind."

Cole rubs his hands together like the sadistic motherfucker that he is, and a wicked smile curls at my lips.

I fucking love my brother's twisted mind. It's the only one that rivals my own.

CHAPTER EIGHTEEN

Remi

I wake with a start. Sitting up, I push unruly curls out of my face and get my bearings. I'm in the pool house still, and it's late. I can tell from the way the moonlight is streaming in through the window.

Ace sleeps soundly beside me, his hand curled possessively around my hip. For someone who likes to repeatedly remind me he isn't a hearts and flowers kind of guy, he's doing a pretty impressive job of pulling me deeper under his spell.

Grabbing my cell off the nightstand, I check the time. One-thirty. Jesus. Mom is going to ask questions tomorrow, a lot of them. But I've already given Hadley a heads up that she's my cover, should anyone ask.

Restless, I check my messages and have a quick glance at social media. I'm about to put down my cell when something catches my eyes.

What the hell?

It's a photo of the beach, where the volleyball court is, and right there, bound, gagged, debagged, and tied to one of the posts is... "Bexley?" I shriek.

"Uh, what?" Ace's voice is heavy with sleep.

"What the hell?" I zoom in to read the marker scrawled across his chest. "I suck Seahawk dick." My eyes fly to Ace. He's still asleep beside me. "Tell me this wasn't you?"

Bexley is already gunning for revenge, and I don't want to think about what he might do if Ace was responsible for this.

"Ace," I snap, grabbing his nipple and twisting.

"Ow, what the fuck?" He bolts upright.

"Tell me you didn't?" I thrust the phone in his face and he frowns, rubbing his jaw.

"What the hell is that?"

"It's Bexley, look..."

He explodes with laughter. "Stupid douchebag had it coming to him."

"So it wasn't you?" I narrow my eyes, looking for any trace of guilt. Before I can make a decision, he flips me onto my back, pinning me to the bed.

"What can I tell you, Princess? I wish it was me. Fuck only knows I can't wait to get him for ever putting his hands on you. But it wasn't me." He runs his nose along my jaw, letting his lips ghost over mine. "How could it be when I was here all night, getting you off."

My stomach clenches. "I fell asleep," I murmur as he begins to grind into me. "You could have... snuck out."

Ace hitches my leg around his waist, driving deeper. Only the thin cotton of my panties and his boxer briefs separate us. “Why would I sneak out when I have you in my bed?”

“It really wasn’t you?” I can’t imagine anyone else is stupid enough to take on Bexley.

“Let me fuck you,” he whispers against the shell of my ear, making my stomach coil. “I need inside you, Remi, baby.” He rolls his hips, showing me just how ready he is.

“Ace, I’m...”

“You’re a virgin?” He doesn’t look surprised, just curious.

I nod. “This, us, I like what we have going,” I slide my hands over his broad shoulders, “but I’m not sure I’m ready to—“

He gives me a tight nod. “I can wait.”

“Geez, thanks.” I drop my eyes. Part of me wants to give it up to him. It isn’t like I’ve been holding onto my V-card for that special someone. I just didn’t ever want it to be something I’ll regret.

Ace grips my chin, pulling my face back to his. “What’s going on in that head of yours?”

“There’s some stuff... stuff you don’t know about me. Stuff I’ve never really dealt with.”

His eyes flash with concern, his muscles tensing. “What stuff?”

I nudge him gently, and Ace rolls off me. He slips his arm around me, pulling me into his side.

“After my mom found out about the affair, she went off the rails. Drinking. Hanging out at bars looking for attention. I guess she needed to know she still had it or whatever. Anyway, she met this guy. She was so smitten, but I never liked him. There was just something about him.

"Things started to get serious, and he started coming around the house. I was so mad at her. We'd barely gotten settled in and she had already moved on, or at least, that's what it felt like." I knew now, that wasn't it at all. She was hurting, and she needed something—or someone—to help numb the pain.

"Anyway, he turned out to be a total jerk. He'd get drunk and order her around as if it was his house. She didn't let him stay over often, but when she did I always dreaded those nights." I inhale a deep breath, blocking out the memories.

"Princess, you've gone awfully quiet over there." I sense Ace watching me. "Did he do something, Remi?"

Anger laces his words, soothing something inside of me. Ace cares. Whether or not he's willing to admit it, I know he does. But like me, he hasn't had a typical upbringing. The people he was supposed to be able to count on, to teach him about love and family and forgiveness, let him down.

And now we're here.

Two lost souls bound together by stolen touches and toxic kisses.

"Tell me about you," I say, changing the subject. I've already said too much about mom's ex. I don't want him to come between any more than he already is.

"There isn't much to say," Ace grunts. "Dad died when we were young. Mom tried, and failed, to hold it together, and I had to grow up fast to take care of my brothers."

"And that guy, Donny? How did that happen?"

"The Heights is a jungle, Princess. If you're weak, you get preyed on. And if you're strong, you have to prove your worth. Lucky for me, I was always strong *and* I had something to fight for."

"Your brothers?"

I feel him nod. "It's why I'm here, for them..." Ace hesitates. "They deserve a chance at something better. Conner is smart, he could do anything he puts his mind to, and Cole has a real shot at football."

"And you?" I lean up to look at him. "What do you deserve, Ace?"

He looks at me and says ten little words that make my heart ache. "There's only one place I'm going, Princess. Straight to Hell."

I wake to the feel of Ace's lips trailing over my collarbone. "It's almost ten."

"What?" I shriek.

"Yeah, we overslept. Conner just texted to say your mom just got here."

"Shit." I bolt upright, catching Ace in the face with my elbow.

"Motherfucker," he grinds out, rubbing his cheek. I duck down to kiss him better.

"I'm sorry, but if my mom finds out I'm—"

"Sorry to burst your bubble, Princess, but that ship has long sailed."

"She knows?" My brows furrow. "And James?" He nods. "Why do you seem so calm about this?"

"Because," Ace flips me, rolling me beneath him, "it doesn't change the fact that I'm going to be doing very bad things to you tonight."

"Yeah?" I grin.

"Yeah." He kisses me, letting his tongue slowly twirl with mine. The news that my mom and James both know about me being here melts away until I'm drowning in nothing but the feel of Ace's lips on mine.

"We should probably go face them."

"Okay." He's acting too cocky, as if he can't wait to see his uncle's reaction.

"You know," I say, climbing out of bed and searching around for my clothes. "James really isn't so bad once you get to know him."

Ace freezes, anger flashing across his expression. He storms into the bathroom, slamming the door.

Okay then.

I let out a small sigh. Maybe there's a way to go before Ace forgives James.

By the time I'm dressed, Ace comes back into the bedroom and pulls on some sweatpants and a clean tank. "Come on." He holds out his hand, and I take it.

We walk the short distance to the house in silence. He says he's not bothered about them knowing, but with every step we take his walls inch down until my Ace is gone.

"Uh oh, the princess and her frog are in trouble," Conner teases as we walk into the kitchen.

"Fuck off," Ace grunts, releasing my hand and going to the refrigerator.

"My mom," I say, "is she—"

"Right here," she frowns. "You have some explaining to do, young lady."

James strides into the room, wrapping an arm around her shoulder. "Conner, you can leave. This doesn't concern you for now."

"Damn, I had my popcorn ready and everything."

I scowl in his direction and he grins, mouthing, 'good luck,' before ducking around his uncle.

Ace leans back against the counter, a bottle of juice in his hand. He takes a long swallow, wiping his mouth with the back of his hand.

"Do you have anything to say for yourself?"

"Nothing comes to mind," he replies coolly.

"I told you explicitly to stay away from Remi—"

"You did?" I gasp, feeling betrayal coil around my heart. Ace never said a word.

"What I think James is trying to say, sweetheart, is that we're concerned about your new... *friendship*."

"We've been hanging out, so? It's not a crime."

"And this weekend," James adds. "Did you stay over in the pool house?"

"I'm almost eighteen—"

"*Not* the point, Remi." Mom frowns. "We're worried about you. Cutting class, stopping out all night and lying to me. It isn't like you, baby."

"You told me to make new friends and to live a little." It's a futile argument, but I feel like I need to defend what Ace and I share.

Because god only knows, he's making zero effort to do it.

"It's one thing to sabotage your shot at something good," James levels his nephew with a hard look, "but to drag Remi down to your level is inexcusable."

"Because of course it's me corrupting the good little princess, right?" He stands straight, animosity rolling off him in waves. "She couldn't possibly want to hang out with me, could she?"

"Ace, that's not what we're saying." Mom's voice

softens. "But Remi needs to focus on school. She needs to make some serious decisions about her future."

"I've already told you, I won't take his money. If I don't get offered a scholarship, I'm done."

"Remi," she gasps, touching the side of her face. "You don't mean that." Her eyes flick between me and Ace as if she knows he's to blame for the change in me.

And maybe he is.

But it isn't that simple.

Ace hasn't changed me—he's just unlocked something inside me.

Something I've spent a long time trying to hide.

"Sarah, you should take Remi home. I need to speak to my nephew alone."

"I won't stop seeing him," I blurt out, because it feels like we're already hurtling toward the end of whatever this is, and I'm not ready for it to be over yet.

"Yes, well, we'll see about that." James' tone is scathing. "I refuse to let Ace taint your future, Remi."

I suck in a harsh breath, and Mom rushes to my side. "Come on, sweetheart. I'm sure James and Ace have lots to talk about." She wraps her arm around me.

Staring at Ace, I plead with him to look at me, but he's fixed on his uncle.

"I'll speak to you later, okay?" My mom says to James as we pass him. She grabs his arm and leans on her tiptoes. "Don't be too hard on him."

With one final glance at Ace, I let Mom lead me away, hoping I didn't just land him in a whole heap of trouble.

When we pull up to the house, Mom cuts the engine and turns to me. "Ready to talk about it?" I'd given her the silent treatment the entire ride home. "Remi, work with me here, please."

"What's to say? You've both made up your minds."

"And just like that, you're going to listen to your mother for once?" Her brow rises, and I press my lips together. "Hmm, thought not."

"So, I like him. Is it really that big a deal?"

"James seems to think it is. He cares about you, sweetheart, and he knows those boys better than you or me."

"Does he?" I sneer. "Because something doesn't add up, Mom."

"Whatever do you mean?"

"He was so excited to bring them to the house, but it's like they can't stand each other. Ace talks about him like he's to blame for something."

"Ace is angry at the world, baby." She reaches over and squeezes my hand. "And he's lashing out at the one parental figure he has left. James told me Ace harbors a lot of hatred toward him over what happened with his mom. But he tried to help. Unfortunately, Maria wouldn't allow it."

"Yeah, maybe." But I didn't buy it. There was something else.

There had to be.

"Does it really bother you so much, the idea of me seeing him?"

"Every parent wants the best for their child, Remi, and honestly, I'm not sure Ace is what you need. Bexley however—"

"Are you kidding me right now? You just found out I like Ace and you're going to sit here comparing him to Bexley?" I reach for the door handle. I need to get out of here.

"Sweetheart, that's not what I meant."

"You know, Mom, you of all people should know that good looks and a charming smile are only skin deep. It's what on the inside that counts, and Bexley Danforth is nothing more than another devil in sheep's clothing."

With that, I stumble out of the car and take off toward the beach.

CHAPTER NINETEEN

Ace

Our stare holds as Sarah and Remi's footsteps get quieter before the front door opens and closes, signaling that we're alone. The vein in James' neck pulsates to the point that I wonder if it's about to burst. He waits another five seconds to compose his words before laying into me.

"What the fuck is wrong with you? I have given you everything you could possibly want or need and yet, you still fuck it up. You still go against the one thing I warned you about."

"No, I'm pretty sure you warned me about parties and drugs in the house. I ignored them too, if you hadn't noticed."

His face turns beet red at my words. "That's it. I forbid you from seeing her again," he bellows.

His eyebrows almost hit his hairline when I just start

laughing. "You forbid me? Come off it, you jumped up prick. I'm a fucking adult, she's almost eighteen. We can do what the fuck we like, and you can do fuck all about it."

He opens his mouth as if he wants to argue, but I don't give him the chance. "I don't need a father," I grit out. "I've managed my entire life without one, and without you. It's too little too late for you to act concerned about my welfare and my future."

"I'm not trying to replace him, Ace. I'm just trying to give you what you missed out on."

"Too fucking late. And replace him?" I sneer. "I can barely fucking remember him. He's been gone almost all my life, but you're fully aware of how long it's been, aren't you?" I narrow my eyes at him, willing him to say more, but all he does is straighten his back and smooth down his fucking tie.

"You're right," he says, sounding much calmer all of a sudden. Funny what happens when you get close to exposing someone's indiscretions.

"I am?"

"I'm just trying to make life easier for you. I know how hard you've had it."

"Yet you left us there in the middle of it. You could have made our lives easier years ago, but you didn't so much as show your face after Dad died."

"You don't think I tried?" he shouts, losing his cool once again.

"Well, did you?"

"That's not the point."

"Well, what is the fucking point then?" I roar. "Because as far as I see it, you're suddenly trying to control my life, and trust me when I tell you that it's the last thing I fucking want. I don't want or need you in my life. I'm only putting up with my bullshit for them," I point above my head to where I assume my brothers are. "They are what's important. It's not too late for them. Me, however, I know I'm a lost cause. And yes, I'm also aware that Remi is too good for me, but so fucking what. Don't you think it's about time I had something good in my life? Something that your money can't suddenly buy?"

He releases a breath and stares at the ceiling for a beat. "If you so much as hurt a hair on her head, I'm warning you, Ace..."

"Why do you care? She's not your fucking daughter. She's only in your life because you're fucking her mother."

"That's enough." His face is bright red now. "I care deeply for both of them, and I will do right by them both."

"And that doesn't include me."

He raises an eyebrow, but I don't hang around long enough to hear what he might have to say.

I can't leave it there, though. My anger won't let me. Stopping when I get to the kitchen, I turn back to him. "Let's get a few things straight. If it weren't for them, then I wouldn't be here. You're a lying, deceitful cunt, and I want nothing to do with you, even less your guilt money. So from here on out, you stay out of my life and I'll stay out of yours. I'll move into the pool house so we don't even need to see each other." I walk away with his mouth hanging open in shock.

I'm done with this conversation and the bullshit about him caring about us that keeps falling from his lips. If he cared, then he wouldn't have left us. Hell, he wouldn't have put us in that position in the first place.

This is all about guilt, all of it, and I want nothing to do with it other than to hurt him just like he did us.

He thinks he's a pro at manipulation, but he's clearly not met the master, because dear old Uncle James is about to get a taste of his own medicine.

I storm up the stairs with such force that both Cole and Conner poke their heads out of their rooms.

"Are you ever going to give him a break?" Conner asks. I get why they're confused—they don't know any of it, and like fuck am I going to tell them now so the truth can fester inside of them like it has me since I discovered it.

"Un-fucking-likely. He's a cunt."

"Really?" Conner asks, gesturing to the house around us.

"His money means fuck all. He's had it all these years and never done shit to help us before now."

"I'm sure there was a reason. He clearly cares enough to do all this. He didn't have to."

"Whatever." I turn my back on them both and continue to my room. "I'm moving into the pool house if you need me."

"You're what? Why?"

"Because I am. All right?"

Conner holds his hands up in surrender. "Okay, fine. Do your thing. Hey, did you see that photo of Bexley that's doing the rounds? That shit is funny as fuck. Any idea who did it?" Cole catches my eye over Conner's shoulder. His sparkle with delight and accomplishment.

"It's the least he deserves."

"Agreed. He's going to get the shit beaten out of him one day."

"Yeah, and hopefully it'll be my fists teaching him a fucking lesson."

"How about you just focus on taking your tension out on your girl, save you getting kicked out of school before Thanksgiving, eh?"

I grab the minimal amount of belongings I have and shove them all into a couple of bags. I avoid the kitchen on the way out to the back yard. The last face I want to look at is his.

It takes me less than ten minutes to find places for everything before I fall down on the couch and stare at my new home.

Why does it feel so cold and empty without her in it?

Pulling my cell from my pocket, I shoot her a message. When I snuck back inside last night, her phone was lighting up like a fucking Christmas tree on the nightstand with news about Bexley's little accident, so I seized the opportunity to take her number.

Ace: You okay?

The little dots start bouncing almost immediately, and a bolt of excitement races through me. Jesus, I need to go back to the Heights and re-grow my fucking balls.

Remi: Mom thinks I should forget you and give Bexley the time of day instead. I walked away and I'm sitting on the beach.

Ace: Shall I come to you?

She waits a little longer to reply this time. It's almost

enough to have me putting my sneakers back on and heading her way.

Remi: I'm okay. Just enjoying the peace before I go back. How did things go with James?

Ace: As expected. I've moved into the pool house.

Remi: How come?

Ace: Because he can't hear you screaming my name from out here.

I can picture her cheeks heating as she reads my message. I don't wait for her to reply this time.

Ace: Can I see you tonight?

Remi: I don't think it's a good idea.

Fuck that.

I'm not giving shit up because of her mom and my uncle.

I wait until the sun has gone down before I set off. I don't take my bike, deciding the run will do me good. I haven't found the time to work out as much since I got here, too consumed with thoughts of a certain brunette to really worry about it, but I need to do something to stay in shape.

It takes me less than thirty minutes to get to her place, and, exactly as I hoped, all the lights are out. Silently, I make my way around to the backyard and look up.

I can't help but smile the second I see her window is once again cracked open. Was she expecting me? Surely it shouldn't be a surprise that I'd show up. I've done it before, and if it means getting another taste of her then I'll do it again.

In seconds, I'm throwing my leg inside and dropping to my feet into her dark and silent room. I slip my sneakers off, quickly followed by my sweaty tank and make my way to her bed. She's fast asleep, and with just the light from the moon shining in through the window, she looks like an angel.

I allow myself a second to take her in before pulling the covers back gently. Her tank has risen up her stomach and is thin enough that I can make out the outlines of her nipples. Her tiny panties are just begging to be ruined.

Dropping down on one knee, I straddle her petite body and press my hands down on the pillow, either side of her head. I breathe her in before brushing my lips over hers. Her entire body tenses beneath me. Her eyes fly open and she lets out a shriek. I move quickly, covering her mouth before she alerts Sarah to my presence.

The fear in her eyes takes me back to what she started telling me about earlier, and the dread that was sitting heavy in my stomach as she confessed about her mom's boyfriend returned. She said she's a virgin... although there are plenty of other things...

Shaking the thoughts from my head, I focus on her.

"It's okay," I whisper. "It's only me. I wanted to make sure you really were all right?"

"So you sneaked in and scared me half to fucking death?"

"Sorry, I thought it would be hot to wake you with my tongue."

"Yeah, if you think getting raped or murdered in your sleep is hot."

I wince. Neither of those were part of my plan. "Let me make it up to you." I trail my fingertip from her neck and down to her already puckered nipple. She might be giving me all the sass, but her body is so on board with my surprise appearance.

"I wouldn't want to stop you." She arches her back and fills my palm with her breast.

"Can you be quiet?"

She rolls her eyes. "Just how good do you think you are?"

Without giving her an answer, I kiss down her body before ripping her panties away.

"You need to stop doing that," she whisper-shouts.

"Why? I like it. And I think you do too, if how wet you are is anything to go by." I run my finger through her folds, and just like I expected, she's soaked for me.

"I'm going to run out. Mom will start asking questions if I suddenly need to buy all new panties."

"I hate to break it to you, but I think they're well aware of what I'm doing to you."

She groans. "Less talk, more action, Ace."

I'm not one to follow orders, but when she's the one dishing them out and her pussy is right in front of my face, I'm powerless but to be a good boy and do as I'm told.

Her moans fill the room as I lick at her until she ends up covering her face with her pillow.

Yeah, baby. I'm just that good.

"You can go back to sleep now. I got what I came for."

She reaches out, rubbing my length through my sweats. "I beg to differ. It seems you might need more."

"I didn't come here for me. I came for you. I can wait." I can, it's true. Although I don't fucking want to.

"Shut up." Sitting up, she pulls me so I'm standing between her knees and shoves my sweats and boxers down my thighs.

"Sure, you can play with that," I say with a laugh.

"Oh, I wasn't aware that I needed permission to do... this," she mumbles the last word around my tip, and it vibrates all the way up my spine.

Shit. She's good at this.

It's going to really fucking suck when all of this comes to an end and I'm left with the likes of Michaela and Lylah to get what I need.

I hate to do it, but once she's finished, I tuck her back into bed and kiss her goodnight. "I'll see you tomorrow. You want a lift tomorrow with Cole and Conner?"

"Why not with you?"

"I don't think that's a very good idea. Do you?"

"Why not?" She gives me a half-shrug. "Mom knows, James knows. What's wrong with everyone else knowing?"

"A lot. Just trust me."

She pouts but doesn't argue.

"I'll get them to swing by."

I give her one last kiss before climbing back out the way I came and jogging to the pool house with thoughts of how she's going to handle tomorrow at the forefront of my mind.

CHAPTER TWENTY

Remi

"We need to talk." Hadley is waiting for me as I climb out of Conner and Cole's car.

"Thanks for the ride," I say. "I'll see you later."

"Don't be a stranger," Conner calls after us.

"Where the hell did you get to all weekend? And don't feed me that 'I was studying' bullshit. You were not studying." Her eyes narrow and then widen. "Holy shit, you got laid... Ace?" His name is coated in disbelief.

"Ssh," I hiss, pulling her away from the crowd filing into school.

"You did, didn't you? You totally gave it up to him."

"Will you stop, already? I did no such thing."

"But you did something?" Her brow quirks up, and I feel my cheeks flush.

"Busted! I knew it. Spill, girl. I want details. All the glorious, dirty details."

"Who are you right now?"

Sadness flickers across her face. "Someone who hasn't had it in far too long."

"Hadley, we're seniors."

"Yeah, well some of us started young." She shrugs as if it's no big deal. I guess she has a point. "So... deets."

"And then can I go to class?"

"Yes," she shrieks with delight.

"Okay," I glance around, checking we're not at risk of being overheard. "I stayed over at the pool house with him... all weekend."

"You did not." Her lips form an *O*, and I nod.

"Holy crap, that's huge. It's huge, right?"

"Something is huge," I smirk.

"Oh my god, you're so bad. I love it." Hadley claps. "So, are the two of you together or casual or..."

"We're... us." It's my turn to shrug.

"What does that mean?"

"It means I don't want to jinx it. Ace isn't exactly the relationship type. But there's something there, Hads."

"And the shit with Michaela was, what exactly?"

"The equivalent of him pulling my pigtails, I guess." The memory of him touching her leaves a sour taste in my mouth, but it wasn't her in his bed all weekend.

"He's probably just scared of his feelings for you. You know how crazy guys can get about stuff like that."

"I guess."

"Your mom is gonna freak."

"She already did. James too. I don't know everything that happened, but Ace moved into the pool house after he and his uncle got into it."

"So now you can sneak in for sleepovers whenever you want."

"You can't tell anyone, Hadley."

"Who am I going to tell? Oh wait," her eyes light up, "I could tell Michaela, knock her down a peg or two."

"Don't you dare." Ace is right. Going public will only paint a bigger target on my back. Besides, there's something thrilling about the idea of sneaking around.

"My lips are sealed. Unlike yours, apparently."

"Hads!"

"Like you don't love it. It's about time you got some. You're a catch, Remi. Don't let anyone ever tell you any differently. Just be careful, okay?"

"Not this again," I grumble as we finally make our way inside the building.

"I'm just saying have some fun, enjoy the perks of being with a guy like Ace," she lowers her voice, "but don't let yourself fall too deeply."

"I know." Heeding her warning would be the sensible thing to do, but Ace makes me reckless. He makes me want things.

Things with him.

"Slow and steady, I promise." I force a smile in her direction.

Even though I'm lying to her.

And myself.

———

My body tingles with anticipation as I stalk the door, waiting for him to arrive.

Ace finally enters the room and everyone falls silent. Even the teacher stops and gawks. I shake my head with silent laughter.

A week later, and he still has that effect on people.

He doesn't take the empty desk beside me. Inside he walks to the back of the room. Disappointment snakes through me, but I know I wouldn't be able to resist him if he were next to me.

The teacher starts the lesson, and my cell phone vibrates in my pocket. I discreetly dig it out, burying it in my lap.

Ace: Are you wearing any panties?

Remi: Behave!

Ace: With you, never.

By the time the bell goes, I'm a tight ball of restless energy. I slip out of the room and melt into the stream of bodies. Ace passes me, his low whisper hitting me right in the stomach.

"Tonight," he whispers, "leave your window—"

"There you are." Michaela's dulcet tone rakes up my spine. "I was hoping we could hang out at lunch."

Forcing myself to move around them, I head for my locker, watching the two of them out the corner of my eye. Michaela is in her full cheer outfit, complete with a Seahawk blue bow in her high ponytail. She looks so sweet and innocent, like butter wouldn't melt. I know she's all salt and acid, though.

Her eyes flick to mine and she shoots me a wicked grin, making a show of curling a perfectly manicured hand around Ace's arm.

And I hate it.

"Hey," Hadley says as she reaches me. "What is... oh. What's that all about?"

"I have no idea."

"And you're okay with that?"

"Of course I'm not okay with it, but what can I do?" Ace isn't encouraging her, but he isn't exactly pushing her away either.

Pulling out my cell phone, I type a message to him.

Remi: Should I wear my old cheer outfit later?

Ace's lip curls as he scans the text.

Ace: Jealousy looks good on you, Princess. Maybe you should steal your step-sister's outfit and I'll eat you out in it later?

Heat floods me as I glance over at him. He's watching me, his eyes dark and hooded, as if he's imagining doing just that.

"Yeah, you're doing a great job of being discreet." Hadley chuckles, snapping me out of it. "Good luck with that."

We head for our next class, and all I can think about is whether or not I should break into the girls' locker room later.

The rest of the day isn't much different. Me and Ace

text back and forth, teasing one another with promises of things to come. There's a constant queue of girls all vying for his attention: Michaela, Lylah, even some brazen juniors follow him around, batting their eyes and pouting their lips. I'd be lying if I said it didn't make me jealous, but I know it's not their bodies he'll be touching tonight.

Conner is waiting for me when I exit school. "Princess." Her smirks. "Your chariot awaits."

"Is Cole at practice?"

He nods. "So it's just you and me."

"I can hardly wait." I roll my eyes playfully as I climb inside.

"So you and my brother, what's up with that?"

My spine stiffens. Conner likes to tease me, but usually Ace and Cole are around to rein him in.

"You should ask him."

He chuckles. "Is that your way of saying you have no fucking idea?"

"We haven't labelled it."

"You know my brother doesn't date, right?"

I'm not sure what we're doing constitutes dating—that would involve leaving the bedroom, which we never do.

But I don't want Conner to know that.

"He took me for pizza," I say, instantly realizing how dumb it sounds.

"Yeah, I heard all about your little trip to the Heights. Dumb move, if you ask me." Conner puts his foot down on the gas the second we're off campus.

"Do you have a problem with me?" I ask.

"Nah, we're good. I've just never known my brother so worked up over a chick. Not even Kelsey—"

"Who is she?"

"You know about Kelsey?"

"Cruz mentioned her."

"Cruz? You're even starting to sound like him."

"I'm not..." The words dry on the tip of my tongue.

"Look, if you two want to bump uglies, that's none of my business, but I know Ace, and he always has a motive. And you seem like a nice girl, Remi. I'd hate for you to end up hurt."

My eyes narrow as I try to figure out if he's being sincere. "So this little TED talk, it's for my benefit?"

Conner shrugs, running a hand down his face. "Just watch your back. It's obvious you like him."

"So what if I do? Is that such a crime?"

"Ace is never going to change. The Heights is in his blood. You don't just leave that behind because you go and get yourself a prep school princess."

His words hurt, but I don't let him see it. Gazing out of the window, I swallow down the building tears.

I know Ace is a dark soul. I know he's done things—scary, inexcusable things. But I also see the boy carrying the weight of the world on his shoulders. He's tough because he's had to fight to survive. He's cruel because no one taught him how to love. And he's cold because it's easier than letting people in.

We ride the rest of the way in thick silence. Conner's words weigh heavily on my heart because I know there's some truth to what he's saying. Society will never accept Ace, and they'll always frown at a girl from Sterling Bay being with the boy from Sterling Heights.

But I don't see things so black and white. I see all the shades of grey.

I see Ace

And none of it changes how I feel about him.

Even if it's foolish.

Even if it makes me a stupid girl blinded by a wolfish grin and a body made for sin.

Conner rolls to a stop alongside my house. "Listen, I'm sorry if I overstepped. I just don't want my brother to end up doing something he'll regret, and I don't want to see you get hurt."

"I appreciate your concern," I say as I shoulder the door. "But maybe you should have a little bit more faith in Ace. People can change, Conner. But you need to give them a chance to."

"Shh." Ace covers my mouth with his hand as he works his fingers underneath my tank top. It's the third night this week he's climbed through my bedroom window. We spend our days pretending we're nothing to each other, saving our truths for moments like this, in the cover of darkness and safety of silence.

"God, I missed these." He lifts my tank, dropping his head to my breasts, licking and squeezing, nipping and stroking. Ace only has to touch me and I melt.

"You only saw them two nights ago." Last night he couldn't come. James insisted the four of them go out to celebrate Cole's spot on the team. Ace hadn't wanted to go, but he did because despite what people think about him, he always puts his brothers first.

I never told him what Conner said to me, and he hasn't mentioned anything, so I'm guessing his brother didn't come clean about our conversation. I still ride with them, but it's not the same. Conner looks at me with disappointment in his eyes, and I reflect it back at him. He thinks I'm foolish for believing Ace can change, and I think he's an asshole for believing his brother can't.

"I almost stabbed Lylah today. 'I'd love you to help me with the assignment, Ace,'" I mock. "Thirsty bitch."

His hand slides up my throat, pinning me to the bed. "God, I fucking love it when you get jealous." Ace stares down at me, eyes full of fire. He works his hand down my body and dips a finger inside me. I inhale a sharp breath at the sudden intrusion. "One day, that'll be my cock. I can't wait to feel you wrapped around me, squeezing me."

"God, Ace..." My eyes roll as he begins dragging his thumb over my clit with so much pressure I don't know whether to scream at him to stop or cry for him to continue.

Lowering his face to mine, he watches me intently. I've noticed it's something he does now. As if he can't quite believe I'm here. As if he's expecting me to disappear at any second.

His intensity is overwhelming, but I'm addicted to the rush.

"More," I beg. "I need..."

"Ssh, Princess." He drags his tongue up my cheek. "I know what you need," another finger enters me, "and I'm going to give it to you. Come on my fingers, Remi, baby."

His dirty words make me shatter, waves of pleasure crashing over me. I cry out as he doesn't let up, but he swallows my moans, pushing his tongue deep into my mouth.

"Fuck, you're so fucking sexy." He strokes my face, planting tiny kisses all over my lips. "I can't get enough of you." His expression darkens, and he shifts his gaze away from me.

"Ace, what is it?" I slide my hand against his stubbled jaw.

"Nothing. I'm just thinking I'm an asshole for not taking you anywhere."

I rear back. "You want to take me somewhere?"

"Well, isn't that what girls what? To go out?"

"I like what we do just fine." But I can't deny the butterflies taking flight in my tummy.

"Don't look so worried, Princess, I'm not suggesting we go to some stuck-up rich people's place. But we could hang with Cruz and D."

"You want to take me to hang out with your friends?"

"Fuck, I don't know... I'm just saying we don't always have to do this..." His eyes are wild, clouded with uncertainty, and it's so cute seeing him like this.

"Is the big bad Ace Jagger asking me out on a date?"

"I don't date, Princess."

"Will you pick me up from my house and bring me home at the end of the night?"

He nods, his Adam's apple bobbing nervously.

"Then," I grin, "it's a date."

CHAPTER TWENTY-ONE

Ace

I release a long breath as I pull up outside Remi's house on Friday night. I'm five minutes early because I couldn't put up with pacing back and forth in the pool house any longer.

I don't date, so why I'm doing this now fuck only knows. But as I was staring down at her last night, all I could think was that I was doing her a disservice. I already know that she deserves better than me. She should have a guy who treats her right, not who just sneaks into her bedroom at night under the cover of darkness and does wicked things to her body. She deserves the hearts and flowers I'm incapable of giving her.

Shaking my arms out at my sides, I notice some movement at the window. I narrow my eyes trying to see her, to see what she's chosen to wear, but when there's no further movement, I figure that it must be Sarah. I wasn't expecting her to be home, or to be aware of this date. It just proves that she and her daughter are closer than James and I will ever be. There's no way he'd stand at the window and watch me take off on a date with his precious Remi.

After a few more minutes, the front door opens and she steps out. My breath catches as she floats down toward me.

She's wearing a black pair of skinny jeans and a loose white blouse.

"Hey," she sings once she's close enough that I'll hear over the rumble of the engine. She stops in front of me and leans forward for a kiss. I hesitate, knowing that Sarah is watching us, and Remi barks out a laugh when my lips connect with her cheek.

"What?" I ask. "Your mom is watching."

"And? I'm my own person, and I know what I want." She places her hands on her hips and stares at me. "Plus, if she's going to stare, then we might as well give her something to stare at."

"Well, when you put it like that." Reaching out, I wrap my hand around the back of her neck and pull her up against me. "Better?"

"Much. I missed you today," she whispers. I'd stayed out of her way, knowing it would drive her crazy for tonight.

I stare at her, amazed that she's willing to spend time with me, let alone come back to the Heights without argument. I was kind of joking when I suggested going and hanging out with the guys, but Remi was all in with the idea. I have a suspicion she's only willing because she's hoping to get an insight into the kind of guy I am.

If that's the case, then she's going to be sorely disappointed, because I've hidden nothing. My past is my past, and I am who I am. I refuse to pretend that it's anything else.

My fingers tighten on her neck as I pull her lips to mine. She doesn't hesitate to open up, and my chest swells, knowing that she's not at all ashamed to openly stand in her street with me like this. My tongue sweeps into her mouth, but I pull back long before I'm really ready to, knowing that we have at least one person's attention on us.

"Ready?"

"To grill your friends for all your secrets? Yes." She grins, and I laugh, my earlier assumption confirmed.

Throwing my leg over my bike, I hand her the helmet. "Come on then, Princess. Time to go to the dark side."

"Hmm... I like it when you take me there."

"You've experienced nothing yet."

Remi wraps her thighs and arms around my body, forcing me to blow out a steadying breath. Will her touch always feel this electrifying?

Not putting too much thought into what the answer might be, I gun the engine and we fly out of her street. She squeals behind me in delight as I speed up on the freeway that heads toward the Heights, and I can't stop the wide smile that spreads across my face.

I feel different when I'm with her. Like for once in my life, I belong, which is really fucking saying something. I feel anything but when I'm at James' or in the Bay generally. She's got some serious fucking magical powers, that's for fucking sure.

The scenery soon changes to the familiar landscape

of my past. The color of the buildings gets darker and the sizes smaller before I have to start swerving around the potholes in the road that didn't exist a few miles ago.

I can navigate through this place with my eyes shut, so in no time we're pulling up out the back of Sinners and I'm killing the engine.

"I never thought I'd be excited to be here," Remi admits when I take the helmet from her and hang it over the handlebars.

No one else would risk leaving something that's not bolted down, but everyone in town knows this is my bike and they wouldn't fucking dare touch it, let alone steal it.

"Come on, then. They've already ordered dinner."

"Good, I'm starving."

Unlike when we were here last, we enter through the back door and head straight up the stairs. Neither Cruz nor D are working tonight; fuck knows how they managed to swing that, but the second I told them my plans they immediately said they'd sort it.

Both of them are a few years older than me. I vaguely remember them from Sterling Heights High, but then to be fair that's probably because I was never really there rather than them being older. I've probably spent more time at Sterling Prep in the last couple of weeks than I did my entire senior year in Sterling Heights High.

"D, get in here," Cruz shouts the second Remi and I walk into the living room they share in the apartment above the studio. "Jag really did bring his girl back."

"Fuck off," I bark as he comes over.

"Ace's girl! It's so good to see you." He holds his hand out for her, and when she slips her fingers into it, he kisses her knuckles and then encourages her to spin for him, which she also does.

He whistles. "Looking good, girl. You're wasted on this motherfucker, you know that, right?"

"Get your fucking eyes off her." I pull Remi into my side and Cruz stares at me like I'm some kind of stranger to him.

"Girl, I love ya, but please, hand my guy his balls back. He's going to think he belongs with the rich 'uns in the Bay at any moment."

"I really don't think he is," she mutters. "You might think he's different, but they're all running scared with just one look." Cruz barks a laugh.

"Nah, they've got it all wrong. He's all bark. There's not much to his bite."

"Oh, I don't know," Remi mutters, and my mind goes straight in the gutter as I recall rebranding last night.

"Whoa, is it getting hot in here?" Cruz fans himself before gesturing toward the couch. "Come on, stop loitering in the doorway, *mi casa es su casa*."

Tugging Remi behind me, we both fall down onto the couch as Cruz brings us over a bottle of beer each.

"This good or do you need champagne, Princess?"

"Fuck you, Cruz," Remi snaps, reaching for the bottle and knocking the top off like a pro.

"Ouch, burn," D says, coming to join us. "Jag, Rem." He nods. "Dinner's on its way."

"So tell us about life in the Bay. What's it like to have more money than sense?"

"I don't remember," Remi says at the same time I reply with, "Fuck knows."

"Okay let's try this another way... What's it like living with people who have more money than sense?"

"Fucking awful," we answer simultaneously, much to both Cruz and D's amusement.

"Jesus, it's like they're a married couple."

"My turn. I want to know what Sterling Heights Ace is like," Remi says, not even attempting to cover up her secret mission.

"Well..." Cruz says, leaning back on his chair and crossing one leg over the other. "Basically as much as a moody fucker as he is in the Bay, I'd imagine. I'd think the only difference is that he spends most of his days planning people's murders rather than actually committing them."

Remi tenses beside me. "He's joking, baby."

"Am I?" Cruz asks, his eyes going wide.

"Mostly."

"Is Kelsey missing him?"

"Fucking hell, does she always ask this many questions?" D asks, sounds way too amused about the situation.

"Nah, she's over it. Got herself a stand in. It was about time she found herself someone better looking."

"Jesus. I knew coming here and letting her spend time with you two was a mistake."

The banter continues long after the takeout arrives, and we all dig into the best Chinese that the Heights has to offer.

"Are you all done?" Remi asks once we're resting back with full bellies and fresh beers.

"Stay put, Ace's girl. Your boy's got this, haven't you?" He smirks at Ace. "It'll do him good to remember what it's like to live without a maid."

"How'd you know about Ellen?" I ask, shocked.

"I didn't, it was a joke." He gawks. "You've got a fucking maid?"

"My uncle has, and I don't want anything to do with him or his life, so I stay as far away as possible."

Remi sits silently beside me but I can tell she wants to say something. Whether that's to defend James or to say something about Ellen, I'm unsure but Cruz doesn't give her a chance.

"Come on then, Preppy. Show us your skills."

The two of us collect the empty containers and take them through to the kitchen.

"I never thought I'd say this," he says when we're out of earshot of Remi, "but that place looks good on you."

"It's not the place," I mutter.

"Yeah, about her."

"What about her?"

"She's too fucking good for you, man."

"Don't I fucking know it."

He stares at me, his eyes narrowing.

"What?"

"I'm missing something. What gives?"

I open my mouth to answer. These guys know me better than anyone, so I'm not surprised he can see something's not quite right.

"You know my main purpose of going to the Bay."

"To take down your uncle," he says without missing a beat. "What's that go to do with Remi?"

I hesitate, not really wanting to vocalize my intentions when it comes to the girl who has managed to bury herself deeper than anyone else. No one other than my brothers get under my walls, but I fear that she's managed to without my knowledge.

"She's really important to James. He's seeing her mother."

"Ace," Cruz warns. "You telling me that this is all one big game?"

I shrug. That was my intention, but I can't help wondering if things have changed too much for that to still be the case.

"I don't know, man. She's..."

"Yeah, I know. I see it. The way she looks at you... You're going to fucking shatter her if you go through with this."

"She deserves better than me. She'll get over it." It pains me to say it, but I can't deny that it's the truth.

"Maybe so, but it seems that you're what she wants."

I hold his heavy stare with my own until my pocket vibrates, demanding my attention. I quickly scan Donny's text before switching it off.

"Problem?" Cruz's brow arches.

"Nothing I can't handle."

"Watch your back, yeah? You know Donny doesn't give two shits if you're living in the Bay now. You run for him, only he gets to say when you walk away."

I'm about to tell him to stay off my back when D shouts, "What the fuck are you two doing in there? Remi is planning her first ink."

Cruz's eyes light up at the prospect of inking my girl's virgin skin before all but running from the room.

"Ace's girl," he drawls. "You getting ready for your first inking? You want the master, right?" Cruz wiggles his fingers at her and she blushes.

"Hey," I mutter, slapping him around the head. "Only I get to make her blush like that."

"Sorry, man. I can't help if she imagines my fingers doing other things."

"I think it's time we left. Neither of these motherfuckers are getting their hands on your body."

"All right, caveman. Calm down." Remi pats the couch beside her, and I have no choice but to sit beside her as she discusses options and where the least painful parts of the body are.

I watch as she soaks up everything he tells her. She continues drinking when they offer us more beer, but I stop. I need to get her home in one piece. I might want to teach my uncle a lesson, but killing us both in the process isn't part of my plan.

When Remi starts yawning, I make our excuses and we head for the door.

"Call me and we'll book that appointment in, girl."

"You've got it." Remi salutes Cruz and he beams at her.

Part of me is glad my friends approve of her and have accepted her in their lives this easily. A bigger part of me hates it. It's only making what I need to do harder and more confusing.

Is it time I focused on myself for once? On what I want, me, instead of plotting the demise of someone else?

"You okay, Princess?" I ask when we come to a stop beside my bike and she sways slightly on her feet.

"Yeah. I really like those guys, and they're not scary at all."

"Like me, you mean."

"You're not scary, Ace." Her voice is slurred, making me wish I cut her off a beer before I did. "I know you'll protect me. Everyone is wrong about you, you know.

You're a good person. You make good choices." Guilt engulfs me as her words rock my body.

"Oh yeah. Who says otherwise?"

"Conner."

My brows pull together as anger swells in the pit of my stomach. If he's in agreement with James and is warning Remi off me, then I'll string him up by his fucking balls.

"And what did Conner say?"

"Shit. I shouldn't have told you that. Whoopsie." She covers her mouth with her delicate fingers and tries to look innocent. "Forget I said anything?"

"Sure," I say with a smile. I can forget until the next time I'm face to face with my brother.

"Come on, let's get you home."

"I don't want to go home." She pouts as I pull her helmet on and lift the visor.

"No? Where do you want to go?"

"To your pool house."

"Isn't your mom expecting you?" She quirks an eyebrow. "Princess, have you been holding out on me?"

"I'm not the only one who can keep secrets, Jag."

I chuckle at her use of my Heights nickname. "Oh yeah?"

"You want to know them?"

"Sure. Enlighten me."

"I want you to take me back to your bed to do wicked things to me. And..." she says before she gasps and blushes.

"And?"

"I want you to fuck me on my birthday." Her teeth sink into her bottom lip, as if she's embarrassed to ask me.

"I thought you wanted a tattoo for your birthday."

"I do. But I also want you," she whispers the last two words, and I nearly come on the fucking spot with anticipation. She's so innocent and sweet.

So fucking sexy.

"If that's what you want, then who am I to deny you, Princess?"

A wide smile spreads across her face.

"Now, let's go and make your first wish come true."

I throw my leg over my bike and wait for her to join me.

With her wrapped around me, I head home, to my pool house, to do almost all the things I've been imagining while sitting beside her tonight.

CHAPTER TWENTY-TWO

Remi

"Morning," Mom says when I enter the kitchen. She's cooking pancakes, but she doesn't wear her usual smile.

"Did Ace take you to Sterling Heights on Friday?" She turns around to face me, disappointment glistening in her eyes.

"I told you he was taking me out."

"Yes, but you never said a word about going to Sterling Heights. Honestly, Remi, do you have any idea how dangerous it can be there?"

"I was with Ace. We went to see his friends."

"That does not fill me with any reassurance."

"Relax, Mom. The Heights isn't that bad." I'd had fun with Cruz and D. Sure, they teased me about me being from the Bay, but they had accepted me as one of their own. Unlike the kids at Sterling Prep, who go out of their way to make me feel like I don't belong.

It's funny, really, that the place I am supposed to fit in is the place I feel most alone, and the place I'm not supposed to fit in is the place I feel most like myself.

"I'm sorry, sweetheart, but I have to agree with James on this one. I would prefer it if you didn't—"

"Don't do this," I say, letting out a frustrated breath. "I like Ace, Mom. And who knows, maybe you'd like him too if you took the chance to really get to know him."

"Well, it seems you'll get your wish Wednesday. James has booked a pre-birthday meal for all of us down at The Blue Bay."

"You're kidding me?" The Blue Bay was expensive, not to mention a favorite hotspot with Sterling Bay's elite.

It was also the last place I could see Ace and his brothers frequenting.

"He knows it's your favorite."

It used to be my favorite, before my dad ruined everything.

"It sounds lovely, Mom," I grimace, "but I'm not sure it's the kind of place Ace and his brothers will enjoy."

"Well it's not their birthday, and if Ace cares about you half as much as you seem to care about him, then there shouldn't be a problem, should there?"

My lips purse. They're testing us. You didn't just turn up at a place like The Blue Bay in your best jeans and shirt. You wore dinner jackets and evening gowns.

"Talk to him, please. I don't need dinner at The Blue Bay, it's not me anymore."

Maybe it never was.

And the thought that James might be setting some infallible test for Ace doesn't sit well with me.

"You really don't want to go?"

"I'd rather do something low key."

"Fine, I'll talk to him. But I can't promise anything. James dotes on you, you know that. And he just wants you to have the things you deserve in life."

I gawk at her. "There's more to life than fancy restaurants and expensive champagne, Mom." It comes out more harshly than I intend, and her face pales.

"That's not fair, Remi."

"Just talk to him, Mom, please. It's my birthday, and I don't want any fuss."

I've already decided what I want. My first tattoo... and Ace.

I still can't believe I was brave enough to tell him I want to have sex on my birthday, but the beers at Sinners might have had something to do with it.

I want him more than I've ever wanted anything.

At first, Ace was just my way of saying 'fuck you' to everything. But he's buried his way under my skin, and I want to give him the one thing no one else will ever have from me.

My first time.

A shiver ripples up my spine just thinking about it.

"What are your plans for today?" She changes the subject, and my shoulders sag with relief. That's the thing about Mom; she never pushes too hard.

"I need to do some homework, and I thought maybe I'd drop by school and see Hadley." I couldn't imagine what it must be like to board at Sterling Prep.

"No Ace today?" Her brow rises.

"We're not joined at the hip, Mom. Besides, I think he and his brothers are spending the day together."

A strange expression washes over her, and I stiffen again. "What is it?" I ask.

"I think of what they had to survive, and it just breaks my heart. And well, I guess it hammers home how different things could have turned out for us." Tears prick Mom's eyes and I go to her, hugging her tightly.

"But they didn't, Mom. You saw the light and kicked his sorry ass to the curb."

"I know, sweetheart, I know." She holds me at arm's length. "Gosh, Remi, you're almost eighteen, and it terrifies me. I'm not ready to lose you, baby."

"Whoa, Mom. Who said anything about losing me?"

"It's senior year." She sniffles. "Then you'll be going off to college and leaving me."

"You have James," I say, glossing over her mention of college. I still haven't decided what I want to do. There's no way in hell I'm accepting my dad's offer to pay for tuition. And if I want a scholarship, I'm going to have to work my ass off.

"I do." Her expression softens. "We haven't talked about the future much..." she hesitates, and I sense she's not being entirely truthful, "but he makes me very happy."

"Are you sure he's what you want, Mom?"

"Whatever do you mean?"

"I just mean we have a good thing going here. You don't have to prove anything to anyone. Especially not Dad."

She gasps. "You think... oh, sweetheart. That's not what this is. James is a good man. But I've wanted to take it slow because I want to be absolutely sure before I rush into anything again."

I stare at Mom and realize I've been carrying around so much hate and bitterness that I've failed to see the truth.

Dad's betrayal changed her. Just like it changed me. But where I became detached and cold, she became desperate for attention. All this time, we've both been feeling the same thing, we've just dealt with it differently.

"Why has James never had a serious girlfriend before, Mom?" As far as I can remember, he's always lived alone in that big house of his.

She brushes the hair off my face, smiling at me the way she did when I was little. As if I'm the most important thing in her life. "We don't talk about it much. But once, he told me there was a girl. She broke his heart and he never really moved on."

"That's sad," I say, wondering who she was.

"It is. You know, Remi, I just want what's best for you. But you're right, you are almost an adult, which means you're old enough to make your own decisions. And despite what I said earlier about Ace, even the most broken souls deserve to be loved." Mom cups my face, placing a kiss on my forehead. Her words sink into me. I know it's not a blessing, not really, but she's telling me to follow my heart.

She's telling me that even if she doesn't like the idea of me and Ace together, she accepts it.

Because I am capable of making my own decisions.

And I choose him.

I choose Ace.

Monday morning rolls around and, as usual, Conner and Cole are waiting for me. I'm barely awake when I pull the car door open and slip inside. "Ace?" I shriek as he grabs me and pulls me onto his lap.

"Morning." He captures my mouth in a bruising kiss.

"Get a fucking room." I glance back at Conner, flipping him off, and notice the nasty bruise around his eye.

"What the hell happened to your face?"

"Ask your boyfriend," he grumbles, pulling onto the street and taking the coastal road toward school.

I slide off Ace's lap and land with a thud on the worn leather. "This is a nice surprise."

"Yeah, well, it would seem Cruz and D were right. You do own my balls, Princess."

His words, although crass, fill me with happiness. "Is that right, huh?" I tease, but Ace crowds me against the seat, staring at me with those frosty eyes of his. "I missed you yesterday."

"I missed you too." I trail a finger along his jaw, loving the way he looks at me with total possession. "Did James grill you about Friday?"

"I managed to avoid him all weekend."

"So... hmm... he didn't mention the dinner to you?" I brace myself, waiting for Ace's reaction.

"What fucking dinner?"

"Princess' birthday dinner. Uncle James wants to take us to some fancy rich place downtown," Conner pipes up.

"You know about this?" Ace grunts, looking to his

brother. Conner nods in the rear view. "You'd know too, if you hadn't moved out to the pool house."

"But you seem to be having so much fun with *Uncle James*." His tone is scathing.

"Hey," I say, sliding my hand against his cheek and making him look at me. "Don't take this out on Conner. I've already asked my mom to talk to him."

"You have?" He blanches.

"Of course. I don't want to go somewhere you'll feel uncomfortable. We could eat at Surf's for all I care."

"You really asked your mom to talk to him?"

"Yeah." I smile. "Why?"

"No reason." He stares past me, and I know he's lying.

Ace isn't used to people taking his side, but I'm determined to show him he's worth it.

"As long as they serve supersize portions, I don't give a fuck where we go." Conner grins at me through the mirror. "Hey, do you think we can bring a date?"

"No," Ace and I say in unison.

"But you two get to—"

"Con," Ace barks.

"Yeah, yeah. Keep my mouth shut," he murmurs, and realization dawns on me.

"Tell me you didn't hit him because I slipped up the other night," I whisper-hiss at Ace.

"He's a fucking traitor."

"Heard that," Conner says.

"Keep talking and I'll black your other eye."

"You need to talk to your guy, Remi, because he's grumpier than a bear with a sore head. I thought you were supposed to be happier when you're getting regular pus—"

He doesn't get a chance to finish his sentence, because I lean over and slap him upside the head.

"What was that for?" he yelps.

"Remi's not wrong," Cole says. "You talk too fucking much".

"Oh it's like that now, you're both taking her side?" I poke my tongue out at him. "That's some bullshit."

A minute later and he's pulling into the school parking lot. Kids swarm the lawns and dread slithers through me. This is the part I hate—the part where Ace and I have to go back to pretending.

"I guess I'll see you later?" I say.

A knowing smirk lifts the corner of his mouth. "For a prep school princess, you really are fucking dumb at times."

"What the—"

"Get out of the car, Princess," he growls, and I do as I'm told, but only because I need space from him before I knee him in the balls.

Ace follows me out, and I'm just about to walk off when he snags my wrist. His fingers slip down my hand, tangling with my own. I gawk at our joined hands and then lift my eyes to his. "But—"

"No buts." He starts pulling me toward the building. "It's time everyone in this fucking school knows who you belong to."

"Ace," I say, trying to push him away from me. He has me pressed up my locker, kissing my neck in the most delicious way. I guess after one class apart he's feeling as needy as I am.

Kids are staring but giving us a wide berth. It's a definite perk of being with the most scary guy in school.

"We have an audience," I whisper, raking my nails over his skull as he grazes the soft, sensitive skin along my throat with his teeth.

"Let them watch." His murmurs dance over my neck, and my breath catches with a soft moan.

"So it is true?" a voice says.

Ace takes a deep breath, standing rigid while I slowly slide my eyes to Michaela.

"The gangbanger and the peasant, how fitting," she snarls.

"What the fuck did you just say?" Ace moves into her space, but I grab his arm.

"Don't," I say, slipping around him, putting myself between them. "She isn't worth it."

Tension ripples in the hall as kids watch, probably chomping at the bit for the long overdue showdown between me and Michaela.

"I'm worth a damn sight more than you," she scoffs, folding her arms over her chest and cocking her hip.

Something explodes inside me. I'm fed up of turning the other cheek when it comes to Michaela and her bullshit opinions about me. It's about time she learned that she can't always get what she wants and watch me fall.

This time, *I* fucking win.

"Whatever, Michaela." I've wanted to watch her fall from her throne for so long, but standing here, seeing the jealousy shimmer in her eyes, I realize no matter how much she has—the big house and expensive car, a line of guys all vying for attention, the trust fund account, and Ivy League school offer—she'll always want more. People like Michaela can never be happy because they spend too much time worrying about things that don't matter.

I might not have the big, expensive house anymore, or Daddy's credit card at my disposal, but the truth is, I don't want or need it. Money doesn't make people happy, it makes them shallow. It makes them fake. And that's not who I am. That's not who I *want* to be.

"That's it? That's all you've got to say?" Her eyes widen.

"I don't need to say anything else." I shrug, a deep sense of acceptance washing over me. "I spent so long wondering what I did to deserve your betrayal. I've cried so many tears over you. Tears that turned to hatred. But now, now I look at you and all I feel is pity."

"W-what?" She jerks back, as if I've physically slapped her. "I'm the head cheerleader. I live in one of the biggest houses in the Bay. I mean, hello, I drive a bespoke Mercedes."

"And yet you're still a vapid bitch."

A collective gasp echoes down the hall.

"You can't say that, you're no one. Nothing. You shouldn't even—"

"Michaela," I snap, and she swallows her words, indignation flaming her cheeks. "I. Don't. Care. You were my best friend. And all this time, I thought I was the one who did something wrong. But now I realize it's you. You're the unhappy one. You thrive in the misery of others. And do you know what? Until you learn to love yourself, you'll never find what you're looking for.

"So yeah, I pity you. Because sure, I might not have a lot, but at least I know the people in my life are in it because they chose it, and not because they want anything from me. Now if you don't mind, me and my boyfriend," the word flies out of my mouth, but I don't want to take it back. Ace is mine. The same way that I'm his. "We're in the middle of something."

I turn into him and throw my arms around his shoulders. "I'm proud of you, baby," he says, leaning down and brushing his nose over mine.

"I'm proud of me too," I say, kissing him right there in front of most of our class.

"But you can tell me the truth," he whispers against my skin. "How much do you want to knock that ugly smile off her face right now?"

"One a scale of one to ten, eleven." I chuckle, sliding my fingers into the hair at the base of his neck and pulling him closer. "You should probably distract me before I really make a scene."

Ace's deep laughter reverberates inside me as he spins me around and pushes me up against the locker. "It would be my pleasure, *girlfriend*."

CHAPTER TWENTY-THREE

Ace

Despite Sarah apparently talking to James about the location of tonight's birthday meal, he point-blank refused to change the restaurant to somewhere a little more low key.

He was testing me I could see that when he took great delight in telling me what I was going to have to wear tonight.

"If you want to be there for Remi, then you have little choice," he said with an evil smile on his lips.

The motherfucker was playing me, and I was falling right into his hands, because he was right. Tux or no tux, I wanted to be there for Remi. I wanted to be there more than I should. But him standing his ground and acting like she's the daughter he never had only proves I was right.

She's his weak spot, and I'm going to fucking smash

it very, very soon. I just haven't quite figured out how it's going to go down. I'm hoping inspiration will strike at the right time—just like the night we stumbled over the IT geeks on our way to meet Bexley, when he needed to be taught a lesson. They didn't take much convincing to send that photograph around the entire school for everyone to see, while ensuring the trail didn't lead back to us in any way.

My lips twitch as I think about that pathetic motherfucker tied naked to that pole. It was the least he deserved, but fuck if it didn't feel good. I'd heard since it was his mother who eventually came to untie him. Seems maybe his team doesn't care as much as he thought, because they quite happily left him there and continued partying without him.

Oh, how the mighty fall.

Although I'm sure he's going to come back fighting at some point. He's been too quiet. I have no doubt he's planning some big revenge as we speak. Whatever it is, he'll lose. I've no doubt.

Standing in the bedroom of the pool house, I stare at my reflection in the full-length mirror. I look fucking ridiculous. I thought my prep school uniform was bad, but this... this is a fucking joke.

I pull at the tight collar of my crisp white shirt. It feels like it's fucking strangling me. My tattoos peek out on my neck and down onto my hands, and I refuse to remove my piercings. James can try to dress me up to look like a preppy douchebag, but he can never remove the truth. I'm bad through and fucking through, and it's about time he had a reminder of that.

Rolling my eyes at myself, I pull a blunt from my

pocket and light up. There's no fucking way I'm leaving dressed like this while sober.

"I feel like a fucking penguin," Conner mutters, coming to join me with Cole following him. They're dressed exactly the same in the tuxes James oh-so-helpfully hired for us.

"This bitch had better be worth it," Cole mutters as Conner snatches the blunt from between my fingers and takes a drag. He makes a show of offering it to Cole, but we both know he can't have any, no matter how desperate he is.

"You got any fucking alcohol in this place?" He stalks toward the kitchen and starts pulling the cupboards open. "Jackpot!" He pulls out the bottle of vodka I'd stashed and lifts it to his lips.

Motherfucker.

"Seriously though, is James just trying to piss us off?" Conner asks, falling down into what he seems to have claimed as his beanbag now.

"No. He's just trying to piss me off. This is a test to see if I really care about his precious Remi."

"Which you do. Evidenced by the fucking ridiculous penguin suit."

"So it would seem."

"Oh, don't be like that. That girl's got you so fucking whipped." I raise an eyebrow at him as I take another drag. "You'd just about do anything for her, I'd put money on it."

"That's one bet I wouldn't take, brother."

"What the hell is that supposed to mean? Do we need to have another little chat about not fucking this up?"

"That wasn't a little chat, asshole. That was me

giving you a shiner for sticking your nose in my business."

"Remember it how you like, but I warned you."

"Whatever." Dropping what's left of the blunt into a used beer bottle sitting on the coffee table, I push to stand and smooth down the front of my pants.

"Come on, let's get this shit over with."

"I can hardly fucking wait."

"Jesus fucking Christ. Does James think she's a real fucking princess or some shit?" Conner asks as we round the corner to find a fucking limo waiting for us. "We're his own flesh and blood, and we don't even receive a fucking card, yet she gets this treatment."

I don't need his reminder of how this differs to our own birthdays over the years. Most of them our own mother didn't even remember, let alone our absent uncle.

My stomach clenches with anger that, while we were barely living back in the Heights, James was here living it up and treating his princess like she's fucking royalty. It's the exact reminder I need for why I'm doing all this.

If this were anyone else's birthday, I would not be here right now. As it is, I'm very tempted to turn around and throw these fucking clothes onto a fucking bonfire.

I don't realize there's anyone inside, so I'm surprised when William opens the back door and a high-heel clad foot appears behind it.

"Fuck me sideways," Conner breathes as Remi steps away from the car and allows us to get a look at her. "Well, that's me suitably jealous. You're in for a good night, lucky bastard."

I barely register his words as all the blood in my body races toward my cock. "Fuck me."

My eyes take in her perfectly curled hair hanging around her bare shoulders, before dropping down to her deep red, skin-tight, full-length dress. Her tits are pushed up in such a way that all I can think about doing is sinking my teeth into them and rebranding her, because that is literally the only thing that could make this sight any better.

That thought is shot to shit when she takes a step toward me and her long, bare leg emerges from behind the fabric.

"Whoa. That thing should be fucking illegal."

"Stop. Fucking. Looking."

"I would if I could make my eyes move."

I elbow Conner in the side, and the little bitch moans as if I punched him again.

"That wasn't necessary," he sulks as Remi joins us.

"That tux looks good on you, Ace."

"Not as fucking good as that dress does on you." I continue running my eyes up and down her body, not really believing she's real.

"Excuse me while I go puke in the flowerbed." We both ignore my irritating brother.

"I really didn't think you'd come."

"It's your birthday, Princess. Where else would I be?"

"I don't know. Running drugs, killing a guy or two." Her brow rises, but there's a smile on her lips. "Anything but wearing that and coming to the most exclusive restaurant this town has to offer."

"I must admit, the first two options do sound more appealing, but sadly, you're stuck with me. And, if you're lucky, I won't even kill anyone."

She laughs, and I smile with her. She likes to joke

about my previous life, but I'm not sure she realizes that almost everything she says is true.

I didn't lie to her the day I told her I wasn't a good person. I guess it says more about her than it does me that she's willing to overlook it all, whereas I'm the selfish motherfucker who didn't give her a chance.

"Come on," James calls, making my muscles tense instantly. "We need to go, we have a reservation."

Heaven forbid we make the place wait for us.

I roll my eyes and slip my hand into Remi's to pull her back toward the limo. Letting her climb in first, I pretend it's because I'm a gentleman. That's bullshit, I just want to stare at her ass as she bends over and try to figure out if she's got any panties on or not. My cock swells as I picture her bare pussy beneath the silky fabric. Biting down on my cheek, I picture laying her out on my bed later and pushing the fabric of her dress up around her waist, eating her until she's coming on my face.

Fuck, this is going to be a long ass evening.

"Have you ever been in a limo before, boys?" Sarah asks politely.

I'm about to bark back an equally dumbass reply when Conner speaks up.

"I'm not sure a limo has ever been to the Heights. If it had, it probably left looking a little different to how it arrived."

Both Cole and I chuckle, clearly both picturing a similar scene.

"Okay, well... I think you'll like The Blue Bay, the food is out of this world."

"Do they have those fancy little portions?" Conner asks skeptically. He cares more about the amount of food he's going to get tonight than he does about having to wear these god awful suits.

"Um... some of them can be on the smaller side. But I'm sure there will be plenty."

The drive across town is awkward as hell, and it doesn't get any better when we turn off the main road down a private driveway leading to the restaurant.

"Fucking hell, that's impressive."

"Language, Conner," James barks, looking anything but comfortable with us all together. He keeps looking between me, Remi, and our joined hands like he's going to shank me any minute.

You're not getting out of this quite that easily, motherfucker.

The restaurant is more pretentious than I expected, and I hate it from the moment we walk through the doors. Everything is either perfect white or chrome. The floor-to-ceiling windows showcase the almost three-hundred and sixty degree view of the Bay beyond, and when I ask for a beer the waitress turns her nose up like I've ordered a glass of shit.

"Champagne for the adults and orange juice for the kids, please," James says, stepping in.

"Kids?" I ask incredulously when the waiter has walked away. "None of us are fucking kids."

"You're under twenty-one, so no alcohol will pass your lips tonight."

I scoff and sit back in my seat. Remi's hand brushes up my thigh, and I reach down to wrap my fingers around it as I try to keep my cool.

I don't want to fucking be here, pretending that we're the fucking Brady Bunch.

It's bullshit, all of it.

"What the fuck is this shit?" Conner asks, his eyes

wide as he stares at the menu before him. It might as well be written in another fucking language for all the sense it makes.

"Just pick what meat you want and the rest can be a surprise," I tell him as James' eyes drill into the top of his head. "What was wrong with a normal restaurant where we can wear normal clothes and eat normal sounding food?"

"It's Remi's birthday, she deserves the best."

"Even though she specifically told you she didn't want this."

"That's enough," he hisses. "Stop trying to ruin it."

"Me? You want *me* to stop ruining it? Un-fucking-believable. Are you really that clueless?"

He stares at me for a beat before the waiter reappears and puts an end to our slanging match to take our orders.

"Remi, I know your birthday isn't officially until Friday, but with Cole's first game and the party I'm sure you'll all attend after, I thought we should celebrate tonight. So, without further ado. Happy birthday, sweetheart." James hands over a perfectly wrapped box.

She's forced to remove her hand from my leg, and I reluctantly let her go, although I miss her calming touch the second her heat leaves me.

"Oh wow," her eyes go wide, "I wasn't expecting anything. Thank you so much."

"You don't even know what's inside yet, baby," Sarah coos, nodding toward the box eagerly, hinting to the fact that she's well aware of its contents.

We all watch in silence as Remi pulls open the ribbon and slides the top off. She pulls back the tissue that hides the contents before she gasps. "Oh my goodness, James. I can't. This is too much."

"Nothing is too much, sweetheart. You deserve it and more."

We all watch with bated breath as she reaches in and pulls out what has her so shocked. The last thing I expect to see when her fingers emerge is a fucking car key.

A tornado begins to swell within me. He bought her a fucking car. I risk a glance over at my brothers, who are also staring at it in utter disbelief.

For years we go without anything, not even a fucking phone call. I might be the only one out of the three of us who's turned eighteen so far, but I didn't get a fucking car. All I got was a fucking OD'd mother and a fucked-up life.

Remi's hand trembles as she places it on the table. She glances my way, her eyes burning into my side of my face as my stare remains on the key.

This is total fucking bullshit.

Is this why he wanted us here? So he could rub everything we don't have in our faces? Are we really that unworthy? That unlovable?

That meaningless?

"That's not all." James eyes the box again, and Remi hesitantly looks inside.

She pulls out an envelope. Assuming it's just a card, I sit back and try to work on my anger not getting the better of me. This is the last place I need to lose my cool with James, but I'm balancing on a very thin edge right now.

As expected, Remi pulls a birthday card from the

envelope, but it's not until something falls from it that I see red. My head spins and my fists clench.

"James, no. I can't accept this."

"You can and you will. It's for the college of your choice."

"This is fucking bullshit."

Gasps sound out around the restaurant as my chair goes toppling back and all eyes turn on me, but the only ones I see are his. The lying motherfucker who's trying to ruin my life with his manipulation and lies.

CHAPTER TWENTY-FOUR

Remi

I can't breathe.

The entire restaurant is watching us, a mix of disgust, curiosity, and surprise swirling in their eyes.

Ace is looming over me, anger rolling off him so dark it's palpable. I reach out for him, staring into his eyes and willing him to calm down. "Sit down, Ace, we can talk about it."

There's no way I'm accepting a car and the check off James. It doesn't feel right, none of it does, and my heart sinks for the three boys around the table who look gutted.

"Ace, I suggest you sit down, son. You're ruining Remi's birthday meal."

I shoot James a pleading glance. He's making it worse. I know he probably didn't mean to rub his wealth in his nephews' faces, but that's exactly what he's done, and now he's driving a wedge between me and Ace so deep I feel like I might fall in and never find my way out.

"Ace, please..." I say, tugging his hand. But his eyes are fixed on James, burning with so much contempt, I feel a tingle of fear. I know Ace hates his uncle. I know there's more going on here than I understand, but I barely recognize the guy standing beside me right now.

"Ace, look at me." I stand up, facing him. His chest is heaving and his eyes are so dark and empty. A violent shiver runs through me.

"Come on, let's eat and try to make the most of it. Please."

"This was a mistake," he grits out. "I should never have come."

Hurt swells inside me. "Hey, look at me." I touch my palm to his face. He's staring right past me. "Ace, please," I beg.

"Excuse me," the manager appears, "is there a problem?"

"Yeah, there is," Ace's tone is ice cold, "but don't worry, the trash will see itself out." He rips his hand away from mine and stalks toward the entrance. I'm about to take off after him, but James leaps from his seat.

"Stay," he says, rubbing his jaw. "I'll go and speak to him. I perhaps didn't handle that very well."

Tears prick the corners of my eyes as I nod. To my surprise, Conner and Cole don't go after their brother. Mom is whispering something to Cole, and Conner is shaking his head as if he can't quite believe what just happened.

"He got you a fucking car," he sneers.

"I didn't ask for it," I choke out, rubbing my throat. My eyes flick to the door Ace just stalked out of. People are no longer staring, instead casting furtive glances at our table while they chat and eat their meals. "I told you this was a bad idea."

Mom's face pales. "I didn't know he was going to give you the check, not here. I swear."

So why did he do it?

It makes no sense.

James isn't malicious. Sure, he might get it wrong sometimes, especially where Ace and his brothers are concerned. But he cares. If he didn't, he would never have taken them in.

I glance to Conner, ready to ask him if he thinks I should go check on his uncle and Ace, but he beats me to it.

"Don't say I didn't warn you."

"What the hell is that supposed to mean?"

"You saw what happened just now." He lowers his voice. "That's the Ace we know. The guy with the short fuse and quick temper. I love my brother more than anything, but he's messed up, Remi. More than you'll ever know."

"I'm going to check on—" I'm halfway out of my seat when James returns.

"Ace won't be coming back."

"What did he say?" I swallow the pain burning my throat. "Maybe I should go after him?"

"I don't think that's a good idea, he needs some space to cool off."

I look at Conner and Cole, hoping they'll back me up. Cole's eyes are narrowed, and I know he isn't happy with what went down, but indecision flickers in his gaze.

Conner looks resigned. His brows are drawn tight, and his eyes hold a sadness that squeezes my heart.

"He's his own worst enemy, Remi," he says. "All he had to do was play nice."

I'm out of my seat before I can stop myself. "I'm going to see if I can talk to him." Without looking back, I hurry out of the restaurant.

But when I get outside, there's no sign of Ace.

I dig my cell phone out of my purse and call him. It rings out, so I text instead.

Remi: We need to talk about this, please.

I stand there, waiting for his reply. Desperate for a sign he's okay. He'd been so angry when the check slid out of my birthday card. Betrayal. Resentment. Hatred. It all swirled in his eyes, radiated from him, but I saw through it. I saw the young boy trying to be a man in a world that only ever taught him disappointment.

A world that had repeatedly told him he wasn't good enough.

Remi: I'll be here waiting, when you're ready.

I hit send and inhale a deep breath. Hopefully, Ace will realize that it's not our differences that define us but how we feel and love and live.

Ace says he doesn't care about anything, but I know he does.

He cares too much.

Ace didn't come back. He didn't call. He didn't text. It's like he's disappeared off the face of the Earth. But Conner didn't need to tell me where his brother had gone off too. I knew there was only one place Ace would escape to when things got too hard.

The Heights.

Part of me wants to go after him, to borrow Mom's car and go down there and demand he talk to me, but I don't. Because I realized something else after the shitshow that was my birthday dinner last night.

I can't be the only one fighting for us.

"Hey, almost birthday girl." Hadley sits down and nudges my shoulder. "Why the frown?"

"Don't ask."

"Wouldn't happen to do with a certain brooding bad boy causing a scene at The Blue Bay last night, would it?"

"News sure travels fast."

"I heard Mr Triskin telling Mrs Gomez."

"Triskin was there? Great, that's just—"

"Relax." She chuckles. "Who gives a shit what Triskin or anyone else thinks? I'm more worried if you're okay."

"He's gone, Hads." Sadness coils around my heart.

"What do you mean, *gone?*"

"He didn't return to his uncle's. He isn't in school today. He won't answer my calls or reply to my messages."

"That's rough."

I nod around a weak smile. "Some birthday, huh?"

"He'll come back. I saw the two of you in the hall the other day. He's just as smitten as you."

"And if he doesn't?" I want to believe Ace will be back once he's cooled off, but part of me worries things will be different now.

"You should have seen him, Hads. He was so angry. I could kill James for doing that."

"What did he do?"

"He bought me a car. A freakin' car. And then as if that wasn't enough, he gave me a check for college."

"Wow, okay, that's huge."

"I know. And to make matters worse, I had no idea. It isn't any wonder Ace hates me. He and his brothers grew up in the Heights with nothing, and then James goes and gifts me a car and a check for college like it's a store card for the Gap. What the hell was he thinking?"

"He probably *wasn't* thinking. That man is completely smitten with your mom, and he adores you. It's just money, and everyone knows James Jagger has plenty of that lying around."

"Which is why none of it makes any sense," I say, something about the whole thing bugging me. "James has all this money, the house, endless resources... and yet, he left his sister-in-law to fend for herself and raise three kids after her husband died? Why didn't he help them?"

"I thought your mom told you he did try?"

"Yeah, but why didn't he intervene?"

"Families are strange things, girl. I know that better than anyone. Perhaps he did try, and in the end he had no choice but to walk away?"

"Yeah, maybe." But I still didn't buy it. There was a piece of the puzzle still missing.

"Your boy will come around, and when he does, you can have crazy wild make up sex."

"Hads!" Warmth spreads through me.

"Tell me you don't want to?"

I press my lips together, fighting a smile. I do want that. Damn, I want it so much.

But first, Ace needs to come to his senses.

"Anything?" I ask, hopeful as I slide into Conner and Cole's car.

Conner grimaces, and I have my answer.

"Well, has he said anything?"

"Just that he needs time."

"Time, right," I grumble.

"Listen, Remi, maybe it's just time you accept that you and Ace are—"

"Con," Cole warns.

"What, man? I don't like seeing her waiting around for him like this. She deserves better."

I flinch. I know he means it as a compliment, but I only hear another strike against his brother.

"You told him I didn't accept the check, right?" I'd wanted to refuse the car too, but Mom begged me to see sense. It was just a car. I could get a part-time job to pay for the gas and insurance, and finally having my own set of wheels would be kind of cool.

In the end, we'd compromised. At the weekend, James is taking me to exchange the brand new Audi for something less flashy and more economical.

"See, bro, I told you." Conner and Cole are having their own conversation.

"You told him what?"

Conner meets my confused stare in the rear-view

mirror. "You're in too deep with Ace."

"I am not—"

"Listen to yourself." He lets out a heavy sigh. "You turned down a check for college, Remi. That's some messed-up shit."

"It isn't... I wasn't expecting that from James. If I wanted someone to pay my way, I'd take my dad's money."

"But that's just it." He slams his hand against the steering wheel, startling me. "You've got options. You have a line of people trying to help you. And you're throwing it all away and for what, a future with my brother? I hate to break it to you, but you're kidding yourself. Girls like you don't end up with guys like us."

"Conner, that's not—"

"Just hear me out. It's cute that you try to shed your rich girl skin, commendable even. But when people see you and my brother together, that's *all* they see. The rich girl slumming it with a guy from the wrong side of the tracks. He's never going to get past that, and one day, you'll end up hating him for it."

I sink back against the warm leather. Is Conner right? Am I just a permanent reminder to Ace of everything they've never had?

Have I been fooling myself this entire time?

"What my dick of a brother is trying to say—" Cole starts, but I cut him dead.

"I get it, thanks." The words get stuck over the lump in my throat.

Needing a distraction from the tension in the car, I dig out my cell phone and check for messages.

But there's nothing.

Deciding to try one last time, I text Ace.

Remi: I won't text again. Maybe you realized I'm not worth it. Or maybe you're just drunk or high and trying to figure out how to tell me you're an idiot for running last night... whatever it is, I want you to know that I see you, Ace. I see you, and I'm still here.

I hit send and close my eyes. I don't expect my cell to ping with a reply. And I definitely don't expect his name to flash across my screen.

Ace: We should talk. Tomorrow night, after the game?

Remi: Yes, where?

A flicker of hope grows inside me.

Ace: Pool house? James is out of town and Conner and Cole will be at the party. So it'll just be the two of us.

Remi: I'll be there.

Ace: Good.

His tone isn't exactly filling me with happiness, but I'll take whatever I can get right now. Because I know that if we sit down and talk, we can figure everything out.

Together.

I'm about to text another reply when my cell pings again.

Ace: Oh, and Princess—wear something sexy. We have a lot of making up to do.

A bolt of desire pulses through me, and I can barely contain my smile. We're going to be okay.

I just know we are.

CHAPTER TWENTY-FIVE

Ace

It might be two days later, but the moment when I saw the figure on that check signed by James fall from the card is on constant replay in my mind.

The second I stormed out of that restaurant, I was gone. It didn't matter what I was wearing, I took off running even before James had a chance to try and dig himself out of the hole he'd already landed himself in.

He tries to make out like he's the decent guy for taking us in, giving us all the things we deserve and missed out on, but the only one he cares about is her.

It should be us. He was the one who ruined our life. He's the one who ensured we grew up without a father and with a junkie whore for a mother.

It. Is. All. His. Fault.

As I walk back into the pool house, the anger swirls in my stomach as if it happened only moments ago.

I don't want to be back here. I want to stay in the Heights and drink and smoke myself into oblivion, but I've got a plan to see through to the end.

James thinks he's winning right now. But it's time to pull out the Ace card and send him tumbling to his fucking knees.

I make quick work of tidying the place up so it looks like I've made an effort. I even put a few fucking candles around the bedroom in an attempt to make it all romantic and shit. Shaking my head at myself, I cuss under my breath. I've never made this much effort for a girl before. Ever.

I usually give them what they need and send them on their way. But Remi is different. She needs more of a gentle touch. And after all, it is her fucking birthday.

Pulling the cake from the bag it was dropped into when I left the store, I push a couple of candles in the top. It's not exactly a brand new car or a free ride to the college of her choice, but it's the best I can do.

Her real present will be here tomorrow.

Conner let slip that Sarah has planned a surprise party for her here tomorrow night. Somehow she's invited our entire fucking class without Remi finding out. Although, I'm not sure why I'm surprised, it's not like she actually talks to any of the kids at school. Sarah's about as oblivious to her daughter's life as James is to what I know. At least she means well; James is just a manipulative cunt.

I shower and dress. I told Remi to meet me here after the game, knowing that everyone will be heading for the first after party at Bexley's. Part of me wants to turn up to that thing just so I can ruin it before his eyes, but I've got my sights set on Remi tonight.

She boldly told me what she wanted for her birthday, and fuck me, am I going to deliver.

My cock stirs at just the thought of what tonight is going to hold. It almost makes coming back here worth it.

I slip out of the pool house ten minutes before the game is going to start. I have zero interest in football or the Seahawks, but there's no fucking way I'm missing Cole's first game. I might keep myself hidden in the shadows where no one else can see me, but I'll be there, and I know he'll know too. It's no easy task keeping my focus on the game, though, not with the anger that's eating me from the inside out as I stand in the darkest spot I can find.

Only a few people see me, but no one dares talk to me.

No doubt the rumors of what happened in that godforsaken restaurant is hot gossip around here. After all, no one behaves like that in a place where dinner costs more than a half-decent car in the Heights.

I shake my head. These fucking idiots don't have a clue what real life is like.

It's not very often I feel anything but anger, frustration, or disappointment, but as I jump on my bike to head back to the pool house to wait for Remi to appear, I swear a little excitement races through me.

It's just because I'm going to finally have her, I tell myself. But I fear it's more than that. And it's that little bit of fear that has me questioning everything I've spent the last couple of days planning.

Remi is the main player in this game she's unknowingly involved in, but equally she's my biggest weakness. With one wrong—or maybe right—move, she could put an end to all of this. I have no doubt she could hold that much power over me if she really put her mind to it.

But I need to resist.

I need to fight her large doe eyes that see more in me that anyone else ever has. I need to resist her kind and encouraging words, and I need to resist her lies that she doesn't want James' car or money, because who in their right fucking mind would turn something like that down?

Someone who isn't like the people of your past.

I push that little voice down and lock the door behind it. Now is not the time for doubts. Now is the time to see this motherfucker through to the final play.

As if on cue, the click of her heels on the path leading to the pool house ring out, and in only seconds she pulls the door open and steps inside.

I'm in the bedroom waiting for her. I'm too fucking impatient to wait any longer than necessary.

"Ace?" she calls, her voice quiet and unsure.

"Bedroom."

Her footsteps draw nearer, and I swear to fucking god I'm nervous for those few seconds. But all the nerves, excitement, and uncertainty fall from my head. "Fucking hell, Princess." My chin drops and my eyes widen at the sight of her.

I know I said to dress sexy, but fuck me sideways, I was not expecting this.

She stands before me with her hair in pigtails, her natural curl twisting the ends, wearing a blue and white Seahawks cheer uniform.

"Do not tell me that's Michaela's."

A shy, mischievous smile tugs at her lips as her hands

come to rest on her hips. "You set me a challenge, Ace. And I do hate to disappoint."

"You stole her fucking uniform."

"Yeah, well, she must have a million seeing as it's the only thing she wears, so I doubt she'll miss it." Remi shrugs.

"Do you have any fucking idea how sexy you are right now?"

Color stains her cheeks, spreading down her neck and onto her chest.

Before I know I've moved, I've crawled off the bed and I'm tugging on one of her pigtails. "No one else had better have seen you like this."

"Why, Ace? Jealous?"

"Fucking right. No one sees you like this but me." Reaching behind my head, I pull my shirt off and drop it to the floor. "I can't fucking wait to get this off you."

"Oh yeah? And here I was thinking you didn't want to see me again." She tilts her head to the side and quirks an eyebrow at me.

"That wasn't about you, baby. That was my shit."

"I know, I just... I needed to talk to you about it."

"I'm sorry," I say, sliding my hand up her neck and gripping onto her nape. Pressing my forehead to hers, I drag in a deep breath.

"I get it, Ace. If I had any idea that James—"

"Don't," I say, startling her. "Please, this isn't about him," I say a little softer, focusing on her touch rather than my festering anger. "This about us. About celebrating your birthday the proper way."

"Oh yeah? You still want to..."

"Oh, Princess. I've thought of nothing else," I lie as I grip onto her ass and lift her to my body.

Her legs wrap around my waist and her heat presses right against my already semi-hard cock.

I brush my fingers over the bare skin of her ass. "You... you're not wearing any panties."

"I thought it would save you a job."

I growl, dropping my lips to the soft skin of her neck and sucking it into my mouth hard enough to leave a mark. I want her to remember this night for a long fucking time.

Throwing her down on the bed, I watch her bounce. The second she settles, she parts her legs and shows me what she's hiding beneath her skirt.

"Ummm..." I dive for her, pushing her thighs apart, wasting no time in pressing my tongue to her clit.

She squeals, her fingers diving into my hair to pull me closer. "Oh fuck, Ace."

"You need this, baby?"

"More than you know."

"Are you sure about that?" Reaching up, I squeeze her breast over the fabric of her top.

"Oh god. So good."

I want to say all kinds of dirty things to her, but my need to keep tasting her, to drive her over the edge with my tongue, to get her nice and ready for my cock is too much to resist.

I keep up the pressure on her clit and slide two fingers into her wet heat. She groans and immediately tries to suck me deeper. Greedy little bitch. Bending my fingers, I find the spot that's sure to make her scream, and in only minutes she falls over the edge and does just that.

While she's still coming down from her high, I pull

her skirt from her hips before sitting her up and dragging her top over her head.

"You seem to have forgotten to visit all your underwear drawers tonight, huh?"

"You don't appreciate the easier access?" she asks cheekily.

"Oh, baby. I fucking love it."

Crashing my lips to hers, I sweep my tongue into her mouth, allowing her to taste herself and to claim her once again.

Fuck. This girl is like fucking kryptonite.

Dragging my lips from hers, I kiss down her neck next before I lick down her chest to my favorite spot.

"Accce," she squeals when I sink my teeth into the same place I did that very first day.

She squirms, telling me that my branding her turns her on as much as it does me.

I kiss down to her breasts and her back arches in my arms as I suck her nipples into my mouth and run my tongue around them teasingly.

"Ace, please. I need more... I need... you."

Climbing from the bed, I push my sweats down my legs and kick them off.

"I'm not sure you were in any position to comment on my lack of underwear," she quips.

"I'm all about an easy life, Princess." I grab a condom from the box I left in my nightstand and drop it to the bed beside her.

She stares at it and swallows nervously.

"Are you sure about this?"

"Yes," she confirms, sounding much more confident than she looks.

"I'll take it slow. Make sure you're ready."

"I'm ready. I need you."

"Fuck. Keep talking like that and there will be no going slow."

"I don't care, Ace. Whatever you give, I'll willingly accept."

"Shit, Remi," I mutter under my breath. How the fuck was I lucky enough to find this girl?

I realize something in that moment as I stare down at her where she's waiting for me with her legs still wide and her chest heaving with desire. I'm going to regret what happens here for the rest of my life.

But even with that epiphany, it's not enough to stop me setting my plan into motion.

I crawl back between her legs and rip the silver packet open with my teeth. She watches intently as I blow the bit I tore off into the room and pull the condom out. Her teeth sink into her bottom lip as she watches me roll it down my length. Her neck ripples as she swallows her apprehension about what's to come.

Taking myself in my hand, I lean over her and take her lips. I kiss her with bruising force as I run the tip of my cock through her wet folds. She's so fucking ready for me it has my cock weeping with the need to sink as deep inside her as I can go.

Fuck, I want to be connected to her in a way that we don't know where I end and she begins. I want to lose everything, forget everything, as I bury myself inside her.

Dropping to her entrance, I push inside ever so slightly. Remi tenses at the invasion, but her kiss doesn't falter as her nails scratch down my back. Her walls ripple around me and I push further, my restraint already at breaking point. She moans, and I know that what's about to come isn't going to be pleasant for her, but there's no stopping it.

"Last chance to change your mind, Princess. If you have any doubts, now's the time to say," I whisper in her ear.

"No. No doubts, Ace. I want you to be my firrrrst." Her final word stretches out as I thrust into her in one smooth glide. Remi tenses beneath me, her breath catching in her throat as she tries to smother the small whimper of pain.

"Fuck, don't move," she says, her eyes squeezed tight as the pain subsides.

She's still for a long, painful second before her eyelids flutter open and her mesmerizing dark eyes find mine. "Okay, I'm good. Do your thing, Ace."

I want to laugh at the determined look on her face, but I can't, because the sensation of her pussy squeezing me impossibly tight is the only thing I can focus on.

CHAPTER TWENTY-SIX

Remi

Ace slides out of me and sinks slowly back in. I clutch onto his shoulders, letting my body adjust to the feel of him.

He's everywhere.

His weight pressing me down into the mattress, one of his hands pinning my wrists above my head, his lips feasting on my skin... It's everything I thought it would be and more.

"Jesus, Remi, you feel amazing," he murmurs against my throat, licking and sucking the skin there. I'm stretched out beneath him, completely at his mercy.

And I wouldn't want it any other way.

"I'm not sure I can go slow," he breathes, rolling his hips in slow, measured strokes.

"So don't." I lock my legs around his hips, arching my back to meet him. It's as if my body knows what to do.

"God, yeah," he croons. "Just like that. You're so fucking tight, baby. So fucking good." The words catch in Ace's throat as he picks up the pace. He leans back a little to stare down at me, watching as he plays my body to sweet perfection. My breasts jiggle between us and he dips his head, drawing one of the peaks into his mouth and sucking, letting it go with a *pop*.

"God, Ace," I pant. "It feels..."

"I know, baby." He grips my jaw, tilting my head to one side and dragging his tongue up my throat. "I know. I'll never forget this," he whispers, so quietly I barely hear him.

"Good thing you won't have to."

Because I already can't wait to do this again.

"Yeah, that's right, Remi. Princess, you're mine now." Ace stares down at me with those cool blue eyes of his and I begin to tremble. It feels different like this, a lingering sensation off in the distance that I can't quite grasp.

"Ace, I need... more." He slips a hand between our bodies, finding my clit, strumming in a rhythm that has me crying his name.

"You should see yourself like this. My dirty little prep school princess giving it up to the big bad wolf." He drives harder, pushing my body up the bed. Our moans fill the space, breathy desperate moans. Our bodies slide together, slick with sweat and drenched in lust.

"I'm close," he groans, kissing me hard. Our tongues tangle as we race towards the edge. His hands are everywhere, in my hair, around my throat, squeezing and kneading my breasts. I can't breathe. Can't think.

Ace consumes me.

He's not just branding me, he's claiming me. He's

ruining me for all other men. Not that I want anyone else.

I only want him.

"Fuck, this will never be enough." He slides a hand underneath my butt and lifts me, slamming into me with brute force. My eyes sting with tears, but I'm too lost in sensation to care.

"Come for me, Princess. Come all over my cock." Ace clamps his teeth around my nipple and I fall, my walls squeezing him tight.

"Fuuuuuck," he hisses, stilling inside me.

My heart beats wildly in my chest, my body sore in the most delicious way. I know he's probably left marks. Bite marks, and bruises where his fingers dug into my hip a little too hard. But I loved every second of it.

Silence envelops us as we both ride the lingering high. Ace buries his face in my neck, tenderly kissing my damp skin. Eventually, he gets up and disposes of the condom. When he comes back to bed, I snuggle into his side.

"Hey," I ask, brushing my fingers through his hair.

He's too quiet.

Too still.

"Are you okay?"

Slowly, Ace lifts his head, giving me his eyes. "Better than fine." He gives me a wolfish grin, but something about it feels off. "Everything is exactly as it's supposed to be."

My brows knit, a strange tingle rolling up my spine. "Are you sure you're okay?"

"Relax, Princess. Everything was great."

My stomach knots at the coolness in his voice.

"Did I... do something wrong?" I whisper. He's no

longer looking at me adoringly—he's looking at me with utter disappointment.

I push away from him and sit up, pulling the sheet up my body. "Ace?" I say when he doesn't reply.

He sits up too, swinging his legs over the edge of the bed giving me his back. His head hangs low as if something is wrong.

"I thought this is what you wanted? I thought—"

He looks over at me and my heart sinks. An evil smirk graces his face. "You made it so fucking easy."

"W-what? I don't understand. I thought we—"

"You thought what, huh? That we'd ride off into the sunset? That I'd follow you to some fancy ass college on good old Uncle James' money?"

"Ace, please." Pain splinters down my chest. This isn't my Ace. It isn't the boy who just made me feel things I've never felt before.

It isn't.

Yet, I see nothing but honesty in his eyes.

"You played me?" I say slowly, the pieces of this surreal nightmare slowly falling into place. "I'm just part of your game to get back at James? You... *used* me." I pull the sheet closer, hating that I can still feel his touch branded on my skin.

"Answer me!" I yell, anger vibrating beneath my skin.

"What can I say, Princess? It was so fucking easy."

"You bastard." I lunge at him, my palm cracking across his cheek. Ace's eyes flare, and before I can stop him he pushes me down on the bed, covering my body with his.

"You were begging for it. Begging for a taste of the bad boy. Don't pretend you weren't using me for your own ends, too."

"You think I used you? I fucking fell for you, you bastard." I try to slap him again, but Ace snags my wrist, slamming my hand down beside my head. Pain jerks along my arm, but I don't scream.

I won't.

"You're lying," I say, ready to call him out on his bullshit. Whatever game he's playing is some kind of cruel defense mechanism. He's hurting over his uncle, and I'm his punching bag.

"There's no way this has all been fake," I grit out. "I've been right there beside you. Every kiss, every touch... you feel it, Ace, I know you do."

A dark chuckle rumbles in his chest, setting my teeth on edge. "I know I get you wet. And I knew it was only a matter of time before you gave it up. You're like a lost sheep, Princess. Starved of attention and ripe for the taking."

Tears burn the backs of my eyes as I try desperately not to cry. "I trusted you," I scream. "I defended you to my mom, to James. I fucking chose you, and this is how you repay me?"

Ace rears back, standing up. His eyes are narrowed, but his expression is clouded with something... indecision... regret, I don't know, because all I can focus on is the pain coiled around my heart.

I sit up, pulling the sheet back around my naked body. "I guess Conner didn't tell you yet, but I told James to keep his check. I never wanted his money." Sadness coats my words. "If I go to college it'll be on my terms and because I worked my ass off to get there."

"Bullshit. You'd be a fool not to take it."

"Not if it costs me you," I admit quietly. He doesn't deserve the words, but I say them anyway. Because I'm tired of pretending. I'm tired of always holding in how I feel, and what I've been through.

"You were right about my mom's ex-boyfriend," I say around a sad smile. "He tried to touch me. It started off as harmless hugs, stroking my hair, telling me what a good girl I was. But then he'd corner me whenever Mom was out of the room. His hands would dig into my hip a little too hard and he'd press up against me, whispering in my ear how much he liked my outfit. How much he'd like to see what was underneath."

Ace's jaw clenches, anger radiating off him. But I don't stop. I need to tell him this.

I need to finally tell *someone* this.

"One night, they came home drunk. Mom passed out on the couch, and I hid out in the bedroom to avoid him. It was too late by the time I realized he was in my room. I've never been so scared in my entire life. I can still remember his fingers slipping under my pajamas and stroking my skin." Bile rushes up my throat, and I take a deep breath. "He was going to rape me, I saw it right there in his eyes. Thankfully, Mom woke up and started causing a fuss. It scared him enough to leave me alone. I started sleeping over at Bexley's a lot after that."

"That fucker tried to rape you?" Ace's eyes are as dark as night, his fist curled at his sides.

I nod. "I closed off after that. The few friends I did have at school started backing off, and I shrank into the shadows. Bexley hit puberty and got hormones and started wanting things I couldn't give him. And then you came along." Bitterness clings to my words.

Clutching the sheet to my body, I stand so that I'm face to face with him. "You're not wrong. Part of me did use you at the start, but not in the way you think." My voice trembles. I want to know what he's thinking. How he sees me now he knows the truth. "You didn't give me time to get in my head about stuff, you just took it. It's messed up, but I think, in a way, I needed that. I needed someone else to be in control."

"Shit, Remi, that *is* fucking messed up. You make me sound like a woman beater."

I flinch at the severity in his tone. I hate that he calls me Remi, as if the future is already decided between us. But it could be worse, he could already be long gone.

"That's not what I mean." I release a weary sigh. "I always knew I could say no to you and you wouldn't push me. But I didn't want to say no, and that's because, whether you want to admit it or not, Ace, there is something real between us. I know you feel it."

He has to. Because I'm not sure what I'll do if he doesn't.

A beat passes, the weight of my secret heavy above us. Ace is as white as a sheet, his body vibrating with rage. "You should have told me," he grinds out.

"Would it have changed anything?"

"Shit, Remi, the things I did to you—"

"I didn't tell you so you'd feel guilty, I told you because I want you to understand that this isn't a game to me. It's the most real thing I've felt in a long time."

He searches my eyes for something, and for a split second, I think I've reached him. But when he takes a step back, his stone mask sliding into place, I know I've lost him.

"You were just a toy to me," he says coldly. "A means to an end with a little fun in between."

"I don't believe you. You took me to your home, introduced me to your friends."

"Who, Cruz and D? Nah." He brushes a finger over his jaw, letting it linger on his bottom lip. "They're not my real crew. My real crew would eat a pretty thing like you alive."

"So that's it then?" Disappointment rolls through me. "You're going to throw away a shot at something real because you're too chickenshit to prove people wrong?"

He takes a big step forward until he's looming over me. "Begging looks good on you, Remi. Maybe I should rethink my—"

Crack.

The sting of palm against his face has adrenaline pumping through me. "Get out."

"Is that it? You're done? I've got to say I'm disappointed. I thought you had a little more fight left in you."

"What's the point in fighting for something you already lost?" I press my lips together, tipping my chin in defiance. I'm one step away from falling apart, but I refuse to give him the satisfaction. "You should go."

"Isn't that my line?" he taunts. My Ace is gone. I realize that now. This imposter is cruel and cold and callous. His words cut, but his cowardice cuts deeper.

"Unless you want me to call your uncle and tell him exactly what kind of piece of shit he's let into his home, I suggest you leave." My eyes flick to my cell phone on the nightstand.

"Have it your way, Princess. I've got places to be, anyway." He starts pulling on clothes.

A rogue tear slips down my cheeks as I hug the sheet to my body. I can't believe this is the same night as when I first arrived.

I trusted Ace with a piece of my heart, and he ripped it out of my chest and crushed it with his bare hands.

And he still. Doesn't. Care.

When he's dressed, he grabs his cell and starts for the door. "So that's really how you want to leave it?" I call.

He pauses at the last second and glances back at me. "I don't think there's anything left to say, do you?"

"I guess not."

"Happy Birthday, Princess." He smirks. "Thanks for the ride."

Ace stalks out of the room without looking back, taking my bloodied, broken heart with him.

CHAPTER TWENTY-SEVEN

Ace

I storm away from the pool house without looking back. I can't. If I so much as glance over my shoulder then I'm going to break.

Something rustles in the trees beside me, but I'm too focused on where I'm going to look if someone's there.

I did what I needed to do. My plan is in motion, and I need to stay strong. This is what it's all about: making James admit the truth and putting together those final missing puzzle pieces from my life.

He's the one to blame for how my life turned out. Things were good... okay, no, things were fine before dad die— was murdered. Or at least that was the plan. I don't think anyone, James especially, expected him to turn up again like fucking a ghost.

If only he revealed all his secrets that day, none of this would have been necessary.

He wanted me to discover the truth myself.

I'm not only doing this for me, I'm doing it for my brothers. Dad might have set this all in motion, but he should be under no illusion that he's next on my hit list, should he ever be brave enough to show his face again.

He might have successfully blackmailed me into handing over the chunk of cash I'd stashed to protect my family, but he went against his promise to stay away. I know he saw my mom, and I know he's the reason she overdosed that night.

When I was a child, I thought he was a God. I doted on him. Wanted to be just like him. But after my most recent interaction with him, I fear my memory might be doing me a disservice.

He is not a good man.

I can't argue that James probably had his reasons reasons for his actions, , but he didn't need to leave us after. Dad might have been an asshole, but at least back then we had two parents and I didn't need to step up to the plate.

Throwing my leg over my bike, I rev the engine and get the hell out of the Bay. I can't be here right now when every little part of this town reminds me of her.

I arrive in the Heights in record time. After stopping for some supplies, I pull up in our old trailer park and bring the bike to a stop. There's a patch of land behind the park, and every weekend it's where everyone heads to get fucked up.

With a couple of bottles of scotch in hand, I make my way down. Nearly everyone ignores me—they're too high and wasted to pay me any attention, let alone recognize me.

I wasn't lying when I said that Cruz and D weren't

my real crew. They're good people. They have honest jobs and mostly live honest lives. These motherfuckers down here? These are real Heighters, and I would never bring Remi here.

"Are my eyes deceiving me? Is that really Ace fucking Jagger walking towards me?" JJ barks after doing a double-take.

"Well, fuck me. The wanderer returns. Decided against living it up with the rich chicks in the Bay, then? Thought you'd come back and have a pop at our pussy?" Dean says, amusement filling his dark and dangerous eyes.

"Talking of pussy, Kelsey is gonna be real happy to see you, bro."

"Not interested," I grunt.

"Fuck. They really are turning you into a stuck-up motherfucker, eh? Kelsey not good enough for you all of a sudden?"

All eyes drill into me as I fall down onto the old couch. "Nah, that's just not why I'm here."

"Why the fuck else would you be?"

I lift the bottle in my hand and make a show of twisting the top and downing mouthful after mouthful until my throat burns for reprieve.

"You motherfuckers got any blow?"

"Sure thing, man. Line 'em up, Pike."

I alternate between taking swigs from my bottle and doing a line of the good shit Pike keeps hidden for special occasions. My homecoming is apparently the perfect opportunity.

"Fuck me, this is good."

My body buzzes as the cocktail of alcohol and sniff takes over my thoughts.

Fuck yes.

Memories of what I left behind start to get hazy, and I settle back into where I belong.

"Well, well, well, if it isn't Ace Jagger." Kelsey's dulcet voice makes my skin crawl, and she blows my escape from reality to shit.

When I don't turn around, she walks directly in front of me. "I missed you, baby."

Just like the last time I saw her, her eyes are blown, her face is gaunt, and as she decides she needs to climb onto my lap, I get a look at her forearms. "When the fuck did you turn into a fucking junkie, Kels?" I snag one of her wrists in my hand.

"About the same time I was left behind with nothing to do."

"Don't you fucking blame this on me. I didn't shoot that shit into your veins."

"I don't need it now you're back," she purrs, settling herself so she's straddling me.

"Not back two fucking minutes and he's got every chick's pussy fucking wet. Jag, man. You need to teach us your secret," one of the guys complains as Kelsey's lips go to my neck.

I swallow down another few shots of scotch as I try to drown the fact that her touch does nothing for me. Electricity doesn't shoot around my body from her kiss. My skin doesn't prickle with excitement when she runs her fingers down my stomach. And my cock does fucking nothing.

Safe to say, in my quest to break the prep school princess, it seems I only went and broke myself in the process.

I'm back in the place I thought I belonged, with the

guys I once thought of as my family, but nothing feels right. I don't feel like I've come back home. I feel like the outsider. The one who left and is trying to claw his way back in.

I never thought I'd say it, but I don't want to be here. I want to drive my ass back to the Bay and crawl into bed beside her hot little body and lose myself in her instead of this bullshit.

I'm just about to push Kelsey off when a shadow looms over me. Glancing up, I find one of Donny's henchmen staring down at me. His face is cold, murderous.

Fucking great.

This night is going from bad to fucking worse.

Kelsey hits the floor as I stand. She complains, but all I do is step over her to find out what the fuck Bruce wants. Donny doesn't send him out for any old reason. He sends him when he wants a job fucking done—and done properly.

"What?" I bark, stepping up to him. I might not be all that happy about his appearance, but there's no fucking way I'm letting him know that.

"Donny's pissed."

"And I care because?"

"Because he needs you, and you're not doing your job."

"I'm done, man. I can't keep up with school and shit." I don't mean for the excuse to come out loud, but as it does, the motherfucker's eyes widen in shock. I swear, even a smile tugs at his lips for a second, before he remembers that he came here for a reason.

"You don't call the shots around here, kid. If Donny needs you, you come running. You know how it works."

"And what if I don't? Then what? Or is that why you're here? Disposal of the unwanted trash." Something flashes in his eyes, but I don't need to see it to know I just hit the nail on the head.

I square my feet, waiting for his first move and praying that I'm sober enough right now to stand even half a chance going up against this guy.

"Come on then, big man. Let's see what you've got."

A crowd starts to gather around us. The only thing more addictive than the drugs in this place is people's need for blood.

I dodge his first few swings. He's not as agile as I once remember him being, and I wonder why Donny didn't send someone younger. He knows I can handle myself. I'd have thought he'd know to send someone who could match me.

Unlike him, I land my first few blows. I ram my knuckles into his ribs, his jaw, and shatter his nose. It's then he sees red and he comes flying at me.

The pain of his fists is nothing less than I deserve and I revel in it, using it to spur me on.

The crowd cheers as we continue. Blood streams from his nose as I spit out what's filling my mouth from the cut in my lips.

"You ready to give up yet?" I taunt as we stare each other down.

He bares his teeth and reaches behind him. His knife reflects the roaring bonfire that's somewhere behind me. I follow his move, but when I reach for my own weapon, it's not there.

I briefly remember the events of tonight, of how quickly I dressed and got out of that pool house. I never leave my knife or gun behind, but because of her I fucking did. And exactly when I need it most.

He takes a step forward, and I prepare myself for what's to come. I can take this motherfucker down easily, but with a knife in his hand I'm much less confident.

The atmosphere around us becomes heavy with tension, and my previous thoughts about being in bed with Remi come back to me.

Why the fuck did I bother with all of this bullshit?

Is my need for revenge really worth all the pain? I remember her face as I said those final words to her. The devastation in her features guts me almost as much now as it did only a few hours ago.

My body moves on autopilot. I no longer feel his blows, nor when my own fists connect with him. The roar of the crowd fades away, and I'm no longer fighting a person but my own fucking demons, my own bad and fucked-up decisions that led me here.

Clarity comes back to me a couple of seconds too late.

I need to get out of here. I need to go back to her. I need to tell her how I really feel.

That's the moment his final blow comes.

Everything goes black as pain shoots from my knees as they hit the gravel beneath me only moments before the rest of my body crashes to the ground.

Before everything fades away, it's only her face I see. But she's not smiling, she's got tears streaming down her face as she watches me leave.

I'm used to pain. Alongside anger, it's what's fueled most of my life up until this point. So coming back around with every part of my body screaming in pain is not uncommon. I'd just forgotten how much it fucking sucked since living the high life for the past few weeks.

I keep my eyes closed, not wanting to discover the reality about where I am and what's happened to me since that motherfucker took me out. It could have been an hour ago, or days ago, I've no fucking clue. All I do know is that the darkness, the nothingness, was a hell of a lot better than reality.

I crave being dragged back under so I don't have to think, so the regret and guilt that's been eating me since walking away from Remi will leave me once again. But it doesn't happen.

My body comes back to me more with every passing second, and when my urgent need to take a piss makes itself known, I risk cracking my eyes open. "What the fuck?"

I blink a few times, not believing what I'm seeing. But each time I look again, my surroundings are still the same. Still familiar.

"How the fuck?"

Pushing up from the bed, I look for evidence of how I ended up back inside the pool house and in my own bed.

Bruce was sent to kill me, or to hand deliver my broken bloody body to Donny, of that I'm sure. He had that look in his eye, so how did I get back here alive?

I know it's not all a really fucked-up dream—the pain is too real and when I push from the bed, and the sight of my busted up and bloody knuckles confirm that the fight really did happen.

I pad to the bathroom to do my thing before resting my hands on the cold basin and preparing to look up. It's been a while since I've seen my face all fucked up. But I deserve it. All of it.

Lifting my eyes, my breath catches for a second as I stare back at myself. No fucking wonder it hurts so much, although I've no doubt it'll look a hell of a lot better once I wash the blood off my skin.

Both of my eyes are black and swollen, my cheeks are bruised, and my lip is still trickling blood. Looking lower, I take in my darkened ribs, although from how easily I walked in here, I doubt they're broken, thank fuck.

I brush my teeth and turn the shower on. Images of her joining me fill my head as I step inside and the regret that's raging inside me only grows.

I shouldn't have done that last night.

With a towel wrapped around my waist, I stalk back into the bedroom and look around. I picture us on the bed as I selfishly took the one thing from her that she can never get back. She's going to regret ever meeting me after last night, and I hate myself even more for it.

I locate the camera I set up for the final part of my plan to bring James to his knees and pull the memory card out. There's no fucking way I can go through with it. I've already done too much. I've already destroyed her.

And in the process, I know I've destroyed a part of myself too.

CHAPTER TWENTY-EIGHT

Remi

"Remi, sweetheart, breakfast."

"I'm not hungry," I yell, pulling a pillow over my face. My eyes are sore and my heart aches as the memories of last night hang over me like a dark storm cloud.

He played me.

Ace played me like a fool.

I can still feel him all over me. His traitorous lips, his sharp teeth, and his treacherous, treacherous touch.

He really is the big bad wolf, and I fell for his ruse hook, line, and sinker.

Bile rushes up my throat and my eyes water as I stumble out of bed and crash into my small bathroom. But I don't vomit. There's nothing left, not after I spent most of the night with my head down the toilet bowl.

Pulling myself up, I stand in front of the mirror. I'm a mess. My chest is covered in hickeys and I have faint bruises around my hips and thighs. But the physical marks are nothing compared to the invisible scars he's left behind.

"Remi?" Mom calls again, and I let out a whimper. If she sees me like this, she'll lose her shit and probably call James, and that is a whole conversation I never want to have.

If Ace wants to use me to hurt James, he'll have to do it himself.

A violent shiver rolls up my spine as I slam my hand against the counter. "Damn you, Ace Jagger."

Even now, standing here broken and bruised and no longer a virgin, I want to protect him. I want to march over to the pool house and demand answers. I want him to look me dead in the eyes and tell me I mean nothing to him.

He doesn't deserve another chance, I remind myself. I've given him enough of those.

Maybe Conner was right all along. Maybe Ace is a lost cause.

Tears roll down my cheeks but I brush them aside. I've been this girl before—scared, weak, alone. I won't be her again.

Ace Jagger was a mistake.

One I vow never to make again.

By the time I drag myself downstairs, Mom is pacing the kitchen. "There you are," she smiles. "I was getting worried."

"What's up, Mom?"

"I could ask you the same thing. Whatever is the matter?" She rushes over to me, brushing the hair from my face.

"I didn't sleep very well."

"Remi, what is it?"

"Me and Ace." I choke over his name. The rest of the words get stuck, and I shake my head, desperately trying to swallow the tears.

"Oh, baby, I'm sorry. Despite my misgivings about the two of you, I could see how much you cared for him. Want to talk about it?"

"No, I really don't." My eyes drop to the floor.

"I hate to ask this, baby, but he didn't—"

"What, no!" I rush out, the instinctive urge to defend him still swarming in my chest. "You were right all along. We're too different. It could never work."

"Oh, sweetheart, come here." She pulls me into her arms. "And on your birthday no less. I'm so sorry."

"Yeah," I whisper. "Me too."

"I know it's probably not what you want to hear, sweetheart, but it's probably for the best. It's senior year, you need to stay focused. And there's plenty of other boys out—"

I jerk back. "I swear, Mom, if you say Bexley's name, I will scream."

"I wasn't going to mention him." But the glimmer of guilt in her eyes tells me otherwise. "I had planned a girls' day for the two of us, but I should imagine you're not feeling in the mood now." Sadness etches into her expression.

"You did?"

"It was supposed to be a surprise, but I booked us in at La Dolce Vita for mani-pedis and facials."

"That's nice, Mom." I fight a grimace.

"I know it's not really your thing, but you used to love getting pampered when you were a little girl. I thought it would be nice."

"Sure thing, Mom." I don't have the heart to tell her no. Besides, maybe it'll give me a distraction.

"Really?" Her eyes light up. "I'm so excited. I had started breakfast," she glances over to the plate of pancakes, "but why don't we go crazy and get something on the way?"

"Are you sure, I don't want—"

"Oh hush, now. I can afford to spoil my only daughter for her birthday. Besides, James is treating us to the pamper session. He told us to get whatever we wanted."

I press my lips together and force a smile.

Of course he did.

La Dolce Vita is exactly as I remember it: spacious and opulent with high ceilings and a rich gold and black color decor. It screams luxury, and reminds me of a time when we didn't have to worry about the price tag of the various treatments on offer.

As it is, we don't have to worry. James is picking up the tab. I realize the second I'm swept away by a glamorous beautician called Shelbie that coming here was a mistake. I don't want to sit and make small talk with a woman who is preened and primped within an inch of her life.

"So sweetie," she sing-songs, "I thought we'd start with the mani and then move onto the pedi. And then we'll get you in the chair for your facial. 'Kay?" Her plump lips curve revealing a set of pearly white teeth.

"Sure."

She gets to work on my nails, filing and buffering. "So you just turned eighteen?"

"I did."

"How exciting. Any big plans to celebrate?"

"Not really."

"I don't believe that for a second." Shelbie leans in and lowers her voice. "A pretty thing like you must have a line of guys all vying for her attention."

"No line, sorry."

Her eyes flick to where Mom is chatting away to her beautician. She's so at ease here, as if she's always belonged in a place like this. The thought stings.

"Your secret's safe with me," she whispers, a conspiratorial edge to her words.

"Hmm, okay, thanks," I say, because it's easier than correcting her.

"Oh to be young again, when everything is perkier and tighter, if you know what I'm saying." Shelbie winks at me.

By the time I'm done, my nails are a glossy black at the base that bleeds into a deep red ombré at the tip. It's the perfect shade to match my mood.

"Right, if you swing your chair around and pop your

feet up on that step, I'll be right with you. The chair reclines, so feel free to sit back and relax."

I do as she suggests, it gives me a reason to close my eyes and avoid any more small talk. But the second everything goes dark, I see him.

Ace.

His icy, soulless eyes staring back at me.

I blink away the fresh tears, staring up at the ceiling while Shelbie sets to work. Off in the distance, the doorbell chimes and voices fill the studio.

"Hey, check it out." I notice Lylah Donovan's dulcet tone and stiffen.

"Girls," Mom says. "I didn't know you'd be here."

"Hi, Ms Tanner," Michaela says, and I can't resist peeking over. Sure enough, Michaela, Lylah and a couple of their other cheer friends stand there, wearing their fake smiles and designer clothes.

"Michaela, it's nice to see you again."

"Ugh," I groan, sinking back into the plush velvet chair.

"Problem, sweetie?" Shelbie asks, but before I can answer, I feel someone approach.

"I didn't realize they let trash in this place." I open my eyes to find Michaela glaring at me. She keeps her voice low enough so no one but me and Shelbie can hear her. "Someone really should speak to the manager about that."

Shelbie keeps quiet as she continues moisturizing my feet.

"Leave it out, Michaela," I release a heavy sigh. "I'm not in the mood."

"I guess you wouldn't be after Ace finally saw sense and dropped you."

"What did you say?" My hands curl around the arm of the chair, digging into the soft silky material.

"You heard me. I'm hardly surprised though. Why have hamburger when you can have steak?"

I vibrate with anger, but it's nothing compared to the pain coiled around my heart.

Ace told her?

He told Michaela about us?

No, I don't believe that. Ace is many things, but he knows Michaela is my weakness.

I can't believe he'd stoop so low.

"How do you know?" I ask, even though it kills me.

"How do you think I know? He told me, of course."

The air *whooshes* from my lungs. "No, he wouldn't"—

"What can I say?" She shrugs, flicking her blonde locks off her shoulder. "But don't worry, I comforted him the best I could."

Bile burns in my stomach, and I swallow hard.

"He was more than—"

"Michaela," Shelbie finally speaks, "don't you think you've done enough?"

"Who, me? I was merely stopping by to wish Remi a belated happy birthday." Her lips curve with malice. "Happy birthday, step-sister." She wiggles her fingers and walks away as if she didn't just deliver the final blow.

"Are you okay, sweetie?" Shelbie offers me a sympathetic smile.

"Yeah, no thanks to you," I bite, and she drops her head.

I know it's not really her fault. Michaela's mom is a regular here—not to mention one of the town's most respected women. Even if she is a home-wrecking whore. Going up against Michaela is just asking for trouble.

But still, I don't apologize.

I can't.

Because there's only so much one person can take. And I've reached my limit with traitorous bad boys and toxic prep school princesses.

"This was a good idea," I say to Hadley before taking another long pull on the bottle of wine we stole from my mom's stash.

"Oh, I don't know about that," she replies. There's something in her tone that makes me sit up straighter.

"Why?" I frown.

"Why what?"

"Why do you have that look?"

"I don't have a look." She averts her shifty gaze.

"Hadley Dove Rexford, you're hiding something."

"Ahh, shit, Remi. Your mom is going to kill me."

"My mom? What the hell does she have to do with this?"

"I'm supposed to be distracting you, not getting you drunk." Guilt flashes in her eyes.

"Oh god." I suddenly feel sober. "Tell me she isn't planning something."

Hadley presses her lips together.

"A party? She's throwing me a party, isn't she?" It all makes sense now.

The pamper session. The new outfit she insisted on buying me afterwards. And the fact that she just so happened to invite Hadley over to keep me company while she went to see James.

"She's crazy. My mom is actually batshit crazy." I bury my face in my hands. This is the worst thing that could happen right now. I don't want a party, let alone a surprise party at James' house.

"She's not crazy. She just wanted to do a nice thing for you."

"Fuck," I breathe. "Tell me she didn't invite the entire class?"

Hadley's silence has me cussing like a sailor. "Calm down," she says, laying a hand on my arm. "It won't be that bad."

"Not that bad?" I grind out. "It's like she doesn't even know who I am. She can't think for a second that I'd want to actually celebrate with any of the kids from school?"

"Hmm, she may have roped in Bexley and Michaela to help with the guest list."

"What the fuck?" I leap up. I don't know where I'm going, but I can't sit. Not when I have all this restless energy zipping through me.

"I can't believe this. The Jaggers' is the last I want to be right now, Hads."

"I know. But if it's any consolation, Ace isn't there."

"What?" My stomach dips. "How do you know that?"

Her expression falls. "I may have helped deliver some stuff to the house earlier."

"Hadley!" I hiss. "And here I was thinking we were friends."

"Hey, we are. But your mom was so excited about it, I didn't have the heart to dash her plans. Besides, I didn't know asshole features was going to do that to you. I'm sorry."

"I know." I flop back down on the couch. "Why would anyone come, though? It's not like I'm friends with anyone."

"People don't need an excuse to party. Besides, it's James Jagger's house. Kids have been chomping at the bit to get a look inside that place for years."

"So people are only coming because it gives them behind the scenes access. Nice."

"You know, not everyone at school is as bad as you make them out to be."

"You mean like Hayden?" My brow rises.

"Not just Hayden. Some people try to be your friend, Remi. But after being constantly pushed away, eventually they stop trying."

She's not wrong.

But it doesn't make it any easier to swallow.

It's been so easy to close myself off. To protect myself. After what happened with my dad and Michaela, and then Mom's ex-boyfriend, I didn't know who to trust anymore.

So I decided to trust no one.

Hadley has always been an exception to the rule. The second she arrived at Sterling Prep in junior year and we got paired together for math, I knew she was different.

"Look, I know you're hurting, and I know a party is the last thing on your mind. But what's the alternative? Sitting here, getting drunk, and crying over Ace? Please, you're better than that."

"What are you thinking?" Because the picture she paints does sound all kinds of lame.

"I'm thinking, you put on the most killer outfit you

can find, you let me do your hair and make-up, we finish that bottle of wine, and we crash your party the way it deserves to be crashed. In total style and with zero fucks given."

I grin back at her. "I knew there was a reason I liked you."

"So you're in?"

Ace, Michaela, Bexley, Lylah... they could taunt me and tease me, hurt me and harass me, but they would never break me.

"Oh, I'm in." A lick of anticipation simmers beneath my skin. "I'm so in."

CHAPTER TWENTY-NINE

Ace

"What the fuck are you doing here?" I ask, stepping from the pool house to find none other than fucking Michaela walking towards me.

Her eyes widen at the state of me, but she doesn't comment. "I'm just helping set up the party." She smiles sweetly at me, and it makes my skin crawl.

I look her up and down. It's weird seeing her out of her cheer uniform, but I can't say losing it makes her any more appealing.

"Why?" I spit. She's the last person Remi would ask to help with the party—the one she probably doesn't want in the first place.

After last night, I can't imagine she wants to be anywhere near the place. Or me.

"Sarah asked me to help." She bats her eyelashes at me.

"And you're coming down here why?"

"We've run out of tape. James thought there might be some—" She glances over my shoulder and I stiffen.

"There isn't."

"I'll just have a quick look."

"No," I spit. "No, you won't. Go to the fucking store if you have to, but you're not going in there."

"Oh don't be so ridiculous. He told me exactly where he thinks it is. I'll be in and out. You won't even know."

I narrow my eyes at her. "I said no."

"What's wrong? Got some poor naive victim chained to your bed or something?"

Rearing back, I snap, "What the fuck is wrong with you? I don't want you near my shit. Now fuck off." Taking her shoulder in my hands, I physically turn her and push her back toward the main house.

I follow her all the way, and once we're inside she turns left to the living room while I go for the kitchen.

I can't remember when I last ate something, and I'm fucking starving.

"Ace, how are... oh my goodness," Ellen gasps, her hands coming up to cover her gaping mouth.

"It's nothing. I'm fine."

"F-fine?" she stutters. "You are not fine. Come and sit down here and let me look at you. You might need stitches."

"I said I'm fine." She pales instantly. "Sorry," I mutter. "It was a rough night."

"So I see. What do you need?" she asks, changing tack.

"Food. Whatever you've got."

She immediately turns toward the refrigerator and pulls a load of ingredients out.

The sound of chatter and crashing about comes from elsewhere in the house, and as I look toward the door, I realize that the counters are full of party food.

"Have you made all this?"

"With my own fair hands," Ellen says, focusing on what she's doing.

"You're wasted here."

"Nah, I spent too many years catering. I love looking after you guys."

"Really?" I ask incredulously. Even our own parents didn't want to look after us, I find it hard to believe that a random woman wants to.

"Really. You're not as bad as you try to make out, you know. I see you," she says, looking over her shoulder and winking at me.

Shaking my head at her, I allow silence to descend as she cooks and the others get the house ready for this fucking party.

I'm in two minds as to whether I should hang around for it or disappear for the night. I do know one thing, though—I'm not going back to the Heights anytime soon. I still have no clue what the hell happened last night, but I'm not risking showing my face for a while. Donny is clearly after my blood for some reason. I know I missed a few messages from him, but sending Bruce after me seems a little much.

"Whoa, aren't you a sight for sore eyes this morning, brother," Conner announces as he and Cole join me at the table. "Remi finally seen the light and tried to knock some sense into you?"

"Oh yeah, this was totally R... her." Fucking pussy, I can't even say her fucking name.

The pain that ripped through my chest when I pulled out of her last night once again slices me in two as I think about her.

"Trouble in paradise?"

"Like you give a shit. You were betting on me fucking up from day one. Well, you were right, brother. Well done. I fucked it up."

Pushing the chair out from behind me, I stalk to the door.

"Ace, your—" Ellen cuts herself off when I look up at her.

"That's it. Run away like a fucking pussy." Not wanting to hear any more from him, I turn the corner. "The girl fucking loves you, man. Pull your head out of your ass for once..." His words die as I get to the front door and fly down the stairs.

I can't fucking be here right now as I watch them all get ready to celebrate her birthday. They're all fucking delusional—Sarah for thinking she wants a bullshit party with people she can't stand. People who make her feel less than she is. Ellen for thinking she can look after us like we're her cute little boys. James for thinking this could ever fucking work.

We don't belong here, and we never will.

Ignoring my bike, I take off across the garden. I take the same route we did the night we had our one and only party here, and before long the beach appears in front of me. Finding a soft bit of sand, I drop my ass to it.

I sit there for the longest time, just watching the waves crash in on the beach. A few people walk past, but no one really pays me any attention. Hell, I wouldn't if I found a guy who looked like I do right now.

My cell vibrates in my pocket. A little bit of hope races through me that she's going to try to fight for me, just like she did the last time I fucked up. But that thought is shattered the second I look at the screen and find Cole's name staring back at me.

Cole: James wants you back before the party starts.

"Yeah, well James can go fuck himself," I mutter to myself. All of this is his fault.

All of it.

I lie back and stare up at the clear blue sky above me. My mind spins as I think about our short time here and the events that led up to it.

I remember that night two weeks before Mom died like it was only yesterday. I was doing a drop for Donny. He'd sent me to some warehouse in the next town over that I'd never visited before. He'd told me to pull up in the parking lot and to wait. Someone would come to take the bag and then I was done until my next phone call.

It was an easy drop. I was relaxed and ready to head home to see what state I might find our mother and the trailer in. The last thing I was expecting was for a fucking ghost to appear from the shadows in front of me.

"Son," he said as my eyes widened and I did a double take.

It had been years since I saw him, and although he was obviously older, I recognized him instantly.

"D-Dad?" He nodded. "But... but you're... dead."

An unamused chuckle fell from his lips. "Yeah, that's what he wants you to believe."

"He? Who's he?"

He leaned into me and whispered, "Give me what I need, and I'll tell you what you want to know."

I should have known better than for him just to turn up out of the blue and tell me all his secrets.

I handed him the bag, assuming that was what he meant, but it seemed he was after more. That's if there was anything other than a couple of bricks in that bag. As per Donny's rule, I never looked.

"Happy?" I asked as a cold, vacant expression washed over his face. I remember the shudder that ran down my spine. He was meant to be my father, yet in that moment I was more terrified than I think I've ever been in my life.

"I need money. Every penny you've got, kid, or I'm coming after the one weakness you have left."

"I don't have one. You're going to need to try better than that," I said, puffing my chest out. It was almost true; I cared about very little in life.

"I'll start with your whore of a mother. And if that doesn't work, I'll move on to your bastard brothers."

I opened my mouth to argue, to tell him that he'd never touch his own sons. I knew he had a temper, but up until that moment I never thought he'd hurt his own flesh and blood.

"All of you are just as worthless as her. Fucking cheap whore who opens her legs for any bloke who looks her way."

"What are you—"

"I'm not your fucking father, boy. I never could have

fathered three pathetic boys like you. You're all nothing to me, fucking nothing. Now get me what I need, or I'll be coming back for her."

I sit up and suck in lungfuls of air. My stomach turns over, making me heave. Thankfully the lack of contents means there's nothing to throw up.

"Fucking lying asshole," I scream into the silence around us. My heart races and my fists curl, the tidal wave of emotions I felt that night as I stared at my dead father, hitting me. The confusion over what he was telling me. The anger that burned through me as he spoke about those I loved like that. The regret that I didn't do more, that I didn't force all of the truth out of him.

He didn't wait for me to give him everything I had. He had already seen our mother and set his plan into action. I have no idea if he drove her to the overdose or if he forced it.

There's a chance I'll never know.

When he'd come back, I had given him the money as requested, hoping like hell he was going keep his promise, unaware that it was already too late. He whispered one single name to me as he disappeared.

James.

I still don't understand it. James wanted him dead. Why? And why couldn't he have found someone capable of getting the job done?

Unable to sit there any longer with my head full of questions and wondering what kind of disaster is happening at James' house, I push up and make the short walk back.

I have every intention of slipping around the edge of the grounds and disappearing into the pool house, but that's all ruined when I find Remi standing around the pool, dressed in a skin tight, short little black dress with her hands on Bexley.

He's standing in her personal space and smiling down at her like a lion who's hungry for his lunch as she rests her tiny hand on his forearm and laughs at whatever dumbass comment he just made.

A red mist descends over me, and before I know I've moved, my feet have carried me halfway toward them. The few people who were loitering around jump out of my way, and a couple of members of the football team shout the motherfucker's name to give him a heads-up about what's coming for him.

I pass the screen that Sarah demanded was here so she could show cute baby pictures of Remi—as if anyone really fucking cares. That woman's heart is in the right place, but she's a clueless idiot sometimes.

"Get your fucking hands off her," I bark, wrapping my arm around Remi's waist and pulling her away from his body.

The music that was booming around the yard is turned down, and more kids spill out of the doors to see what's about to kick off.

My skin burns the second Remi's angry stare lands on me, but instead of ripping me a new one like I'm sure she was intending to do, a gasp falls from her lips.

"Oh my god, Ace." Remi gasps. "What the hell happened?"

"Leave it," I bark, taking a step toward Bexley.

His shoulders widen as he tilts his head up. He's a fucking stupid motherfucker for going up against me.

"Looks like the odds are in my favor this time, Jagger. You seem to have got your ass handed to you.

Now it's my turn to prove you're not as fucking scary as you think you are."

I take another step toward him, a growl rumbling up my throat.

"Okay everyone," someone shouts over the noise. "Remi's mom has a video she'd like to play."

Remi groans behind me, but I doubt anyone's attention turns to the fucking screen with Bexley and I about to go at it.

"Go on then, big man," he taunts. "Fucking hit me.

I pull my fist back, ready to do just as he suggests when my voice from behind me stops all my movement.

"Last chance to change your mind, Princess. If you have any doubts, now's the time to say." I turn slowly, and my heart plummets.

My video.

The one I was going to play.

The one I was going to use to ruin her.

The one I changed my mind about.

"No. No doubts, Ace. I want you to be my firrrrst," Remi's voice sounds out all breathy and needy.

"You motherfucker," Bexley roars.

Remi screams as the reality of the situation hits her. I turn to her, wanting to tell her that this wasn't me. That I changed my mind. I wasn't going to play it. I took the card out of the camera and was going to throw it away.

The next few seconds happen so fast that I'm not entirely sure what happens.

Bexley puts his entire weight behind the punch that comes hurtling my way, but at the last minute a head full of brown curls flashes in front of me. The pain from his fist never comes, but a cry of agony comes from elsewhere.

I glance to the side to see Remi falling, her body limp as it tumbles toward the still water of the pool behind us.

Jumping onto action, I race to catch her, but I'm too late. Her head collides with the tiled edge and the water engulfs her.

I don't think, I just act.

Diving in after her, I gather her body up in my arms and as fast as I can get her above the water. By the time I reach the top step, silence surrounds me as our entire class, including my brothers, watch in horror as I lower her lifeless body to the ground.

Pushing her hair from her face, I drop my eyes to her chest to see if she's breathing. "Come on, Remi, baby." I gently shake her body. "Princess. I'm here. It's okay."

Something catches my eye, and when I look down the water dripping off her body is red.

"Someone call a fucking ambulance."

I pull Remi on to my lap and hold onto her, praying that it's not the last time I'm going to get the chance.

Remi and Ace's story continues in *Tame Him*, releasing on August 27th 2020.
https://bit.ly/TameHimGR

Two angsty romance lovers writing dark heroes and the feisty girls who bring them to their knees.

SIGN UP NOW
To receive news of our releases straight to your inbox.

Want to hang out with us?
Come and join CAITLYN'S DAREDEVILS group on Facebook.